A
ROYAL VISIT
TO VICTORY
STREET

BOOKS BY PAM HOWES

A
ROYAL VISIT
TO VICTORY
STREET

PAM HOWES

bookouture

Published by Bookouture in 2022

An imprint of Storyfire Ltd.
Carmelite House
50 Victoria Embankment
London EC4Y 0DZ

www.bookouture.com

ISBN: 978-1-80019-794-7
eBook ISBN: 978-1-80019-793-0

Dedicated to the memory of the wonderful Ronnie Spector (Aug '43–Jan '22). Thank you for the fantastic music and the fabulous memories of The Ronettes. Reunited with sister Estelle in rock'n'roll heaven. I treasure the memory of the day I met you in 2016. It's a memory I will treasure forever.

ONE

Mary Robinson dropped the phone receiver back onto its cradle and fanned her hand in front of her face in a flustered fashion. She stared at her bemused expression in the hall mirror for a long second and shook her head. She'd just been summoned to a very important meeting at two o'clock prompt with the Wavertree Women's Institute. The institute's current president, Eva Thompson, had taken up the reins a couple of years ago when Mary's late friend Fenella Jenkins had to resign from the long-held position due to her ongoing ill health.

Madam President Thompson had insisted that Mary arrive on time as the meeting was to discuss an, as yet, undisclosed top-secret matter that would need a great deal of careful planning. *What the heck could be so important to warrant a phone call at two minutes past nine on a Tuesday morning?* Mary thought, as she hurried into the bedroom to get dressed. Good job she'd had the foresight to wash and bobby-pin her hair up after her bath last night as that would save her a bit of time today. She unfastened her blonde locks and ran her fingers through the sleek waves that fell naturally to her shoulders. A quick brush through any unruly areas later and she'd look like she'd just strolled out of Madame Hettie's hair salon.

Mary rooted through her wardrobe and lifted out her smart blue two-piece wool suit, adorned with a navy velvet collar and cuffs, and her best white cotton blouse. *Those would do nicely*, she thought. The blue complemented her eyes, so she'd been told many times by her daughters. She hung the clothes on their hangers from the picture rail to air for later. She'd look smartly dressed for whatever might be dropped on her plate, anyway. Her navy court shoes and handbag would match the outfit perfectly.

But before she could think about getting all dolled up, Mary had some housework to do this morning. She pulled on her old brown cleaning skirt and fawn, bleach-splashed cardigan, tied a turban loosely around her curls and set to, stripping the sheets off the bed. Her husband Martin had recently bought her a fancy Hoover washing machine with an electric mangle attached and the difference it had made to washdays was unbelievable. Such a time saver and it even heated the water which saved lighting the floor-standing gas boiler and steaming up the kitchen. Most women round here did their laundry on a Monday morning, but Mary had been too busy yesterday. She'd stepped in to look after her daughter Molly's two young children, both of who'd woken up with a bit of a tummy bug, while their mother attended to some business in the city centre.

Mary wasn't needed for grandmother duties today. Young Patti was in the nursery this morning and Harry was back at school, both having made a miraculous recovery by teatime when the ice cream van turned up on their road. Mary had been looking forward to getting stuck in and finishing her housework before Martin arrived home for his tea. And now, darn it, there wouldn't be time to make the steak and kidney pie she'd promised him either.

It would have to be sausage and mash, instead. Not that

Martin would mind, he'd eat anything she put in front of him. She'd bake the pie tomorrow. She liked to spoil him, after the years she'd spent as a war widow and him as a single man who'd fended for himself following the death of his mother. It was so nice to have a man in her life to look after again, and a good one who looked after *her* equally in return.

* * *

Bella Harrison anxiously chewed her lip as she listened to the caller and agreed to get there as soon as she possibly could. She took a deep breath and hung up, oblivious to the concerned stares from receptionist Emily who had just walked in at the front door after a mid-morning visit to the bank to deposit yesterday's takings.

'Won't be a minute, Emily,' Bella called over her shoulder as she dashed upstairs to the Bold Street Studios rehearsal room. She rapped loudly on the door, hoping the occupants weren't in the middle of a recording session.

A voice called, 'Come in.'

She pushed the door open and hurried inside. 'Sorry to disturb you but I need a word with Bobby,' she said. 'It's urgent.'

Her husband was sitting at the control desk alongside Basil Jenkins, his stepfather, and they both turned to face her.

'You look a bit upset, love, what's the matter?' Bobby asked, pushing his chair back from the desk on its squeaky castors and reaching for Bella's hand.

'I've just had a call from our Lizzie's teacher,' she gasped. 'Lizzie's fallen in the school playground and they think she's broken her wrist. But she's hysterical and they can't get her to calm down.' Lizzie was Bella and Bobby's seven-year-old daughter who was deaf. They relied on sign language to communicate with her. 'I'm going to go and pick her up and take her to the hospital. She'll be frightened and in pain and won't understand what's wrong.'

'I'll come with you,' Bobby said, getting slowly to his feet and reaching for the walking stick he relied on. Bobby had lost his lower right leg during the war and although he managed fine with his false limb, when he first stood up from a sitting position, the stick helped him to steady his balance.

'Earl's due back in the studio in a few minutes,' Basil announced. 'I'll drive you both to the school to pick Lizzie up and then drop you at the hospital. Emily can hold the fort until he arrives. We've no one in for a session until later and I'll be back to help him by then.'

Basil and Bobby took the small lift down to the ground floor and Bella ran down the stairs and put on the lightweight beige jacket that matched her pencil skirt and picked up her handbag.

'You'll be okay on your own for a while, won't you, Emily?' Bella asked the young receptionist. 'If anyone comes in to book studio or rehearsal time just make a note of it and get a phone number if they have one so that we can give them a call later. Earl won't be long,' she said, referring to her sister Molly's husband and the third partner of the Bold Street entertainments' business. 'He was meeting our Molly and then coming back here.'

'I'll be fine,' Emily replied. 'You get yourselves off and I hope Lizzie isn't too badly injured. The poor little love.' She saw them out and shut the door behind them.

'I'll just bring the car to the end of the street,' Basil said. 'You two make your way over to the church side and I'll pick you up there. Saves Bobby having to walk too far.' He hurried off up Bold Street towards the car park and Bella clutched Bobby's arm as they walked towards St Luke's church; or what was left of it. The stone-built outer walls miraculously still stood proudly but the building inside was a ruin from bomb damage received during the war years.

'Here's Basil,' Bella said as he drove up the street towards them in his shiny black Rover saloon. He stopped beside the kerb. Bella opened the front passenger door and helped Bobby into the seat. She made sure he was comfortable and then climbed onto the back seat behind him.

Basil drove to Woolton village as fast as he could and turned onto Out Lane. He pulled up outside Woolton primary school and turned to speak to Bobby. 'I'll hang on here and then I can run you all to the hospital.'

'Thanks, Basil,' Bobby replied. 'We'll be as quick as we can.'

Bobby took Bella's arm as they made their way across the playground and into the reception area where they were shown to a room just off the main corridor. They could hear poor Lizzie screaming before the door was even opened. Their little daughter was sitting on a chair and her teacher was kneeling in front of her trying to sign words.

But Lizzie was having none of it and ignored her, her right arm, looking red and swollen and with bruising already starting to show around the wrist area, hanging loosely by her side. Bella dropped down beside the teacher and took Lizzie's left hand in hers. Lizzie paused her crying and her eyes opened wide and her chin quivered when she saw her mother and father. Bella let her hand go and quickly signed to her as well as speaking slowly and directly, and Lizzie nodded, big fat tears tumbling down her flushed cheeks.

Bella got to her feet and turned to the teacher. 'I've told her we're going to take her somewhere they will make her feel better and stop it hurting. I think she understands.'

Lizzie's teacher nodded and handed Bella a carrier bag that contained Lizzie's blazer and her satchel. 'Everything she brought to school today is in there. Will you let us know how she gets on? She was skipping quite happily with some of the other girls at playtime, tripped and put her hands out to save herself. It all happened so quickly.'

'Unfortunately accidents do,' Bobby agreed. He smoothed Lizzie's blonde curls from her tear-stained cheeks. 'We'll report back as soon as we have some news, it might be tomorrow though, by the time we get seen at the hospital.'

'Not a problem, Mr Harrison,' the teacher said. 'Good luck.' She signed 'Bye bye' to Lizzie who gave her a watery smile and accompanied them all to the double front doors.

* * *

'I'll go back to the studio,' Basil said as he pulled up outside the Royal Liverpool Hospital entrance. 'Ring when you need picking up.'

'It's okay, Basil really,' Bobby said. 'We'll get a taxi, save you coming all the way back. We'll go straight home from here and will ring you later when we're sorted.'

After booking in at reception and explaining about Lizzie's disability, Bella and Bobby were told to take a seat in the busy accident and emergency department and eventually Lizzie's name was called. She was examined by a gentle nurse who patiently signed how she was going to help her and make her feel better.

They were sent to the X-ray department where Lizzie's swollen limb was declared broken in two places. Her wrist was put into a plaster cast up to her elbow and then gently placed into a sling. She was given a barley sugar lollipop for being such a brave girl. Bobby and Bella thanked the staff who had been so kind and gentle with Lizzie and then Bobby asked the receptionist if she would call them a taxi. They went to wait outside.

'Phew,' Bella said. 'Well that went better than I was expecting. We were so fortunate that the lovely young nurse who helped us has a deaf brother. She was really good with sign language. It made all the difference.' She looked down at their daughter and then handed the bags she was carrying over to

Bobby. She swung Lizzie up onto her hip. 'She's nearly asleep,' she announced as Lizzie's head drooped onto her shoulder. 'Must be the pain relief they gave her that's making her a bit dopey.'

'It's at times like this that I feel completely useless,' Bobby said, a catch in his voice. 'I can't even offer to carry her or I'd end up falling over and injuring us both.'

Bella shook her head. 'Oh Bobby, you're far from useless, love. She's only little and no weight for me to carry. Anyway, look,' she pointed to a vehicle that was pulling up in front of them, 'here's our taxi. Let's get her home and comfortable and we can have a much needed cuppa.'

* * *

As Bobby slid his key into the front door of their bungalow home in Woolton village he frowned and raised his eyebrows at Bella who was still carrying a sleeping Lizzie and looking as puzzled as *he* felt. They could hear music, but where was it coming from? The place should be empty, everyone either at work or school. He could hear male voices chatting and laughing and the sound of an acoustic guitar being strummed.

He put his finger to his lips and led the way down the long narrow hall, following the noise to the door at the end. He turned the knob slowly and quietly pushed the door open. Three young lads were sitting on the floor in front of the tiled fireplace, their backs to him and Bella. Their son, Levi, was the guitar-strumming culprit; a second boy was drumming in rhythm by patting on his legs and banging an upturned saucepan with the handle of a wooden spoon, and the third boy was singing along in harmony with Levi.

The threesome were so engrossed in what they were doing they were oblivious to anything else. Smiling, Bobby held his hand up to silence Bella until they had finished their song. He clapped slowly as three heads whipped around, looks of guilty horror written all over their faces. Bobby quickly dropped his smile and tried hard to keep his tone firm as he spoke. 'Well, that was great, lads – but – why aren't you at school?'

Levi jumped to his feet; his hands flew to his mouth, guitar hanging loose around his body from the strap. 'Er, erm, erm, sorry, Dad, Mam,' he stuttered. 'But why are you home?' He stopped speaking as he looked at his sleeping sister in Bella's arms. 'Oh my God! Why is Lizzie wearing a sling? Has she had an accident? What's happened to her?'

Bella carried her sleeping daughter over to the sofa under the window and laid her down. Lizzie snuggled into a cushion and sighed but she didn't wake up.

'She's had a fall at school and she's broken her wrist and a small bone in her lower arm,' Bella explained, pointing to the area on her own arm. 'We're just back from the hospital. But never mind about Lizzie for now, like your dad just asked, why aren't you at school?'

Levi hung his head, seemingly lost for words. He looked at the other two boys who also remained silent.

Bella shook her head. 'Your mam will go mad, Kenny Falmer,' she directed at Levi's red-haired friend from his early school days, who had been responsible for doing the drumming on her saucepan. He'd passed his eleven plus at the same time as Levi, and his mother had been over the moon when he was offered a place at Quarry Bank High School. 'She's got high expectations of you, young man. After all the sacrifices she's had to make to kit you out with your uniform, you don't want to disappoint her, do you?'

Kenny shook his head. 'No, I don't, Mrs Harrison,' he replied, chewing his bottom lip, his face as red as his hair. 'And you're right; me mam will go mad with me. But it was just a dead boring history lesson this afternoon and we wanted to do some singing. We fancied having a go at skiffle but we need a washboard and some thimbles and me mam won't lend us hers.'

Bella pursed her lips. 'I won't tell tales to your mothers this time,' she promised. 'But no more playing truant or you'll be in big trouble. And if the school decides to send the school board man round to your houses then your parents will know soon enough. So you'd better just keep everything crossed that they don't do that.'

The three boys hung their heads and nodded. Bobby tried to stifle a grin but lost the battle. 'Right, well seeing as you're here and it's too late to go in now I suggest we all go to my music room and have a chat.'

Bella smiled. 'Go on through to your music room then and I'll bring some refreshments to you in a few minutes. I need to make a phone call to my mam first. Take all your stuff in with you, boys, so that no one trips over it. I think we've had our fill of accidents for today.' She watched as they all picked up their school bags and blazers and trooped after Bobby into the garage he'd had converted into a music room shortly after they'd moved into their new bungalow.

She shook her head after their departing backs. It bothered her at times that Levi paid more attention to music than his schoolwork. It was all very well hoping to see your name in lights, but as she knew herself, when life took over and the need to get a proper job came into force, a few qualifications wouldn't go amiss. She'd never had the chance to go to college as she'd had to leave school when war broke out and get a job to help her mam support the family. She'd like Levi to have the educational opportunities the war had robbed her of. Still, he seemed determined to do his best to try and gain a little bit of fame for himself and his pals. Maybe in time he would realise he could do both if he put his mind to it. She was pretty certain her mam still had an old washboard that she no longer used since Martin had bought her a fancy new washing machine, and she could pick up some thimbles from Betty Dawson's wool and haber-dashery shop in the village. She'd ask her mam to save the wash-board for the lads, if it hadn't already been chucked away. She put the kettle on the stove to boil and then dialled her mam's number, but the phone rang and rang.

Frowning, Bella dropped the receiver back onto the cradle, wondering where she was. She knew she'd had things to catch up with at home after looking after Molly's kids yesterday. She'd said so last night when Bella had spoken to her. *Ah well, something must have cropped up*; she'd try her again later. She took the biscuit tin from a shelf and laid some chocolate bourbons and lemon puffs out on a plate, poured three glasses of orange squash for the boys and made a pot of tea for her and Bobby.

TWO

Mary chewed her lip as she listened to the excited chatter of several of her fellow Wavertree WI members. They were all seated around a large oblong table in the church hall on the dot of two as requested, a notepad and pen on the table in front of each of them. She took a deep breath as they waited for Madam President to arrive. True to form, Eva Thompson was running late, even though she'd insisted her members were to get there bang on time.

That was something Fenella would never have done, Mary thought, keep people waiting. Her late friend's timekeeping, like her appearance, had always been precise and impeccable. The woman sitting next to Mary glanced at her watch, rolled her eyes and shook her head.

'Blooming typical,' Joyce Andrews muttered as the doors were flung wide open and, in a flurry of activity, Madam President swept into the room, carrying a file and throwing out apologies for her late arrival. All to do with a last-minute phone call that she simply had to take, she announced importantly.

Mary's neighbour raised an amused eyebrow and shuffled

round in her seat. 'Anybody'd think she'd been speaking to royalty,' she said with a smirk.

Mary smiled and turned her attention to Eva Thompson who took her place at the top of the table. Eva's eyes roamed over the seated women and settled on Mary. 'Mary, my dear, would you mind coming to sit beside me please? I shall require your assistance with this project.'

Mary felt her cheeks heating as Joyce Andrews gave her a nudge and whispered jokingly, 'Teacher's pet.' She got to her feet and walked around the perimeter of the table to take the empty seat next to Eva Thompson.

'Thank you, Mary,' Eva began. 'And thank you, ladies. Well, now I'm sure you're all wondering why I have called this rather urgent meeting.' She paused and took a deep breath. 'Well, I've been informed by a person of authority from Saint George's Hall, that after their most successful tour of our cities and towns following her coronation a few years ago, Queen Elizabeth and Prince Philip, the Duke of Edinburgh, are planning a short tour of certain cities again. Liverpool being one of them, and they have decided on a number of areas they would like to visit.'

She paused once more, looking at her attentive, wide-eyed audience, and then continued. 'Wavertree has been chosen for our city and one street in particular has been mentioned. That street is Victory Street and this is the reason I have asked Mary to join me up here. Mary lived on Victory Street for most of her life until her house suffered damage during the war years. I know she has fond memories of her time there and also is still in touch with many of the residents.'

Feeling shocked, Mary looked around the faces staring at her. She smiled and nodded. She did indeed have the fondest memories of living on Victory Street. She had given birth to all three of her daughters in their little terraced home, but there were sad memories too as she had lost her youngest, Betty, to diphtheria, and during the war it was also the final place she'd held her late husband Harry in her arms before he went off to join his regiment. She'd never set eyes on him again. She blinked rapidly, took a deep breath and focussed on what Eva was saying.

'I think we are all aware that Prince Philip had a particular soft spot for our wartime songstresses, the Bryant Sisters,' she was saying with a smile as Mary tuned her attention in again. 'It's my belief he's chosen this street for that very reason, having probably been informed that it's their home ground.'

Heads nodded and all eyes turned to Mary. Her eldest daughter Bella was the lead vocalist with the popular trio and sang alongside her best friends, Edie and Fran, both of whom still lived on Victory Street.

'The powers that be at the town hall have left it in our safe hands that we ladies will organise a street party complete with entertainment,' Eva finished with a smile. 'I know we've managed to put on some good shows inside this church hall, but do we feel we can pull this off between us outside on the street? It really must be the best we can manage. It is a very special privilege to be asked to entertain our dear queen and her husband, as I'm sure you will all agree.'

Mary spoke up first. 'Well you could blow me down with a feather after hearing that news. How exciting! We've organised parties before, both on the street and on the nearby Mystery Park, so I don't see why we can't manage to do it again. We need a plan of action in place. I suggest we divide into three or four groups, and then various tasks can be split between us so that each group is responsible for taking on and organising its own task list.'

'Oh, Mary, you are always so organised, I knew I could rely on you,' Eva gushed. 'We should write down all the things we need to think in depth about: decorations, food, flowers to be presented to Her Majesty, etcetera.'

Mary nodded. 'And you can leave the entertainment side of things to me. My sons-in-law Earl and Bobby, along with Basil, will be able to get the acts booked through their entertainments agency. Do we have a date for this special event yet?'

Eva looked at the sheaf of papers she'd pulled out of her file and screwed up her eyes as she scanned the first page. 'Ah, here we are. The royal tour is scheduled for the end of June. Saturday the thirtieth is Liverpool's turn. So I make that six weeks away.'

Mary smiled at the sharp intakes of breath and mumbles of 'We'll never do it.' But they would. Once she'd got her family involved they would soon have a marvellous plan in place. Maybe it would even bring back the wartime spirit of a few years ago. The men were used to putting on shows at theatres with just a few weeks to arrange them and she knew that most of the Victory Street residents would be eager to help organise the street party as soon as she was allowed to let them know that it was happening.

'We will,' she assured the doubters. 'Just leave it with me and by Thursday's usual WI meeting I will have all the planning lists you'll need. I know we have to keep this under our hats for the time being, but I'm going to need my family's help with the musical side and the artistes will of course need to start rehearsing to get their performances polished in time. I will speak to Basil and the boys and see what acts they suggest as suitable.'

She paused for a moment and then continued, 'My daughter Molly is the best one to consult over decorations and flowers so I will also let my girls into the secret but I will make sure they keep their lips sealed. Just write down the date in your notebooks, and also make a note of any helpful thoughts and ideas you have over the next few days. When we see you all on Thursday night back here, your heads will be buzzing.'

Mary smiled as everyone clapped and cheered. What an

exciting time they were all going to have, getting ready for this wonderful and totally unexpected event. Mary knew it had to be the very best they'd ever done – and if it was anything to do with her, it would be.

* * *

Bella raised an eyebrow as Bobby passed her in the hall where she was standing with the phone in her hand. 'Yes, Mam, of course, and thanks, we'll see you after tea then.' She put down the phone and followed Bobby into the lounge where Lizzie was still tucked up on the sofa, enjoying a cheese sandwich.

Bobby smiled. 'What's up? Is your mam all right?'

Bella chewed her lip and nodded her head. 'I think so. She sounded a bit odd though; sort of out of breath and she wouldn't tell me where she'd been all afternoon. But she's coming over in about an hour with Martin and she's asked if Basil can be at ours as well. Oh, and apparently Molly and Earl are joining us too. She's already spoken to them. God knows what that's all about but no doubt we'll find out soon enough.'

Bobby raised an inquisitive eyebrow.

Bella shrugged and continued, 'She also wanted to know if Levi would be out at his boxing club so I told her he'd already left with his pals. From that alone I gather she has something to tell us that she doesn't want the kids to hear.' Bella put her hand to her mouth, a worried look crossing her face. 'Oh heck, I hope it's not bad news and there's nothing wrong with Mam or Martin's health.' She sat down next to Bobby who slipped an arm around her shoulders and gave her a squeeze.

'I'm sure they're just fine,' he reassured her. 'They both looked and seemed okay at the weekend. Might be something nice they have to tell us. Perhaps Martin has won the pools. Littlewoods treble chance. You never know,' he added as Bella rolled her eyes at him and laughed.

'I doubt it. He always checks his pools religiously on a Saturday teatime when the football results are on the wireless. He'd have said something on Sunday when they came round for their dinner if that was the case. Right, if our Lizzie's finished with her tea I'll get her washed and into bed. Just look at her, she's still half asleep, bless her. Mind you, Mam will want to see her. She was upset when I told her about the accident. I don't suppose it really matters if she stays up anyway; she won't have a clue what anyone is saying for most of the time. I'll just wash her and change her into her nightdress for now.' Bella picked up her daughter and carried her into the bathroom, calling over her shoulder, 'You ring Basil and let him know to come over for seven.'

'Will do,' Bobby called back.

Lizzie was almost flat out by the time she'd got her ready for bed so Bella decided to tuck her up and quietly closed the bedroom door behind her. Mam would just have to peep in on her later.

* * *

Molly and Earl were first to arrive closely followed by Basil. Bella took them through to the sitting room and left them with Bobby while she made everyone a cuppa. She brought a laden tray in and then sat down next to her sister on the sofa while Bobby, Earl and Basil took their mugs into the music room for five minutes.

'So what do you think it's all about?' Molly mused, taking a sip of tea and cradling her hands around the mug. 'This sudden meeting, I mean.'

Bella shrugged. 'No idea. But Mam sounded quite strange when I spoke to her earlier.'

'Hmm, I wonder. Hey, you don't think she's expecting, do you?' Molly grinned. 'A late baby isn't all that unusual, is it? I've heard that a lot of women get accidentally caught when they're on the change.'

Bella choked on a mouthful of tea and spluttered as it snorted back down her nose. Molly fished a hanky from up her cardigan sleeve and handed it to her sister who started to cough. She thumped her on the back and laughed. 'Would it be that much of a shock to you?'

'I suppose not,' Bella said, wiping her eyes and laughing. 'But anyway, I don't think Mam's on the change yet. She's never mentioned it. She's not that old really and nor is Martin. But I can't see them having kids somehow.'

'Nor me. Ah well, we'll find out soon enough,' Molly said. 'How's our Lizzie? I presume she's in bed? Poor little mite, having a nasty fall like that. Is she asleep?'

'She is,' Bella replied. 'She's doing okay, but she's worn out. She coped really well at the hospital. The nurse who helped us knew sign language so it made things a little easier to cope with. How are your two now? Mam said they'd had tummy upsets yesterday.'

'They're fine thanks. Don't know what made them sick, but they've made a miraculous recovery. Dianna's babysitting for us tonight. She's such a help with them and they love their big sister. I'll miss her when she gets married and moves out.'

Dianna was Earl's eldest daughter from his first marriage, and she and her fiancé Stewart were saving up to get married. She was currently living with her dad and Molly and her two half-siblings.

'Can't believe how quickly all the kids are growing up,' Bella said. 'It doesn't feel like five minutes since Dianna was only ten and she and Earl had just emigrated from America. By the way, how did your business meeting go today?'

Molly smiled. 'I know. Time's flying. Ah, there's the door. That'll be Mam and Martin. I'll go and let them in and I'll tell you later about the meeting. But just a snippet to be going on with; everything has gone well.'

* * *

Mary glanced around at her family, gathered in Bella's lounge, all looking curious as to what was going on. She smiled and took her WI notebook from her handbag. 'Right, well I bet you are all wondering what the devil is happening,' she began, her lips twitching with amusement as they leant forward in their seats and stared at her.

'Er, yes, we are,' Bella replied. 'We've got several possible theories in mind though,' she teased. 'Just wondering who will win the bet.'

Mary laughed, looking at her daughters who were as dark as she was blonde; both the image of her late dark-haired husband, and with the same big brown eyes. You'd have thought she'd had nothing to do with their creation. 'Have you now? Well go on then, tell me and I'll let you know who's right or wrong.'

'You're in the family way, Mam,' Molly blurted out as Mary and Martin stared at one another and then bent double with laughter.

'Er, no,' Mary spluttered, wiping her eyes. 'Oh my God, you're a million miles off. Anyway, don't you think we have enough of flipping kids with all your lot? Not that we don't love them,' she added. 'No, try again.'

'You've won the pools?' Bobby offered, crossing his fingers behind his back.

'Oh, lad, how I wish,' Martin said, shaking his head. 'Now that *would* be something to celebrate.' He and Bobby exchanged glances, wishing it were so.

'Any more guesses?' Mary said. 'No? Right, well you're miles off, although a pools win would have been very nice. I can see you haven't a clue, so let me get on with it. Victory Street is going to receive a royal visit.' After shocked gasps and applause had died away, she explained about the details and how the Wavertree WI had been put in charge of organising the event.

'Blimey,' Bella said, her eyes wide. 'That's a task and a half, Mam. Are you sure you're up to it?'

'Well that's where you lot come in,' Mary said. 'I couldn't do it without you.'

Basil nodded in agreement. 'And we'll do our very best to ably assist you, Mary my dear. Well what an honour it is. My darling Fenella would have been made up to be involved with an important event like this.'

Mary smiled and leant over to pat Basil on the hand. 'She most certainly would. And do you know what, Basil; we'll be doing her proud. She'll be watching over us like a strict guardian angel and we won't dare put a foot wrong!'

'I'm sure she will, Mary, I'm sure she will.'

Mary pulled herself together and consulted her notebook. 'Basil, you and the agency will of course be in charge of entertainments. Apparently, Prince Philip was a big fan of our girls during the war, so the Bryant Sisters must be top of the bill.'

'Well that goes without saying,' Basil said, nodding his agreement. 'This is so exciting. I can't wait for us to get the plans in place.'

'We'll need to close off one end of the street,' Mary said. 'Can I leave it with you to get permission from the council or whoever it is you get that from?'

'I'll sort that out,' Basil assured her.

Bella puffed out her cheeks. 'Can I tell Fran and Edie?' she asked her mam. 'Six weeks doesn't give us a lot of time to sort out new outfits. We'll need to have them made so the sooner we start the better. I'll phone them later and arrange to pop round to Edie's tomorrow and we can have a catch-up and make a few plans. They'll be absolutely made up to be included. Well we all are. '

'Yes, of course, you can tell Fran and Edie. But make sure they keep it to themselves for now,' Mary replied. 'I realise you'll have things you'll need to discuss and plan as it's a while since you sang together. Molly, I'm putting you in charge of decorations and flowers, chuck. I know we can rely on you to do us proud with your skills.'

Molly beamed and nodded. 'Well seeing as I was going to announce that the new shop plans will be going ahead and me and Earl have signed everything we need to today, this event will be our first big job.'

'Oh, Molly, congratulations,' Bella cried, giving her sister a big hug. 'Everything went well then?'

'It did. The old jeweller has closed completely now so the premises are all ours. We'll be joining you in the city in our Bold Street shop within the next couple of weeks.'

Mary smiled proudly. Her Molly had always had the gift of making a table look nice for special occasions and decorating rooms with her hand-made bunting. A while ago it had been suggested that she start her own business as the entertainments agency were often asked to supply musical acts for wedding parties and other occasions. Many times they'd also been asked if they knew anyone who could decorate the rooms or supply flower displays. Now Molly and Earl's children were a bit older, her dreams of starting her own business were about to come true.

'Dianna is also going to work alongside me,' Molly announced. 'She'll still be singing with her cousins from time to time of course, but she's asked if she can help in the shop too. It's all working out so perfectly; and how fabulous that we can actually boast a royal event as our first job.'

'It's going to be a busy time for you,' Earl said, putting an arm around Molly's shoulders. 'We pick up the keys on Friday and then it will be all hands on deck to get the place ready to open. It's in quite decent condition. The old guy looked after the premises well. It just needs freshening and brightening up a bit. When we went to look around he remembered me going in to buy Molly's engagement ring. Can you believe that?' Earl smiled. 'We'll rope in Levi and his pals to do some painting. They'll be glad to earn a few bob in their spare time.'

Mary nodded. 'Good idea. But remember, apart from Fran and Edie being told, keep quiet for now about the royal visitors, until I let you know it's okay to spread the word.'

They all agreed to the total secrecy pact and Bobby reached into the sideboard cupboard for some small glasses. He opened a bottle of sherry to toast the wonderful news, and Molly's exciting new business plans.

'Thanks, Bobby,' Molly said as he asked everyone to raise their glasses. 'We just need a suitable name now. Any suggestions are welcome.' She beamed at them all. 'That's something else for you to be thinking about.'

THREE

Bella draped Lizzie's pink angora cardigan around her shoulders and fastened the top two buttons. 'There you go. It's like a cape now and it'll keep you warm while we go and catch the bus to Aunty Edie's house.' She signed the words to her daughter while speaking slowly and directly to her.

Lizzie beamed and nodded. 'Granny's new cardie,' she said, stroking the front of the soft fluffy garment.

Bella smiled and picked up her handbag. Mam was always knitting cardigans for Lizzie and Molly's Patti, and this was the latest creation. Lizzie was talking a lot more lately. She seemed to understand almost everything, even though she couldn't hear what people were saying. And at least she could make people aware of her needs. After the shock of learning their daughter was deaf, and Bobby swearing she would not be institutionalised as many deaf people were, both he and Bella had learnt to sign to communicate with her.

Levi was brilliant at sign and patient with his little sister. Most of the family tried their best and after a fashion signed to Lizzie as well as speaking slowly and clearly, directly facing her.

Bella was convinced that lip-reading now played a big part in Lizzie's understanding of what people were saying to her.

They set off to walk down to the bus stop on Menlove Avenue, Bella holding Lizzie's uninjured hand. She seemed to be happy enough this morning but Bella and Bobby had decided that a few days off school, while she got used to her arm being in plaster, was a good idea.

They didn't have too long to wait for a bus and Bella settled Lizzie near the window and sat down beside her. She really must learn to drive, she thought for the umpteenth time this year. It had been suggested several times by Bobby who was unable to drive due to his disability, but although Bella had had a couple of lessons last year, she still felt very nervous about the idea and kept putting off booking further lessons.

They relied on Basil a lot for lifts but that couldn't go on forever. He wasn't getting any younger and one day would maybe need to depend on other people to take him out and about. Molly was already driving, which was as well now she was opening her own business. She'd passed her test late last year and Earl had bought her a little car. Bella was envious of Molly's independence. But that could also be hers if she just put her mind to it. She looked up as the bus conductor came to stand beside her.

'Been in the wars, little 'un?' he said to Lizzie.

'She has,' Bella replied for her daughter. 'She had a nasty fall at school yesterday. She's deaf,' she explained to the man as Lizzie continued to stare out of the window. 'She's not being rude and ignoring you. We're getting off at The Mystery Park stop,' she said.

'Ah, bless her,' he said, tapping the little machine hanging around his neck and handing Bella her ticket. 'I've not charged for her, poor little mite. Hope her arm gets better soon.' He dug into his jacket pocket and pulled out a small wrapped slab of Cadbury's Dairy Milk chocolate. He handed it to Bella. 'Give her that later. I was saving it for me tea break, but she'll get more pleasure from it, I'm sure.' He touched his cap in a salute and moved down the bus.

'Thank you so much,' Bella called after him and slid the chocolate into her handbag. *What a lovely man*, she thought, settling back into her seat. And what a nice treat for Lizzie. She gazed out of the window as the bus turned onto Queen's Drive and trundled past Molly and Earl's house. Molly's garden looked lovely. As did the bold and bright colours from the display of spring flowers growing in the attractive white-painted window box.

Her sister would do well with the new business. She had such a flair for putting even the simplest things together and making them look beautiful. As the bus slowed down on approach to The Mystery Park stop and she made to stand, the conductor signalled to Bella to stay in her seat until it stopped. He came and helped her to walk Lizzie to the open platform at the back of the bus and lifted the little girl down.

'Thank you. You've been so kind,' Bella said, taking hold of Lizzie's hand. Lizzie smiled at the man who put his hand to his heart.

'She reminds me of Shirley Temple, all them blonde curls,' he said, a catch in his voice. 'Take care now, little 'un.'

Lizzie was studying his face as he spoke. She pulled her hand free from her mother's and blew him a kiss. Bella laughed and waved the bus off. The conductor hung onto the pole on the platform and blew Lizzie a kiss back. 'She's stolen my heart,' he called, waving goodbye.

'The park!' Lizzie exclaimed, pulling Bella through the gate and onto the grass. 'Swings please.' She pointed but Bella shook her head and got down to Lizzie's level.

'Not today, sweetheart,' she said and explained: 'You can't hold on tight and you might fall again.'

Lizzie nodded and then squealed excitedly and pointed to a

little dachshund dog ahead on a lead. His owner, a tall black woman, waved and hurried towards them.

'Bella, Lizzie,' she said arriving beside them, puffing slightly. 'How lovely to see you both. Oh my goodness, what on earth has happened to you, little Lizzie? Were you coming to visit us, Bella?'

Bella greeted Ruby, Earl's sister, with a hug and explained about Lizzie's accident. 'How lovely to see you too. Yes, we'll pop in for a few minutes. We're on our way to see Edie and Fran for a catch-up, but we're a bit early.'

Ruby's face lit up. 'Come on then. Dolores is at home, she's not on duty until this evening. She'll be thrilled to see you.'

Bella and Lizzie followed Ruby and an excited Lucky out of the park and across onto Saint Alfred Road. She led the way up the stone steps to the glossy dark green front door of a smart white-painted three-storey Georgian house.

'Dolores, come and see who I found on the park,' she called as they made their way into the hall, Lucky's claws clattering on the polished wooden floorboards as he scuffled around.

Dolores came hurrying out of the dining room at the bottom of the hallway. 'Oh my goodness, little Lizzie, what have you done?' She dropped to her knees and signed and then gave Lizzie a gentle hug.

Bella again explained what had happened. 'I was hoping we might see you yesterday but we were in and out of the accident and emergency department and into X-ray and plastering before we could catch our breath.' Both Ruby, and Dolores who was married to Earl's brother Scotty, worked at the Royal. Dolores was a midwife and Ruby was a sister in the accident and emergency department.

'Oh, what a shame,' Ruby said. 'We were both off duty yesterday. Dolores is in later, like I told you earlier, and I'm off until tomorrow now. Come on down to the dining room and have a seat for a while until you're ready to go to Edie's.'

Bella followed Ruby into the dining room where the big window overlooked the park. As she'd walked past the door of the front sitting room her heart had beat a little faster as a million memories rushed through her head. This house used to be Bobby's family home and that large front room had been their bed-sitting room as Bobby couldn't manage the stairs.

Bella and her young mixed-race son Levi had moved in with him after their marriage, alongside her widowed mam and Molly. Their terraced home on nearby Victory Street had been damaged during the war and Bobby's mother Fenella, who had also been widowed, offered them a roof over their heads. Levi was the result of a very brief fling with Earl Franklin Junior, an African-American pilot whom she'd met while on a tour of air force base camps with the Bryant Sisters. With Earl's permission Bobby had adopted Levi and brought him up as his own child.

Earl kept in touch for updates on his son, and following his divorce he eventually emigrated to Liverpool with his daughter and sister. He met and fell in love with Bella's sister Molly. Eventually his brother Scotty and family also came to live in England and they too chose to make Liverpool their home, buying the large old house from Fenella when she decided to sell it. The sale freed up enough money to buy two new bungalows in nearby Woolton and Bella and Bobby had lived in one of them ever since, with Basil still living in the other.

Bella smiled to herself as she thought proudly of their large multicultural, musical family and how they all got along just fine. Dianna loved having her cousins Tammy and Ebony living nearby after years of being the only black girl in school. The three girls sang as a trio and Earl had chosen the name Dianna and the Crystalettes for them. He had big plans for the girls and had promised to make them famous one day. Bella was interrupted from her daydream as Ruby asked if she'd like a coffee.

'I won't thanks, Ruby. I'll be no doubt having a brew at Edie's soon enough.'

'Have a seat.' Dolores pointed to a sofa under the window. 'You looked miles away just then.'

'Memories,' Bella said as she sat down and lifted Lizzie onto her knee. Lucky curled up by Bella's feet and looked up at Lizzie who wriggled down and sat beside him on the rug where he snuggled up close to her. 'There are so many memories in this house.'

Ruby nodded. 'I'm sure there are. We love it here. I feel at times like I've never lived anywhere else, and it's not even my home, it's our Scott and Dolores's.'

Dolores laughed. 'What's ours is yours, Ruby. We wouldn't have it any other way and you know that. Your brother loves having you living with us and so do the girls.'

'Have you heard from your parents recently, Ruby?' Bella asked. Grammy and Grandpa Franklin, as Dianna called her grandparents, still lived in New Orleans where the Franklin family had settled after emigrating from South Africa many years ago. They had visited for Christmas two years ago and the whole extended family had adored them.

'Not for a couple of weeks,' Ruby replied. 'I expect we'll hear something soon. Otherwise Scotty will need to call them to make sure they're okay. I do wish they'd think seriously about coming to live with us. Mom loved her visit here but Dad likes New Orleans and I can't see him ever wanting to leave. He's too set in his ways now.'

Bella nodded. 'I know how he feels. I couldn't ever leave Liverpool to go and live abroad.'

Ruby smiled. 'Well I must admit, nor could I now. This is my adopted home and I love it. By the way, how's Molly getting along with her plans? Earl tells me everything is all signed up for the shop now.'

Bella grinned. 'Yes, she's all ready to get cracking once they collect the keys later this week.'

'She'll do well,' Dolores said. 'Tell her to let us know if we can help in any way. Both of us are a dab hand with a paintbrush.'

'I will. She'll be glad of the help. Well, I'd better make tracks across to Edie's place. Come on, Lizzie,' she signed. 'Say "Bye bye" to Lucky and your aunties.'

Lizzie smiled and waved and blew kisses and Ruby and Dolores hugged and kissed the little girl they'd taken to their hearts.

* * *

Edie was standing on the pavement wiping her red-painted windowsill down as Bella turned into the top of Victory Street. She waved at her friend and her daughter and smiled as Lizzie let go of Bella's hand and skipped towards her.

'Be careful you don't trip,' Edie signed, getting down to Lizzie's level. She gave her a hug and got back to her feet to greet Bella. 'How's she doing?'

'Okay, thanks. But it's early days so we're keeping her off school for the rest of the week until she adjusts to using one hand.'

'Come on in and I'll give Fran a knock. Blooming pigeons made a right mess out there earlier.' She threw the rag she'd used for cleaning onto the fire. 'Wish they'd go and do it across the road at Net Curtain Nellie's house. Her windows are always filthy anyway so a dollop or two of pigeon muck won't make much difference over there.'

Bella grinned as Edie popped out the back and banged on Fran's door. The neighbour opposite was a bit of a scruffy devil and let the street down, or so all the other residents who were extremely house-proud thought. Bella shuddered and felt pity for Miss Clancy, the gentle elderly lady who lived next door to her, and who had to share an outside toilet with the family.

Nellie was always at the window, fag in hand, twitching her filthy nets and spying. The woman had told countless tales and lies about the other neighbours in the street and had earned her trouble-causing name soon after moving in. She'd caused problems for Fran in the past, who now avoided her like the plague.

'I can't believe Nellie's family haven't been moved by the corporation yet,' Bella said to Edie who hurried back into the sitting room with the news that Fran was on her way.

'I know, me and Fran have said that,' Edie replied. 'I'll just pop the kettle on.' She dashed into the kitchen and then rejoined Bella. 'There are eight of them in that two-up two-down. God knows where they all sleep. They must be struggling. She told Miss Clancy next door that the corporation don't have a big enough house for them at the moment. If they stopped blooming well breeding it might help. She only had two kids when we moved in here. Now she's got six and another on the way. And that idle bugger she's married to is never in work. Says he's got a bad back. Miss Clancy has asked to be moved to a new flat. She's fed up to the back teeth of the noise, kids fighting and screaming and Nellie and the idle sod arguing and yelling, and it goes on at all hours. They've no consideration for anybody.'

'Well his back's obviously not that bad if she's expecting again,' Bella said and shook her head as Edie's back door opened and Fran's voice called out, 'Only me.'

Fran stepped into the sitting room, a big smile on her face and her four-month-old baby boy Gary on her hip. 'Good to see you, Bella and how's the little invalid?' She handed Gary to Edie and dropped down to Lizzie's height to speak to her. 'You okay?' she signed, giving Lizzie a hug.

Lizzie smiled and nodded. 'I want to play with 'Raine and Dennis.'

'They are at school,' Fran signed. 'You can sit with baby for me and look after him. It's a big girl's job. I think you can do it better than Lorraine can.'

Lizzie's face lit up and she nodded. 'Okay.'

'I'll just nip back home and bring his trolley in and then he can sit in that while she minds him,' Fran said, dashing back out of the house. She returned in a flash with the trolley and strapped Gary into the seat with a cushion behind him to help keep him upright. 'That'll keep her occupied and him too,' she directed at Bella. 'He's not taken his eyes off her since we came in. Bless him.'

Bella smiled. 'Thanks, Fran, it's nice of you to give her a bit of responsibility. She'll feel important.'

'Kettle's boiling so I'll make us a pot of tea and get her some milk and biscuits,' Edie said. 'Then you can tell us what's going on. We're both curious after your phone call last night.'

With Lizzie settled on the hearthrug, chatting to Gary who was staring wide-eyed at her, Fran poured tea into three mugs at the table, and Bella began her tale. Her friends stared open-mouthed as she explained that their street would be the one visited by royalty and that the Bryant Sisters would be the main event on the show that would follow.

'Wow!' Fran exclaimed. 'That's fabulous news. So Victory Street, out of all others in the area, is the one?'

Bella nodded. 'Mam said she thinks it's because Prince Philip had a soft spot for our songs during the war. Not sure how true that is, but it'll do for me.'

'And me,' said Edie with a grin. 'Oh my God, can you imagine the neighbours once they're told? They'll all be so thrilled to bits. Well, all except for her across, of course. They'll be out painting the front steps and tarting up their window boxes.'

'Maybe someone could do hers in secret when it gets dark,' Fran suggested.

'Maybe, we'll see,' Edie said. 'You never know, she might even be willing to help, although pigs might fly. I've just bought new nets for the front room so she can have the old one. At least it will be clean.'

'Well, apart from worrying about Nellie and her mucky steps, we need to think about what we're going to sing,' Bella said. 'It's a few months since we last worked together, since before Gary was born, in fact. We'll need new outfits and I'll arrange us a meeting with Basil. Can you two sort out getting the kids minded or picked up from school one day soon and let me know what day suits you both best and then I'll book us in with Basil to discuss this further? Mam's got another WI meeting tomorrow afternoon so I'll have a bit more information after that.'

Fran and Edie nodded in unison. 'Our mams will help with the kids,' Edie said. 'But obviously we will keep this to ourselves until it's all confirmed properly.'

'Let's raise a toast,' Bella said, lifting her mug of tea in the air. 'To Her Majesty Queen Elizabeth and Prince Philip, and our own Victory Street.'

'Hear, hear,' Fran and Edie said, clinking their mugs with Bella's.

FOUR

LIVERPOOL, MAY 1956

Friday morning, Molly opened the door to her new Bold Street shop and stepped inside, Earl and Dianna on her heels. They'd just been to collect the keys from the estate agency and it was now all theirs. She smiled as they looked around; taking in what work needed to be done to freshen the place up. The wooden-topped counter was in a good position, almost directly opposite the door, and could stay there. The glass counter frontage would be useful for showing off any small displays she made, so that could also stay. The double windows were a good size for displaying her larger floral arrangements.

'Well apart from painting all the walls and woodwork white I think it will be fine,' Molly said, nodding her head slowly. 'We can get that done this weekend maybe and then get someone in to put some new floor covering down early next week. The carpet is worn and grubby so needs chucking out. I quite fancy some oilcloth that looks a bit like light parquet flooring. And maybe have a large rug just in front of the counter, a grass-green shade would look lovely and fresh and go with the flowers. The floor will be easy to mop clean. We can get a couple of second-hand chairs for our customers to sit on while they decide what they want to buy. The sink in the little back area will be great if we can fix a worktop next to it so I can do the flowers in there. I'll need a few shelves putting up in there too.'

Earl nodded his agreement. 'I can arrange to get those jobs done. It all sounds just right to me. What about you, Dianna? Do you think that all sounds okay?'

'Sounds perfect, Dad,' Dianna replied, nodding her head, her glossy dark brown ringlets bouncing on her shoulders. 'But I think the wooden shelves in the alcove would look nicer painted in green to match the rug when we get it. Gives a bit more contrast against all the white. And if we can find two old wooden chairs with arms we can paint them green too and put contrasting cushions on them; maybe in a nice gingham fabric. I bet Aunt Dolores will have some suitable scraps in her work cupboard. She never throws any fabric bits away.'

'That's a great idea, Dianna,' Molly said, giving her stepdaughter a hug. 'I can see you will be a brilliant assistant to me. We'll go for the green paint then and you can ask Dolores for some scraps to make a couple of nice cushions.'

'I'll get the guy that did our studio signs to come and measure up for the sign outside as well,' Earl said. 'Have we got a name in mind yet?'

'Nearly,' Molly said. 'We'll have another discussion tonight and settle on something.'

'Okay. That's a deal then. I'll drop you two back home and go and pick up some paint and brushes and stuff and I'll speak to Levi later. Get him to round up a couple of his mates for painting sessions on Saturday and Sunday. With a bit of luck you can be ready for opening the following weekend.'

Molly nodded. 'I need to order some supplies from the wholesalers and we'll be ready to start. We'll be very busy for the next few weeks, that's for sure. Actually, Earl, drop us off at Mam's and we'll have a brew with her and see how the meeting went last night. We can get the bus back to Queen's Drive when we're ready.'

* * *

Mary welcomed her daughter and Dianna inside and they followed her into the sitting room where the coffee table was covered in bits of paper with notes scribbled on each one.

'Excuse the mess,' Mary apologised. 'I'm just trying to co-ordinate everything into little piles so I know where I'm up to. Sit down and I'll make us a cuppa.'

Molly smiled and she and Dianna took seats on the sofa under the window. Mary came back through with a tray of mugs and slices of her home-made Victoria sponge.

'Just clear a bit of space for me, love,' she directed at Molly who stacked the papers to one side.

'Hope I haven't mucked up your filing system,' Molly said with a grin.

'Oh, it'll get sorted later,' Mary said, handing them their mugs. 'It's just nice to have a break and to see you two. So, how did it go today? I know you said you were picking up the shop keys this morning.'

Molly nodded. 'We did and it's all good. Earl's getting the paint organised and we'll make a start tomorrow. It's not too bad really. We'll probably be open by next weekend. Well that's what we're aiming for anyway. We just need to agree on a name so the bloke can get the sign made up.'

'Anything in mind?' Mary asked, holding out the plate with the cake on to Dianna who smiled and helped herself to a piece.

'Hmm, sort of. Still not quite sure but it's a choice between *Bold Street Blooms and Bunting* which ties in with *Bold Street Enterprises*, of course, and we hope to get a fair bit of work from them. When they book wedding acts they can refer clients to us if they ask about flowers and decorations. So it does make sense.

The other name was *Molly's Floral Creations*, but that title doesn't say enough about the business really. They might just think it's a flower shop but we want to be much more than that.'

'Oh of course you do,' Mary agreed. 'You'll get asked to do displays for funerals and all sorts; as well as weddings.'

Molly smiled. 'Yes, no doubt, but I'll feel really sad making up funeral sprays and wreaths.'

'Well someone has to do it, chuck. Might as well be you. You can show compassion where others can't. That's very important to somebody who's been newly bereaved. '

Molly sighed. 'Yes, of course it is. I'm sure we'll cope. How did the meeting go last night?'

'Okay, love. I've asked them all what jobs they feel they will be best at. Some have offered to make cakes and other food related stuff so that will be the street party buffet sorted. A few are good at sewing so they can help with making bunting. We'll need a heck of a lot of it this time, more than we had for the coronation do's we put on. Some of that bunting is in the cupboard at the church hall but it got left outside in the rain and looks a bit tired and mucky. I'll fetch it back here and give it a soak in my new washer. A bit of Omo soap powder will brighten it up. There are a couple of large Union Jacks as well so I'll give them a rinse and an airing.'

'You could ask the ladies if they have any red, white or blue items they no longer use or wear or even scraps of fabric lying around,' Dianna said. 'We can ask my aunties to help as they love sewing and will happily make some bunting for us.'

'I'll do that, love,' Mary said. 'We're having an extra meeting again next Tuesday so I'll put that on my list. Might as well as make good use of old clothes if they've anything to get rid of rather than waste money buying yards of stuff. We can always get some yardage from Paddy's market as well if we need to. I think we're going to make a few leaflets to put through all the doors on Victory Street next week and then word of mouth will no doubt tell all the surrounding streets. Although I believe we'll have to limit the actual royal visit to the residents only. The rest will see them when the car arrives and departs. There has to be a few rules for safety's sake. But people can come to the party later and watch the last bits of entertainment too.'

'Well it looks like everything is under control, so far so good,' Molly said. She finished her mug of tea and smiled. 'Would you be able to keep an eye on Patti and Harry tomorrow for a few hours, Mam, while I supervise the work in the shop?'

'Of course I will, chuck. Bring them round when you're on your way down to Bold Street. I need to have a word with Basil this weekend as well, just so I can report back to the ladies what he's planning to do with regards to the entertainment side of things. Madam President wants a brass band that will play the national anthem. I suggested the boys' brigade as they are quite good, I've heard them rehearsing. But she pulled a face at that; I think she's expecting a bit more. However, we can't run to the Queen's Guard with their red suits and bearskin hats.'

Molly laughed. 'One of the forces bands might be a good plan. They'll look great on stage in uniform. That's a job for Basil, definitely. I'll give him a call when we get home, Mam. He and Earl might be able to get some of the guys from RAF Burtonwood to help us. Earl's still in touch with some of them. They could back the Bryant Sisters too. Right,' she said, getting to her feet. 'I think we'd better be making tracks, Dianna. Got to pick the monkeys up from nursery and school. We should just make it if we catch the next bus. See you tomorrow, Mam. Thanks for the tea and cake.'

* * *

Basil sat back on his seat and crossed another item off his long list. He'd just spoken to Bella and she and the girls were going to pop in to see him and run through a couple of songs next week.

They had also booked an appointment at the dressmaker's down Bold Street so that was them sorted out with their outfits. They knew what suited best so he'd leave the choice to them. Molly had also called him to let him know that the WI president wanted a brass band.

He was one step ahead on that and was waiting for a call back from a forces band leader he'd remained friendly with since the days of his Entertainments and National Service Association tours; commonly known as ENSA. He reckoned that the royal entourage wouldn't be staying around too long but there would be time for the girls to entertain them with a couple of songs and make sure they met the residents of Victory Street.

It was also usual to present a bouquet of flowers to Her Majesty on these types of occasions, usually handed over by a little one, so Molly could see to the flowers and he reckoned he knew the perfect little lady to present them. He'd need to speak to her parents first of course, to make sure they felt she would be up to it. He'd do that tonight when he got home.

Meantime he'd try and contact a few more of his stable of artistes to see if they'd like to perform for the Victory Street residents later in the evening. He smiled as he thought about his beautiful Fenella and, although he wasn't one for fanciful thinking, he was sure her spirit was guiding him at times. She'd make sure he got it right, you could bet on it.

* * *

Bella felt her eyes filling as Basil asked her and Bobby if they'd agree to let Lizzie present a bouquet of flowers to the queen.

'Oh, Basil, that would be wonderful. She'll be so thrilled to bits. As soon as Mam says we can start to mention it we'll sit her down and explain things to her. We'll have a few practice sessions, maybe she could pretend Ethel was queen and get her to curtsey and hand the flowers over nicely.' Ethel was her mam's best friend from schooldays onwards. She was also Basil's good friend and the two kept one another company at weekends since Fenella had passed away.

Basil laughed. 'Et would be tickled pink to play queen. She'll be made up when I tell her.'

'Well there's no point in Mam doing it because Lizzie knows she's her granny and not the queen, but we can pretend Aunty Et is for a day or two until she gets it right.'

Bobby grinned. 'That'll be fun. But thanks Basil, Lizzie will love meeting the queen, be it Aunty Et or the real one. It'll be so exciting for her and such lovely memories for us to treasure as she gets older.'

'Lizzie is the perfect choice with her cute smile and blonde curls,' Basil said. 'I think she has a look of Princess Anne and I bet the royal couple will see that too. Now as you know we're putting a bit of a show on in the evening for the residents,' he continued. 'I think it would be nice if Levi and his two mates could sing something for them. Maybe a bit of the skiffle music they seem to like. That Lonnie Donegan's "Rock Island Line" seems to be a top favourite right now with the young ones.'

Bobby nodded. 'I caught them doing that the other day when they skipped off school. I'm sure they'd love to sing it in front of an audience.'

'Well, get them into the studio and we'll have them learn a couple of songs this next week – once we can tell them, that is. I hope Mary has some news very soon as it's not easy to keep our traps shut when there's so much to do and so little time to do it in.'

'Molly said it should be next week,' Bella said. 'She called me earlier. And the Victory Street residents will be getting told then as well. They can start to get their street ready. They'll be so proud, they honestly will. I know most of them will pull their weight in getting it ready. And you know what Fran's like. She'll soon sort anyone out who doesn't.'

Bobby and Basil laughed. 'I wouldn't like to be in any shirker's shoes with Fran on the job,' Basil said. 'Well, it's all coming together.'

Bobby nodded. 'That'll be thanks to my mum watching and guiding proceedings from her heavenly throne.'

Basil raised an ironical eyebrow and grinned. 'Now it's funny you should say that...'

FIVE

WAVERTREE, JUNE 1956

'Put one through each letterbox,' Mary said to Fran, pointing to the small stack of handwritten leaflets sitting on Edie's dining table. 'I think it might be a good idea to have a bit of a residents' meeting as soon as possible. Most of them are nosy enough to see that it's you and Edie pushing those through the doors so you will be collared no doubt and questions will be asked. Perhaps we can get everyone to meet on The Mystery Park on Sunday afternoon about two thirty for a planning committee meeting.'

'That's a good idea,' Edie said. 'Then we can just give them a run-through of what the plans are and ask everyone to make a bit of effort in getting the street looking as nice as we can make it. Weeding between the cobbles and freshening everything up, that sort of thing.'

Mary nodded. 'Just get the word out there. There'll be them that are dead keen and the usual moaners who are not. We can offer help to the older residents in whatever way they need it. Right, well I'll leave this with you two and I'm going to take myself into the city now and visit our Molly's new place, see how she's getting on with the decorations for the street. I'll be in touch about Sunday and I'll see you on the park. Let's hope the weather stays nice and bright this month. June's usually decent, fingers crossed.'

'See you Sunday, Mary.' Edie gave her a hug and a peck on the cheek and Fran did likewise. Edie saw her out and rejoined Fran in the back sitting room. 'Shall we have a quick cuppa and then make a start?' Edie asked. 'Get it done before we pick up the kids from school. Gary will probably fall asleep while we're out so that'll kill two birds with one stone.'

Fran smiled and picked Gary up from the rug where he was trying his hardest to roll over. 'Might as well. We're out with Bella at the studio tomorrow so best we do the posting today then it's done with. I'll just go and pop this little man in his pram and meet you out on the street. Bring Max for a walk as well, it'll do him good.'

'Good idea.' Edie nodded and rooted in the sideboard drawer for Max's collar and lead. 'He's getting a bit too chubby, he needs more exercise. He's been at my mam's most of this week as you know and she feeds him too many treats.'

The little Welsh corgi pricked up his ears at the mention of his name and looked at her as though disagreeing with her comment. He got up slowly from his basket, strolled across the room and with a huge sigh dropped down by her feet.

'Oh, Max, don't look so fed up,' Edie said, laughing. 'You enjoy a walkies once you make the effort and just think of all the lampposts you get to sniff while we're out there.' She slipped his collar and lead on and tickled his ears. 'Come on, lazy bones.' He trotted after Edie down the hall and out onto the street.

Fran was already standing outside with Gary in his pram, talking to Miss Clancy from opposite. 'Morning, Miss Clancy,' Edie greeted their older neighbour who was smartly dressed in a two-piece, olive-green suit, her wavy grey hair neatly styled. 'You look very nice.'

'Good morning, Edie and Max, and thank you.' Miss Clancy bent to stroke Max's ears. 'Fran said you have something really nice to tell us all. I'm intrigued, my dear.'

'We do indeed.' Edie handed one of Mary's hand-made leaflets to the old lady who peered over the top of her spectacles as she read it. Edie often wondered why she wore them if she couldn't see to read through the lenses. But she smiled as Miss Clancy gasped out loud.

'Oh my goodness, this is wonderful news. Their royal highnesses are gracing us with their presence.' She shook her head in amazement. 'Why us though? Out of all the streets to choose from in Liverpool, why choose Victory Street? I mean, it's not as if it's the grandest street in the city.'

'Well that's just it,' Fran replied. 'It's to visit ordinary folk in an ordinary street. *And*,' she continued with a twinkle in her eye, 'Prince Philip is a fan of the Bryant Sisters, apparently. We're going to sing a couple of songs while they're here.'

'How wonderful,' Miss Clancy said, beaming from ear to ear.

'Join us on The Mystery Park on Sunday at two thirty and we'll reveal the full plans to you,' Fran said. 'Bella's mam Mary from the WI is in charge and of course she used to live on this street many years ago when her family were growing up.'

'I will most certainly be there and I'll help spread the word,' Miss Clancy said. 'This involves our street only, I presume?'

'That's correct,' Fran replied. 'The rest of the area will be invited later to the show we are putting on, but for the royal visit the numbers need to be kept to Victory Street residents only.'

'Are you going to put one through *her* letterbox?' Miss Clancy inclined her head backwards in the direction of her next-door neighbour's house, wrinkling her pert little nose in disgust.

Edie nodded. 'We'll have to, but I doubt they'll come. They never join in anything. We need to do something about the state of the front of the house, even if it has to be done in secret. Leave it with me; I'll be as discreet as can be.'

'God help you, love,' Miss Clancy said. 'I've just come back from seeing a man at the Wavertree town hall housing department. That's why I've got me best suit on. They've promised me a flat in Allerton later this year. I'm top of the list for one in a new block. I love Victory Street but it's never been the same for me since *they* moved in next door. My nerves can't take it anymore. I'll only turn down the offer, when it comes, if they've moved them before me.'

'Oh I'm sorry Miss Clancy, I don't want you to be pushed out,' said Edie.

'Ah bless you chuck. Really I feel sorry for whoever gets that house after me. The landlord will need to get it fumigated before he rents it out to anyone else. This week I've had big black beetles coming through from under the gap in the skirting boards in the front room. They call them black witches. They've got white powder on their backs and I know it's DDT. No doubt she's trying to get rid of them, but cleaning the place up might help a bit. They wouldn't come into her house then in the first place. Anyway, that did it for me so I marched in that town hall with determination today and they actually said they were about to write to me about the new flats. So I've saved them a job and it gives me a bit of peace of mind to be going on with.'

'I'm sure it does,' Fran said, patting the old lady's shoulder and inwardly shuddering at the thought of black beetles invading her home. 'It will all work out for you and if in the meantime you are frightened or worried about anything, you know you only have to knock on mine or Edie's doors for help. Good luck with everything and we'll see you on the park on Sunday afternoon.'

* * *

Mary strolled up Bold Street towards Molly's new shop. Her daughter was busy arranging bunches of colourful flowers and green foliage in buckets standing on wooden platforms outside on the pavement under the two front windows. Dianna waved at her from inside the shop where she was artistically placing a few plants in painted ceramic pots along with some pottery figurines of little animals. The shopfront looked bright and cheerful and the freshly painted name sign hung above the door. Mary felt a rush of pride and gave her girl a hug as Molly stood up to greet her.

'It looks beautiful, chuck,' she said and Molly beamed and gave her mam a hug back.

'Thanks, Mam. We're getting there. I need a bit more stock for the shelves inside but it's deciding what to buy. Come on in and we'll make you a nice cuppa.'

'I've brought you a flask of tea,' Mary said, patting her shopping bag, 'and some cake. I wasn't sure if you'd have anywhere to make yourself a brew yet.'

'Ah well, we got a lovely new kettle from Basil as an opening gift,' Molly said. 'It's one of those new electric kettles that you plug in. Saves us having to keep going over to the studios and begging a brew.' She laughed. 'Think we were driving them mad. But we might as well drink yours seeing as you've gone to the trouble of making it for us. Thanks, Mam.'

'Them electric kettles worry me,' Mary said, following Molly into the shop. 'Water and electric don't mix in my opinion. But it seems to be the way forward. I mean, look at them new irons, where you put water in and they puff out steam. I'd be worried about getting electrocuted. It's not natural. Better pressing stuff while it's still a bit damp or using a wet cloth and a flat iron.'

Molly laughed and got three mugs down from a shelf in the little back kitchen area. She filled them with tea from her mam's flask and put the cake slices onto a plate. 'It's what they call progress, Mam. All meant to help make life simpler for the modern housewife. I mean, look how much you enjoy your new washing machine after saying for months you didn't want one because you thought they were dangerous.'

'Hmm,' Mary said, pursing her lips. 'I'm still a bit wary at times but you're right, it does make life easier on washdays and it's done me no harm yet. I'm still here to tell the tale.'

'There you go then. Shall we take these through to the shop? There are a couple of chairs near the counter so you can take the weight off your legs for a while.'

Mary followed Molly and parked herself on one of the chairs. She looked around, smiling. 'It all looks so fresh and clean. The green and white paintwork looks lovely, just right for a flower shop. Who made the cushions on the chairs?' She picked up the one from behind her and took a closer look. The intricate patchwork design in green, white and yellow fabric with a neat frill around all four edges of the cushion was perfect for the wooden Windsor chairs that were painted in a dark green gloss.

'Aunt Ruby made them,' Dianna said. 'She's an expert at patchworking, Grammy taught her.'

'Well they look lovely,' Mary said. 'I bet if she made some to sell in here they'd go down a treat. I'd buy four to go on my three-piece suite.'

Molly nodded. 'That's a good idea, Mam. We need a few different things to fill the shelves with. People could buy them for gifts or to use at home. I'll see what Ruby says and if she has the time to do that. She's busy making us some bunting in the same fabrics to hang in the shop to pretty it up a bit and so people can see that we will make and supply for their parties. After all, it *is* in the name!'

Mary smiled. 'So you made a choice then?'

Molly laughed. 'We did. Welcome to Bold Street Blooms and Bunting. Me and Dianna are in the throes of cutting out hundreds of V-shapes for the street party bunting in the red, white and blue scraps that have been given to us so it's been a big help having Ruby do the cushions for us. She and Dolores will help us with the party bunting too as they have two sewing machines at their house. Scotty got us the chairs for free from a place that he's renovating to sell on and Earl painted them for us. They're just the job for customers to rest on while they decide what they want to buy.'

Dianna beamed. 'I've just had a thought. Aunt Ruby can make gorgeous rag dolls too. You know the ones she made for Patti and Lizzie for last Christmas, well she made them for me and the twins too when we were small. I still have mine. She's in brown fabric and I called her Topsy. But she can make white dolls as well like Lizzie's is.'

'Now a couple of nice rag dolls would look lovely sitting on the shelves,' Mary said, nodding her approval.

'I'll have a chat with her about it,' Dianna said. 'I'm sure she'll be thrilled to be asked. She loves being involved in anything to do with our families.'

Molly smiled. 'That will be great, Dianna. Thanks, love.'

'I'll just finish this tea and then I'll get on my way,' Mary said. 'I've that much to do; I'm meeting myself coming backwards at the moment. I've got our Lizzie in the morning while Bella comes down here with Edie and Fran for a rehearsal and to get fitted for their new dresses for the show.'

'It'll all be worth it, Mam,' Molly said. 'Just you wait and see.'

* * *

Basil picked up Bella, Fran and Edie from their respective addresses to take them all into the city for their rehearsal and dress shop appointments. He'd taken Lizzie to Mary's earlier to be looked after for a few hours; dropped Bobby off there at the same time and then Martin was running him down to the studio.

Mary had told Basil she'd just come off the phone to that woman who'd taken over from Fenella at the WI. Eva Thompson had been panicking like a headless chicken, according to Mary. Eva had been informed by the powers that be, whoever they were, that British Pathé News would be filming the royal visit and subsequent events as they had done previously during the 1954 visits. It was good news as far as Basil was concerned as all publicity helped their businesses and his acts were sure to get a mention.

But that dozy Eva one couldn't organise a piss-up in a brewery and she seemed to be leaving most of the hard work to Mary as far as Basil could see. Poor Mary was wearing herself out trying to pull it all together. She'd told him that Eva was good at making notes and giving orders but was totally useless at doing anything practical. Basil thought it was time that Mary was promoted to president; she could do the job blindfolded. Ah well, there may come a day in the not too distant future when that could happen. If anyone deserved it, Mary certainly did.

* * *

Fran and Edie were waiting on the front as Basil pulled up with Bella in the passenger seat. Nellie's grubby nets twitched as the girls got into the back seat and Fran gave her a royal wave as they pulled away. She grinned and settled back into her seat.

'Nosy bugger,' she said. 'Oh I'm so excited about this. I'm so pleased the war is over at last but I miss singing together, it feels like years.'

'It nearly is,' Bella said, turning to talk to Fran. 'We really do need to do a bit more. I know it's hard to find the time with the kids and running a home and what have you, but we always enjoyed performing and it's doing something for ourselves that will help keep us young.'

'We need to get you recording again,' Basil said. 'There's that upcoming trio of sisters who are actually related, The Beverley Sisters, and they seem to be doing okay. They had quite a big hit record at Christmas.'

'Hmm,' Edie said, nodding. '"I Saw Mommy Kissing Santa Claus". I really liked the way they sang it. Maybe for next Christmas we could do something similar, get us back into it again.'

'Yes,' Basil agreed. 'Let's see how things go with this show and then we can talk about it.'

SIX

LIVERPOOL, JUNE 1956

'Cast your eyes over this.' Basil handed a sheet of paper to the girls. On it he had listed five songs and asked them to choose two to sing for the royal couple, the rest, he said, they could perform later in the day.

Bella scanned the list and looked at Fran and Edie. 'One of these has to be "Boogie Woogie Bugle Boy",' she said. 'It was always every audience's favourite and I bet Prince Philip will love it.'

'Oh definitely,' Fran agreed and Edie nodded. 'Then something more modern for our second song. What about Kay Starr's "Rock'n'Roll Waltz"?'

'Yeah,' Edie agreed. 'I think most people like that. It's such a sweet song.'

Bella nodded. 'That's okay with me. There you go, Basil. That didn't take us long.'

'Good choices,' Basil said. 'Right, I've got half a band set up for rehearsals today, the rest will be here later in the week, but at least we've got a bugle player. Your Sam will be playing the drums, Fran, but he's working today and Edie's Stevie has offered his services as sax player. Earl's going to sing a couple at the evening show and hopefully Levi and the lads and Dianna and her cousins will also perform. So this show is a real family affair.'

'It should be a really good night,' Bella said. 'And there will be some younger people in the audience who will appreciate a few newer songs than we normally do. Levi wants to do a bit of skiffle Lonnie Donegan style *and* he's been singing a couple of Elvis songs in his bedroom this week. He sounded pretty good actually. We've sorted them a washboard out and some thimbles. Mam had kept her old one so she's given it to them and some of her ladies at the WI came up with a few spare thimbles so that's them sorted.'

'Right, girls, let's get these songs sung, see how they sound and then you can go and get yourselves sorted out with your new dresses.'

'It's all go from now on,' Bobby said. He smiled at them from his seat by the desk and pointed behind them. 'You'll have to share the microphones; and I've set some up for the band members.'

'Okay, boys,' Basil raised his hand and counted the band in. The bugle player blasted out the opening notes and the girls began to sing, transporting Basil back to his days as an entertainments manager for the ENSA group. He'd taken his artistes to most of the military and air force bases in the country during the war years. He couldn't have wished for a better job. They'd had their ups and downs over the years but it was a time in his life he wouldn't have swapped for any other line of work. As the girls finished the song he and Bobby clapped, and Earl, who had just arrived, whistled through his fingers and shouted, 'More.'

'We haven't sung the next one before, so be gentle with us,' Bella said with a laugh.

They started to sing the lovely "Rock'n'Roll" waltz and Earl grabbed hold of their receptionist Emily who had just popped up the stairs and whisked her around the floor. She laughed and hummed along. As the song ended Earl bowed and thanked her.

'I've just come up to see if anyone is ready for a brew yet,' she said, grinning. 'But I can see you're all a bit busy so I'll come back later. I wasn't expecting to have a dance as well. Thank you, Earl.'

'My pleasure, young lady,' Earl replied. 'That was great, ladies,' he said. 'The Bryant Sisters are back in business.'

'Well, for now we are,' Fran said. 'We'll have to see what the future brings. But it's my guess the young ones will steal the show in the evening with all this new-style music that's coming our way from America.'

Bella nodded her agreement. 'Levi informs me that he and his mates are now called teenagers. That's a new word to get your heads around. They were down at the docks last week after school and the sailors from the States are bringing in loads of new records.'

Earl smiled. 'The Cunard Yanks are bringing across some good stuff. I love it. We're in the throes of a whole new sound in music and we may as well get used to it because it's coming over here in a big way. Our kids are going to love it.'

Basil sighed. 'Maybe the younger generation is what we need to concentrate on once this royal show is behind us. I know Dianna and the twins are itching to sing more modern music when the twins have finished their typing courses that my brother insisted they do, just in case. We need to write more songs for them. I suggest we listen to everything we can that's popular right now and Fran and Bobby start thinking about working on a few new songs with Di and the twins in mind.'

Fran smiled. 'I'm up for that. Bobby?'

Bobby nodded. 'Count me in. Let's get a foothold on this new sound before others beat us to it.'

'Right, girls, just run through those other songs on the list, particularly that Dream Weavers' "It's Almost Tomorrow" as it's one you've never done before, then Earl can do his songs and then you three are free to go to the dressmaker's.'

'What are you singing, Earl?' Bella asked.

'Erm, Dean Martin's "Memories Are Made of This" and Jimmy Young's "Unchained Melody", I believe,' Earl replied. 'Although I know the songs reasonably well, I haven't performed them before, so be prepared for a few mixed-up words today.'

'Here,' Bobby said, rooting in a desk drawer. 'I've got you the sheet music, so you've no excuses now.'

After performing the songs chosen for them, the girls perched on chairs and listened to Earl singing his.

'Earl's voice gives me goosebumps,' Fran whispered to Bella as "Unchained Melody" came to an end. 'It's so rich and deep.'

'It is,' Bella agreed. 'They'll love him as they always do when he performs.' She got to her feet. 'Right then, let's go and sort out our outfits. I've not had a new dress for ages, so I'm looking forward to this. We'll pop our heads in Molly's shop and say hello to her and Dianna while we're down that end of the street.'

* * *

After their visit to the dressmaker's, Fran and Edie decided to do some shopping in the city while they had the chance without carting their kids along. Bella wanted to get back home so she said goodbye and got on a bus to go to her mam's to pick up Lizzie. She felt very happy with the choice of dress they had all decided on, a full-skirted, buttoned bodice with a sweetheart neckline and short sleeves in a bright blue cotton fabric with white spots. Very fashionable at the moment with the more mature ladies as well as the younger generation, so they'd been told by Sarah who owned the dressmaking business. She'd shown them pictures in magazines of girls wearing the style for dancing and theatre-going. Well no matter what, it would be a nice summer dress to add to her wardrobe.

She had also enquired about taking Lizzie into the shop and having a new dress made for her to wear when she presented Queen Elizabeth with the flowers. She'd ask Molly what colours she was putting in the bouquet and have Lizzie's dress made up in similar colours. They were popping into the dress-maker's next week for a measure-up. Lizzie's arm would be more comfortable a week down the line so her sling could be removed without causing her any discomfort.

As the bus approached her stop she lifted the bag Molly had handed to her and made her way to the platform. Molly had asked if she had the time could she cut out some V-shapes for the bunting that was to decorate Victory Street. Bella had laughed and said of course. Cutting out was no problem to her but sewing the pieces together was another matter. Apparently, Dolores and Ruby had volunteered for the sewing side of bunting making. Dianna and her fiancé Stewart would collect the prepared pieces from her tomorrow night and take them to her aunties. Molly had a good production line going.

Bella jumped off the bus and walked the short distance to her mam and Martin's bungalow. She could hear Lizzie's piping voice and her high-pitched laughter as she opened the gate.

'Here's your mammy,' she heard Martin say and Lizzie hurtled down the path from the back garden.

'Be careful you don't fall again,' Bella gasped as her daughter banged into her legs in her haste. She dropped down to Lizzie's height and gave her a hug while signing a warning to be careful. Martin came around the side of the bungalow and gave her a wave.

'Your mam's got the kettle on,' he said. 'Lizzie's just been helping me in the garden. Sorry she's a bit mucky but she's enjoyed herself.'

'I'm sure she has and thanks for letting her play with you.

Let's go inside now and see Granny,' she signed to Lizzie who nodded eagerly.

'Granny's made cake,' she announced.

'Well in that case, how can we say no?'

Mary popped her head around the corner. 'Come on in and have a cuppa. Martin will run you back to yours in a bit,' she said, leading the way into the kitchen. 'Sit down while I pour and then you can tell us how the rehearsal went and what dresses you've decided on. More things to tick off the never-ending list, but we're getting there.'

'We are, Mam, everything is going just great. And it's all down to you and your great organisational skills.'

Mary beamed. 'Well if it wasn't for my talented family I couldn't have done this job and I'm not sure anyone else could either.'

'We need a name for our group,' Levi said to his friends Kenny and Jimmy as they made their way to the Bold Street Studios for their after-school rehearsal. 'It's gotta be something different, but I'm not sure what. Maybe Dad can help us think of something. We'll ask him when we get to the studio.'

'Which dad do you mean?' Kenny asked. 'Bobby or Earl?'

Levi shrugged. 'Either of them. They'll both be there and they're both my dads.' He swapped his guitar case to his other hand and smiled. 'I know you two think it's a bit weird, but it works for my family.'

'I think you're dead lucky that they both encourage you in playing your guitar and singing,' Kenny said. 'I have to keep quiet when I'm at home because of my dad.'

Levi nodded. He was very lucky and he knew it. Kenny's dad had been injured during the war and had been badly disabled ever since. He'd been unable to work and was now bedridden in the front room of the family's tiny terraced house. Sharing a bedroom with his brothers meant Kenny had nowhere that he could enjoy making music except at Levi's parents' places. Both sets always made him welcome and he'd told Levi he loved being a part of his big, and sometimes noisy, family.

'Same here,' Jimmy said. 'I'm not allowed to make any noise either in case I wake me little sisters up. Mam won't let me have the wireless on after seven. She wouldn't even let me finish listening to *The Goon Show* the other night because our Sheila had a flipping earache. It's dead boring and they're all driving me crackers. That's why it's always nice to be at yours, Levi. And I'm really looking forward to having a go in the studio today. It's dead good that your dads are giving us this opportunity. Be great if they can help us decide on a name for our group as well.'

Levi nodded as they walked into the shop to be greeted by Emily who told them they were expected and to go straight upstairs to the studio. 'I'll bring you up a glass of squash each in a few minutes,' she said. 'I've a couple of calls to make first.'

'Thanks, Emily,' Levi said, leading the way upstairs.

'Hey, boys,' Basil greeted them. 'Thanks for getting here on time. I know the buses are not always easy to get on from school.'

'We were dead lucky,' Kenny said. 'A full one left as an empty one turned up right behind it. We were first on.'

'Right, well get your blazers off and make yourselves comfortable. Ah, here's Earl with the list of songs you suggested to him.'

'All right, boys?' Earl greeted them, closely followed by Bobby who nodded and smiled a friendly welcome. 'We've got the room ready for you back there. Washboard and thimbles are waiting for Kenny and we've also got a tea-chest bass for Jimmy to play. One of our band members made it for you. Now I know "Rock Island Line" is the top favourite and I agree you should give it a go. Bobby tells me you do it really well.'

The boys all smiled proudly.

Earl continued. 'Maybe choose one of the Elvis songs next

and then finish with "See You Later Alligator". We will have a full band backing you, like Bill Haley's Comets, so that should be good, and people will join in and sing along. You can finish the night at the street party, do the whole finale. Once the royals have left we'll be joined by the other streets nearby for refreshments and I think there will be a lot of kids of your age who will like your kind of music. That new dance style is taking off so give them something to jive to. How does that sound? Dianna and the girls will do a couple of numbers before you but we'll use you boys as the finale.'

The three boys beamed. 'Sounds great to me,' Levi said as Kenny and Jimmy nodded their approval. 'We need a name. Will you help us to decide please? The lad in the class above us that plays skiffle with his mates, that John Lennon, who lives around the corner from us on Menlove Avenue, he's called his group The Quarrymen after our school. We think that sounds really good. So we need something catchy but God knows what.'

'We'll get our heads together,' Earl said. 'By the time you leave the studio, I promise you will have a name to be proud of.'

* * *

Basil drove the boys home after their rehearsal and the conversation in the car was charged with energy. He smiled, wishing he himself were fifty years younger. What an exciting time to be their age. So many changes since the war and a lot more opportunities for young people now. 'So, boys, what do you think of the two names Earl and Bobby thought up for you?'

Levi, sitting in the front passenger seat, beamed. 'We like them both. But we've decided we prefer The Sefton Trio rather than The Falcons. It's keeping the Liverpool theme like The Quarrymen. And all three of us love to go to Sefton Park, so it seems fitting to have that name.'

Jimmy and Kenny nodded their agreement. 'I love it,' Kenny said. 'It's perfect.'

'I prefer that name too,' Basil said. 'Yes, it's definitely the right choice. And if the night goes okay for you I can see us getting a few bookings from some of the social clubs around the area. Fingers crossed now, boys.'

* * *

On Sunday afternoon Mary and Bella were taken to The Mystery Park by Basil in readiness for the residents' meeting. Bella waved as Fran and Edie came into view, accompanied by Miss Clancy their neighbour from opposite Fran's house. They exchanged greetings while Basil went to park the car outside Scotty's house on Prince Alfred Road. He joined the women who had commandeered a couple of benches while they waited for more people to arrive.

'I hope it's a good turnout,' Mary said. 'We need their support to pull this off.'

'It will be,' Basil assured her. 'Once I've explained that shutting the street off at one end will only be for a few hours, they'll realise it's not going to inconvenience them too much.'

Mary nodded and looked relieved as people started to arrive. Children were sent to play on the swing park while the adults sat down on benches and some on the nearby grassy mound. Fortunately the weather was warm and dry with just a gentle breeze on the air. *How lucky we are to have such a lovely place to meet up*, Mary thought. It had been kindly donated to the area of Wavertree by a mystery benefactor many years ago, earning itself the name of The Mystery Park. She got to her feet, clutching a sheaf of notes and cleared her throat.

'Thank you all for coming along this afternoon,' she began. 'It's much appreciated. Now, I would just like to clarify a few points to add to the leaflet that you will have received through the door.'

A few heads nodded and one lady spoke up. 'Pleased to meet you, Mary. My name is Joan Finn and me and my Alfie here are fairly new to the street. Please let us know if we can help in any way at all. This is such a privilege for Victory Street. I think we're all in shock with the news.'

Mary smiled. 'Thank you, Joan, that's just what we need to hear. It is indeed an honour and something we'll never forget and nor will our children. That's why we want the day to be really special for everyone concerned.'

A man who was seated beside Joan, who Mary took to be Alfie, said, 'We'll make a start on clearing the cobbles of weeds and me and Joe, my neighbour here,' he pointed at the man sitting next to him, 'we're both handy with joinery jobs and we can get our hands on enough wood to make window boxes for them that don't have one.'

'Thank you so much,' Mary said. 'That is very kind of you and I'm sure people will appreciate the gesture.'

'I've an allotment,' another man spoke up. 'I can help fill them window boxes up with plants once they're made. Got some lovely colourful stuff on the go right now.'

Mary smiled. 'This is great. What a kind and helpful community Victory Street really is. As most of you know, it was my home for many years and it's lovely to see some new faces among the usual suspects. And it's so nice that you all have such pride in your street.'

'Well most of us do,' Joan Finn spoke up. 'But there's one that lets us all down. Miss Clancy knows who I mean, don't you, queen?'

Miss Clancy sighed and nodded her head. 'Sadly, yes, Joan, I do.'

'Well look,' Alfie Finn said. 'What we plan to do is get the outside of her house looking a bit tidier. We'll paint her sill and doorstep in the dark one night, wash her front door down and she'll be none the wiser as it'll all be dry before they show their faces midday. Then when they go out, we'll attach a window box to the sill and fill it with plants.'

Edie smiled. 'And I've a length of white netting she can have for her window to replace the mucky one. I'll put it in a bag and leave it on her step anonymously. If she decides to use it then that's good, but if she takes umbrage then there's not much else we can do.'

'I'm sure she'll be glad of it,' Joan said. 'I know there's very little money going into that house and with all those mouths to feed, I don't suppose there's anything spare for fancy stuff, however it costs very little to keep clean, but there you go. If we get her house front all tarted up for the special day, what she does after is her own business. She might even start to show a bit of pride in her home.'

'Hear, hear,' a few voices shouted in agreement among a few mumbled 'And pigs might fly' comments.

'What about bunting and decorations?' Joan asked.

'All being taken care of,' Mary said. 'Once the street is ready and freshened up then my daughter Molly will come and hang miles of the stuff from the lampposts. She's seeing to flowers for the queen as well. Basil here has arranged for the top end of the street to be closed for the day and a stage will be erected there. We've got acts and a band who will entertain while the royal couple are here and then when they leave we'll be setting up a buffet for the street party.'

'We can all help to provide food for that,' Joan said. 'If someone can let us know what's needed, we can muck in with baking and what have you.'

'Thank you,' Mary said. 'I'll be sure to be in touch the week of the visit and let you know what we need. Well, I just want to thank you all so much for coming today. I know there's not a lot of notice but this was dropped on my plate with very little warning. I'm just truly grateful that you are all as thrilled as I am that Victory Street has been chosen.'

'And then we've also got entertainment lined up for the evening,' Basil said. 'All in all I think we're in for a very grand day. And it's all down to this lovely lady here who was thrown in at the deep end. But if anyone can pull this event off, it's definitely our Mary,' he finished as a cheer went up and Mary blushed and smiled her thanks.

EIGHT

When Mary and Molly arrived on Victory Street on the Thursday evening, two days before the royal event, they were thrilled to see the changes already made and the residents waiting on the street to help them put the bunting in place. Molly had filled her car boot with decorations and picked up her mam on the way back from the shop after closing time. Earl was coming later to help and had taken Dianna home from work to look after Patti and Harry. Basil was here instructing the men, who were setting up the stage, on where to put things. An electricity supply was generously being supplied by two nearby houses and the residents had been informed that a fee would be coming their way to help with the costs towards their bills.

Joan and Alfie Finn greeted them as they climbed out of the car. Joan beckoned to Mary to follow her down the street. Mary hurried after her looking at all the immaculate weed-free cobbles and white window boxes, displaying colourful blooms.

'It looks so very smart,' she said. 'What a great job you've all done, Joan.'

Joan smiled proudly. 'Do you know what, Mary, it's brought

us closer as a community,' she said. 'It's been lovely, really getting to know our neighbours, and they are such a very kind and caring bunch of people. We've had that wartime spirit back this last couple of weeks with everyone helping each other.' She stopped outside Fran's house and nodded to the house opposite. 'What do you think?'

'Blimey, that *is* an improvement,' Mary said looking at Net Curtain Nellie's house with Edie's gifted nets shining white behind the gleaming glass. The steps and sill were painted in cardinal red like the rest of the street and even the brass letterbox and door number were shinier than usual. The window box was planted with colourful flowers like every other box in the street.

'Yep,' Joan agreed. 'Just shows what a bit of gentle persuasion can do to achieve results. She's actually not all that bad when you get to know her. Her real name is Glenda and she's on her own now as that shiftless article she was married to cleared off with a right floozy from one of the dockside pubs last week. He's left poor Glenda with not a penny to her name and all those kiddies to look after and another one on the way. Told her he doesn't believe the one she's carrying is his as his back was too bad to perform when she got caught. He's accused her of going with another bloke. As if she's got the bloody time. What a horrible man.'

Mary's hand flew to her mouth in shock at what Glenda had been enduring behind closed doors.

'She came out to help us when we were all busy on the street and her two eldest boys, who are twins but don't look alike, pulled a lot of the weeds from between the cobbles. That's when she got it all off her chest. I think she just needed someone to talk to. She really opened up to me and said she's actually glad he's gone now. He knocked her about a lot and she didn't like his mates who came to the house. They were mainly ex-convicts and drunken bad lots.' Joan nodded at Fran's house and continued. 'He's very pally with that young lady's ex, and she didn't like the things her bloke made her do on behalf of Frankie that caused a lot of trouble for Fran in the past. Glenda feels really bad about it now.'

Mary shook her head. 'Oh, he's another bad lot, that Frankie. Thank goodness he's locked up for years and Fran finally got her freedom from him. He was a bully and treated her badly, and he and a couple of his mates nearly killed our Molly's husband, Earl, in a racist attack. That's what he's gone down for.'

'I read about that in the paper at the time. I'm so glad your son-in-law survived the attack. Terrible that was, just because of his colour. And Fran's new husband Sam is a lovely young man. She seems very happy with him and their baby is a beautiful little boy.'

'Sam is very good to Fran and he's just what she needed to get her confidence back,' Mary said, smiling as a car pulled up and Earl and Stewart, Dianna's fiancé, and Levi, got out and waved. 'Here's the cavalry. We'll soon have that bunting up now they've arrived. Perhaps Glenda and Fran can have a bit of a chat soon to sort out any bad feelings.'

'Maybe they will,' Joan said, nodding. 'Well I'm going to go inside and make several pots of tea. I've borrowed a couple of teapots from the neighbours and some extra mugs. So when it's all sorted, we'll celebrate with a brew and one of the ladies has made a mountain of scones this afternoon so I'll go and cut and butter a few for us. Just give us a knock when you're ready, Mary, and I'll fetch it all outside. My Alfie has set up a trestle table ready.'

Mary laughed. 'You've got a good one there.'

'Oh I have that, most of the time anyway,' Joan replied, with a grin.

* * *

Mary smiled with pride as she watched the bunting being draped from lamppost to lamppost and then what was left was fixed to the upper windowsills of the houses.

'Oh, it looks a treat,' she said to Basil. 'I was a bit worried when they were climbing those ladders and leaning over though. My heart was in my mouth for a moment.'

'It really does look good,' Basil agreed. He smiled and pointed up to the sky. 'I knew they'd be quite safe though. See that cloud up there?'

Mary nodded, her head on one side as she studied the cloud he was pointing at.

'What does it look like to you?' he said.

Mary felt a little shiver go down her spine. 'An angel I think, I can see big white wings.'

Basil nodded. 'That's my Fenella. I told you all she's watching over us. Bet she came out as soon as Earl started swaying on the ladder near that first lamppost. She had him in her safe hands.'

Mary gave him a hug, fighting to hold back tears. 'That's a comforting thought, Basil. She's never far away from any of us. I feel her all the time. I even talk to her as I'm going about my daily chores. I've told her all about this event. It's one thing she wouldn't want to miss out on.'

Basil smiled. 'She'll be with us on the day. That's one thing we can rely on.'

Mary sighed. 'Well that's more than I can say for her lady-ship, Eva Thompson. Wouldn't you think she'd have popped down here and shown her face tonight? A bit of moral support for the residents and all that. Just to see how things are going if nothing else. It's not as if we'd expect her to climb ladders or weed the cobbles. You can bet your life she'll be here for the royal visit though. Pushing her way in like she'd done it all single-handed.'

Basil snorted. 'She might show her face but she'll get no

praise from these good people. They don't know her from Adam. They'll wonder who the devil she is and she'll get short shrift from the likes of Joan if she tries taking over.'

Mary laughed. 'Well we'll have to wait and see what happens. Right, let's go and enjoy Joan's hospitality before we leave. This is it now until Saturday morning. It's been hard work but I'm sure it will be well worth it.'

'I'm sure you're right, Mary,' Basil said. He waved to the cloud that was now dispersing in the distance. 'See you Saturday, Fen, my dear.'

* * *

'Now just try it one more time,' Bella signed to Lizzie. 'Give Aunty Et the flowers and curtsey nicely like Mammy showed you.' She looked at Bobby and raised an eyebrow as he stuck up a thumb in a gesture of support.

'She's nearly there,' he said. 'Just a bit more concentration and you'll have cracked it.'

Bella nodded as Ethel sat on the armchair ready to get to her feet as Lizzie approached with a hastily put together bunch of garden flowers. This was the final bouquet-giving rehearsal as tomorrow would be a busy night with them all adding the finishing touches to their songs down at the studio.

'Okay, Lizzie,' she signed. 'Walk slowly to Aunty Et and give her the flowers. Hand them over more gently than you did last time. Then curtsey nicely. You ready, er, Queen Elizabeth?'

'As I'll ever be, chuck,' Ethel said with a grin. She smiled at Lizzie who walked carefully towards her and handed the flowers over before holding out her skirt at the hem with her good hand, and curtseying.

'Thank you,' Queen Ethel said, smiling as regally as she could manage while trying not to laugh out loud as the little girl stared bemusedly at her, head on one side as though trying to work something out.

'Bobby, jelly babies, quick,' Bella said as Bobby rooted in his jacket pocket and handed a paper bag of sweets to Bella. She tapped Lizzie on the shoulder and handed her the bag as she turned around. She signed, 'Well done and thank you, go and play with your dolly now until bedtime.' Lizzie clutched her sweeties and smiling broadly left the room. 'Distraction tactics,' Bella said. 'God knows what she was about to say to you, Aunty Et, but best to take her mind off things and she'll have forgotten by the time she presents the flowers to the real queen on Saturday.'

'You hope,' Bobby said with a laugh. 'Anyway, the queen is used to little kids so I'm sure it will all be fine.'

'Molly's dropping Mam off here shortly and I think Basil is going to run you home, Aunty Et, when he takes Kenny and Jimmy back. I'll just go and give Edie a call to see how it's all going down on Victory Street and then I'll get Lizzie ready for bed. The boys shouldn't be too long now. Levi's got homework to do tonight so he'd better not be too late.'

* * *

Levi, Kenny and Jimmy were on their way home from boxing class. They stopped near Calderstones Park gates and waited for the bus that would take them the two-mile journey back to Levi's place. From there Basil would give Jimmy and Kenny a lift home to Wavertree.

'Right,' Levi began, 'you know that we have to go straight to the studios after school tomorrow for one last run-through of our songs.'

The others nodded. 'And that's it then,' Kenny said. 'Saturday is *the* day. I feel nervous even thinking about it to be honest, but I'm sure we'll be fine.'

'We will be,' Levi assured him. 'And like Basil said, if it's a success then I know what *I'm* doing after we finish school. I know my mam and dad want me to go to college and Mam even mentioned university, but that's not what I want. I want to be a musician. Fingers crossed it all goes well and we get a chance to do some more shows.'

Kenny shrugged. 'Mam said I've got to get a job as soon as I finish school. She needs the money. No college for me. But I might be able to work in the day and then still be able to play in our group at night. I can earn a bit of spending money for myself that way. I doubt I'll see a penny of my wages; it'll all go on the family.'

Jimmy nodded his agreement. 'And that's pretty much the same for me,' he said. 'It would be good if we can find jobs that allow us to be free at night and weekends so that we can do some musical work – if anybody wants to hire The Sefton Trio, that is.'

'Let's see what happens this weekend,' Levi said as the bus came into view. 'You never know what's around the corner, as Granny Mary always says. Hopefully, for us three, it will be the start of a musical career.'

NINE

Mary woke up early to hear the phone ringing in the hallway. She slid out of bed, pushed her feet into her fluffy pink slippers and hurried out of the bedroom, closing the door behind her. Martin was still sleeping and he might as well have another half hour while she made them some breakfast. But first, who the devil was this mithering so early in the morning? She glared at her grumpy face in the mirror that hung above an oak console table where the phone sat, and stuck out her tongue.

'Smile,' she instructed her reflection.

Patting the hairnet that covered her freshly set hair she cleared her throat before picking up the receiver and putting on her posh telephone voice, as Bella and Molly called it when they were teasing her. 'Good morning, Wavertree 9410,' she said, with a slight emphasis on the 'o'.

'Mary, is that you?' an anxious voice enquired.

Mary rolled her eyes. Flipping Eva Thompson; she might have known. 'Yes, good morning, Eva, of course it's me. What can I do for you?' Who the devil did the woman *think* would be answering Mary's phone first thing in the morning?

'I just need reassurance that all is in order for today,' Eva said. 'I've been awake half the night worrying.'

'Why? Everything is just fine. I told you it would be. There's nothing for you to worry about at all. We've got it all in hand.'

'You are aware that the royal couple will be arriving in Wavertree at twelve prompt, aren't you?'

Mary gritted her teeth and tried to remain calm. 'Yes, of course I am, we discussed the timing last night at the meeting. We are all set up and ready. You could have come down to see that for yourself on Thursday evening. I did invite you, Eva, remember.'

Eva coughed before speaking as though delaying her reply while she thought about what to say. She cleared her throat and then coughed and spluttered again. 'Oh, do excuse me; I don't know where that little tickle came from. It quite took me by surprise. But I, erm, I was very busy on Thursday evening, as you know I had things to do for last night's final WI meeting before the event.'

Mary bristled and took a deep breath, willing herself to stay calm. They'd all been blooming busy, none more so than Mary over the last few weeks. She'd been dashing around like a blue-arsed fly. The woman had turned up at last night's meeting like Lady Muck, late as usual, and had sat silently staring into space, away with the fairies, for most of it, contributing very little while leaving Mary to brief her team on what time to bring the buffet supplies round.

The kindly Joan Finn had offered her kitchen to store all the prepared food for the party. Eva hadn't even offered to bake a single scone, never mind help to provide supplies of sandwiches and cakes. Still, Mary thought, they'd done well enough without her and she was sure today would be a great success whether Eva turned up or not. Although she was in no doubt she would be there, best swanky hat on her head and all, to pose in front of the cameras while the event was being filmed by the British Pathé News team. She took another deep breath, refusing to rise to the bait. It would only shoot her blood pressure up and she needed to stay as calm as she possibly could today.

'Look, Eva, I have to go; I'm very busy right now. See you down on Victory Street later, goodbye,' she said firmly, replacing the phone on its cradle and strolling into the kitchen to put the kettle on. She spooned tea leaves into the pot and opened the curtains and stared out at the bird table that Martin had made. A few sparrows were squabbling over some breadcrumbs. She'd put some more out later then there'd be plenty for them all. While she waited for the kettle to boil she busied herself cutting and buttering bread and trimming some of the fat off two slices of bacon. That could go out on the bird table as well. She turned to smile at Martin as he strode into the kitchen and slipped his arms around her waist, dropping a kiss on top of her head.

'You okay, queen?'

She nodded. 'I think so, love. You heard the phone ringing then?'

'I did. And I heard your side of the conversation. Sounded like Eva was flapping again, no doubt.'

'She was.' The kettle started to whistle as it came to the boil and Mary filled the teapot. 'From the word go she's been as much use over this event as a chocolate fireguard,' she said with a sigh. 'Thank God the rest of the WI team have got their heads screwed on right.'

'It'll all be fine, chuck. You just see. It'll be a credit to all your hard work, and your family's.'

'Let's hope so,' Mary replied. 'Right, do you want tomato on your bacon sarnie?'

Martin grinned. 'Is the pope a Catholic?'

'I'll take it that's a yes then.' Mary laughed and threw a

sliced home-grown tomato into the frying pan with the bacon rashers.

* * *

'Hold still while I fasten the bow in your hair.' Bella tried to stop an excited Lizzie jigging from foot to foot. 'There, that's lovely,' she signed, tweaking the pink ribbon into place around her mop of blonde curls. The ribbon matched the pink fabric of the new dress that Lizzie was wearing. 'Let's put your shoes on now and then you're ready.' She fastened the black patent ankle straps onto Lizzie's slender foot and straightened her white ankle socks. 'Now sit on the chair while Mammy goes to get dressed. Stay there,' she signed.

Lizzie nodded and Bella dashed into the bedroom where Bobby was putting his suit on. Basil was picking them all up and running them to Victory Street where they would all meet at Edie's house. Then he would return to collect The Sefton Trio members, who were in the music room with Levi's guitar, doing a bit of a last-minute practice, and Aunty Ethel, who was going to help Mam with serving the buffet at the party after the royal couple left the street.

Edie had told them they could use her bedroom as a changing room to put their new dresses on for their early slot in the show. Bella's dress was already down there to save getting it creased in the car so she slipped a cotton summer dress over her head to be going on with. Her hair had been set yesterday and she ran her hands through the shiny dark locks, flicking the wavy ends out over her shoulders. She'd already done her make-up so another quick slick of lippy at Edie's would do just fine.

Fortunately the weather looked as though it was going to be nice, the sun was shining and just a few fluffy white clouds floated in a bright blue sky. *No dark rain clouds in sight thank the lord*, Bella thought.

'Right, Bobby,' she said as he fastened his tie and brushed his blond hair. 'Let's go and wait in the sitting room for our lift. God I feel so excited, but also really nervous about performing in public again. It's been so long. Let's just hope we don't disappoint the royal couple.'

* * *

By eleven thirty the residents of Victory Street were ready and waiting. The buffet supplies were stored in Joan's kitchen as arranged. The Bryant Sisters were getting ready in Edie's bedroom. Earl was sorting out the younger entertainers in Fran's borrowed front room and keeping his eye on Lizzie and his own two little ones with the help of Aunty Ethel, while Molly did some last-minute tweaking of decorations into place on the street.

Each resident, following Basil's instructions, was lining the street, standing on the pavement outside their own properties, flags on sticks at the ready to wave, small children at the front of the line-up. The regimental band with members from various troops, including Fran and Edie's husbands, were seated on stage, smartly uniformed. Many of them had served in the war and felt like they were back at an ENSA show. They were all ready for the nod from Basil, and the British Pathé News crew were standing to one side of the stage, cameras and equipment at the ready.

The members of the Wavertree WI were all lined up near the stage in readiness to help set up the trestle tables for the afternoon tea, looking smart in the green uniforms they'd all agreed to wear at last night's final meeting. There'd been no sign of Eva Thompson yet, much to her team's annoyance. Just before eleven thirty Mary gasped as a large shiny black car turned the corner and stopped at the bottom of the street. Her hands shaking, she tugged on Basil's sleeve and he whipped around and then shook his head.

'Relax; it's not them arriving early,' he said. 'It's the Lord Mayor's car. I expected him to be here, but who the devil is that getting out of the car behind him? She can hardly move with that contraption on her head.'

Mary stared and then pursed her lips. 'I don't believe it. It's Eva Thompson, the president of the WI. Why the heck didn't she tell me earlier when she phoned that she was coming with the blooming mayor? We've been expecting her here all morning to help. Typical. Trust her to wrong-foot me when she must surely know I'm bound to be feeling so very nervous as it is.'

Mary glared at the woman as she struggled to maintain her balance and get out of the car with dignity while the chauffeur did his best to guide her head out without knocking her hat off. Mary caught the eye of her fellow WI member, Joyce Andrews, who was trying hard not to laugh. Mary raised her eyebrows in response and Joyce whipped a hanky from up her cardigan sleeve and pretended to sneeze into it. Mary knew that once Joyce started laughing there'd be no stopping her and her laugh was infectious. The street residents were looking puzzled and muttering among themselves. Joan Finn caught Mary's eye and came hurrying over.

'Who's that woman with the feathery dustbin lid on her head?' she asked Mary. 'It's not the mayor's wife, as I'm sure she's an older lady.'

Mary tried not to laugh at Joan's description of Eva's monstrosity of a hat, which indeed was the size of a round dustbin lid adorned with peacock-blue feathers and a large matching blue chiffon bow.

'Believe it or not, Joan, she's the president of the WI,' Mary explained. 'She's supposedly in charge of all this.' She waved her hands around and lowered her voice. 'Except she's done very little to help and left it in the main to me and the other members over there.'

Joan's mouth fell open. 'What, and she's come to claim all the praise for doing sod all?'

'Something like that,' Mary said, sighing wistfully as Eva was finally hauled out of the car, the hat, the same colour as her two-piece suit, still miraculously in place, just about.

Joan shook her head. 'Well I never. The blooming cheek of it. And what the heck does she think she looks like, arriving with the mayor like she's his fancy piece. Ooh, wait till I tell me neighbours. She'll get short shrift from me and them if she starts trying to take over now. We thought you were the president, Mary, what with you doing all the organising and coming to talk to us and what have you. They're all staring at her, wondering who the heck she is.'

Mary nodded. 'Exactly. She should have made herself more available and then people would recognise her. And she's supposed to be wearing our uniform as well. Ah well, what's done is done. Nothing I can do about it right now. Let's enjoy the day.' She shook her head, feeling really annoyed with Eva. 'Right, she's coming over, I'd better go and present myself and see what she has to say. Time's getting on and they'll be arriving very soon.'

Mary hurried back to Basil's side and waved for Eva to join her. She quickly introduced her to Basil who shook Eva's hand and then he looked across to greet the mayor whom he already knew from previous functions. The mayor and Eva were shown to the side of the stage as excitement rose in the waiting residents and a shout of, 'They're on their way,' rose from a man on look-out duties at the end of the street. The mayor's car was now parked to one side leaving the street free for the royal vehicle to arrive.

'The main roads in the area are lined with people,' Eva

whispered to Mary. 'We struggled to get through at times. There are a lot of policemen on duty as well as some soldiers.'

Mary nodded, her eyes glued to the top end of the street.

'I'll go and bring the girls down now and make sure Molly's got Lizzie sorted with the flowers,' Basil whispered. 'The young folk can watch through Fran's front window. Best we just keep to residents on the street for now. It's rather crowded out here at the moment.'

He dashed into the house and within seconds he was leading the Bryant Sisters out onto the street, all dressed in their new matching blue and white spotted dresses. Bella handed Lizzie over to Mary along with the beautiful bouquet of pink and white blooms that Molly had put together. Fortunately they were arranged in a spray style and not a heavy bunch, which made it easier for Lizzie to hold with her good hand, and Mary rested the length of the spray on her arm in the sling.

Bella, Fran and Edie took their places at the side of the stage for the time being. Mary gave her daughter a little wave and Bella waved back. All eyes were glued to the end of the street as the church clock struck twelve in the distance and two black cars pulled onto the cobbles. The first car looked to be transporting official-looking men in suits who, Mary thought, were most probably to do with security or royal aides or whatever they called them. The people who made sure the royals were safe, anyway.

She wondered if they had guns in their pockets and then dismissed the idea as silly and fanciful. This was Liverpool, and there wasn't a war on here now. She gave herself a mental shake and focussed on the slender figure of Queen Elizabeth as she exited from the rear of the second car, and the very handsome Duke of Edinburgh in his military uniform. A roar from the crowd sounded as the band struck up the national anthem and everyone joined in, singing 'God Save the Queen' at the tops of their voices.

Mary smiled as the anthem came to a striking end and the royal couple strolled up the street on a length of red carpet that Basil and Earl had laid down earlier this morning. Mary hadn't a clue where they'd got it from and she hadn't had the time to ask them, but she was glad they'd had the foresight to think of it as the queen was wearing white peep-toe, strappy shoes with a decent-sized heel. Not practical for walking on cobbles, that was certain.

Her stunning dress was made from a beautiful sky-blue shantung fabric with a button-through bodice, topped with a contrasting white collar, three-quarter-length sleeves, a full skirt and little peplums that accentuated her slender waist. On her beautifully waved hair sat a small blue tri-cornered hat. Mary smiled to herself as she compared the classy little hat to the ridiculous creation being worn by Eva Thompson today.

The cheers as the anthem finished were heartwarming. The mayor stepped forward to welcome the couple and handed over to Basil as master of ceremonies. Basil bowed and took Lizzie by the arm, gently steering her to stand in front of the royal couple. He signed to the puzzled little girl who was holding the bouquet of flowers that she should hand them to the queen and then step back and curtsey. Lizzie smiled and nodded, she thrust the flowers into the queen's hands, said, 'There you are,' in a little voice and stepped back, did a little curtsey and added a twirl.

The Duke of Edinburgh laughed out loud and thanked Lizzie, using sign language. He patted her gently on her unin-jured arm. Lizzie beamed and looked at the queen who was also smiling at her. Mary thought she was maybe thinking how like her own little girl, Anne, Lizzie was, and how very thoughtful that the prince used sign language. Everyone cheered and clapped and Lizzie, who could hear certain loud noises, laughed and ran over to her mother.

'Well done,' Bella signed, 'I'm proud of you. Here's Daddy now. You stay with him while Mammy sings for the queen.'

'Good girl,' Bobby signed. 'The guy with the camera closest to the stage caught all that,' he quickly told Bella. 'Hope we get a photo or see a film of it eventually. Good luck, love.' He kissed her on the cheek before she headed on stage.

Bobby led their daughter to the pavement to watch, and Bella joined Fran and Edie on stage as Basil announced, 'The Bryant Sisters are now going to perform two songs for our royal visitors.'

A loud cheer went up and as the bugler played the opening chords the girls launched into the wartime favourite "Boogie Woogie Bugle Boy", which had always been a crowd-pleaser in their shows. Everyone joined in, singing along, and Prince Philip watched their performance with a big smile on his face. The girls took a bow and after thanking their audience who were cheering and clapping Fran announced their next song.

The trumpet player played the opening and the girls started to sing Kay Starr's "Rock'n'Roll Waltz". A loud cheer went up and several men grabbed their wives and waltzed them up and down the best they could on the crowded pavement. Mary observed that all the time the girls were singing the news team had cameras on them as well as filming the royal couple's reactions. This would be wonderful publicity for the Bold Street Studios and hopefully would relaunch the Bryant Sisters' career. She turned as a hand fell on her shoulder and Basil pointed to the sky above the chimney pots.

'What did I tell you?' he whispered as an angel-shaped cloud floated gently above them. 'She's here. I knew she would be.'

'Oh, Basil.' A sob caught in Mary's throat and she gave him a hug. 'I'm sure she is.'

TEN

As the royal couple took their leave, after shaking hands with Basil and Mary, to loud cheers, flag-waving and clapping, Mary and her team quickly took charge of getting the trestle tables set up on the street ready for the party. Basil and Earl rolled up the red carpet and put it at the back of the stage behind the band that were playing a few background tunes amid the hustle and bustle.

'I recognise this,' Joyce Andrews said. 'My son plays the record on our gramophone all the time. Think he said it's called "Zambezi".'

'You're right, it is called "Zambezi",' Mary said. 'Makes me feel like I want to dance.' She wiggled her hips and laughed. 'Hopefully we'll get a chance later.' She spotted Eva standing alone looking like a spare part and shook her head. 'Oh dear, she looks lost. We need to find her something to do,' she whispered to Joyce. 'Madam President,' she called at the top of her voice, waving to catch her attention. 'Can we have some help over here please?'

Eva's eyes opened wide and she smiled. She strolled across

the street in Mary's direction. 'Yes, Mary, you need some help, you say?'

'We do,' Mary replied. 'All our spare hands are busy on deck and everyone is already doing what they can. I need someone to put these on the tables.' She handed over a stack of white cotton sheeting that had been cut into tablecloths and hemmed by Ruby and Dolores who were here helping on the street now the royals had gone.

'Can you put a cloth over each table as Earl and Scotty over there put them in place please? Make sure they are level with equal sides and ends hanging down. It needs someone with an eye for detail to do that properly. Thank you.' She turned her back and winked at Joyce, who stifled a grin.

'That'll make her feel useful,' Mary said.

As each cloth was put in place the WI recruits carried laden trays from Joan's house. Ethel passed by with a tray of fresh scones and shouted to Mary, 'Those girls are still as good as they ever were. I hope they decide to start up their singing careers again.'

Mary laughed. 'So do I. Shame to let talent go to waste. They've had a long enough break. Basil needs to keep on at them now.' Hearing her name being called, she turned. Molly came hurrying over, her arms full of small floral displays.

'Those are beautiful, chuck,' Mary said. 'You are clever with your hands.'

Molly smiled. 'Thank you, Mam. I'm putting them on the tables. I thought rather than chuck them away at the end of the night it would be a nice idea if we raffle them off. I've brought a few other bits from the shop to donate as well and a book of raffle tickets. Dianna says she'll take them round when everyone is sitting down eating and easy to get hold of. How much do you think we should charge, threepence a strip?'

Mary nodded. 'That's a lovely idea, Molly. Most people have got the odd threepenny bit in their purse or pocket. Saves mucking about with change then. And if they've only sixpenny bits handy, try and sell them two strips.'

'We will, Mam. Well I think that all went down very well, don't you? The queen looked beautiful. Her dress was stunning. Gorgeous shade of blue. Our Lizzie was a star. She made us all laugh. And our Bella and the girls' dresses looked lovely. It was good to see them back singing together again. Hope they do more later on if there's time.'

'They might do. Dianna and the twins are doing a few songs, then Earl, and of course Levi and the boys, so we'll have to see how long the band can stay on for. They might be needed back at their bases. Although we've got Sam and his drums and Stevie and the saxophone as well as Levi and his guitar, so we'll probably manage if the others *do* have to leave. But yes, love, the queen's dress was really nice. She always looks lovely though. Very smart.'

Molly nodded. 'Right, I'll go and put these on the tables now the cloths are on. Think your president could do with sticking that hat somewhere safe for the rest of the day as she keeps bumping into people with it. She's an accident waiting to happen if you ask me.'

Mary sighed as Eva came towards her with a pained expression on her face. 'What's wrong?' she asked, folding her arms as more team members rushed by carrying food to the tables.

'Erm, you seem to have everything under control, Mary,' Eva began. 'Maybe I should go. I feel a bit in the way. A child over there just threw something at my hat. I hope it's not damaged it. This was a very expensive gift from my late husband, you know.'

Trying to keep a straight face, Mary walked around and examined the hat. 'Nope, can't see any damage at all. Why don't you just take it off and I'll ask Joan if you can pop it into her front room out of the way for now. None of us have got hats on. I'm sure you would have been much more comfortable in your uniform like the rest of us.' She tried to say it kindly but she was annoyed.

Eva frowned. 'Well, I was travelling in the mayoral car and thought it would be more appropriate to dress smartly for the occasion.' She glanced over her shoulder and then to her left and right. 'Oh dear, it would appear that the mayor has left me stranded. He's gone.'

Mary sighed inwardly, feeling at the end of her tether now with the woman. 'Eva, you're not stranded. There are regular trams and buses to the area and you don't live that far. Everyone is too busy right now to offer you a lift or they would. We've worked hard to put this day together and give these good people a party. They deserve it after all the time they've spent making their street look so attractive. All the entertainers are giving their time freely as well. Take your hat off, try and relax and enjoy yourself. Here, Joan,' she called out as Eva reluctantly removed her headgear. 'Can we store this hat in your front room for now?'

'Of course.' Joan smiled sweetly, taking hold of the hat and walking away with it as Eva looked on anxiously.

'Right, if you follow Joan she will show you where the plates and trays of food are,' Mary said to Eva. 'You can help to carry them out. The younger children are getting impatient, waiting. Poor little mites are hungry and they've been promised a party.' She smiled as Eva nodded and followed Joan indoors. *A bit of firm handling never went amiss*, Mary thought and went over to the microphone on stage to announce that people should now be seated as the tea party was officially ready.

'You boys help yourselves,' she said to the members of the band. 'Take a break and get some food while you can. There's enough to serve an army here,' she joked as a couple of them grinned and saluted her.

* * *

Dianna smiled as she passed out the raffle tickets and collected in the money. 'Thank you very much,' she said to a lady who handed her a shilling and got four strips in return. Following a quick discussion with Molly and Granny Mary, the suggestion that any money they made should go to a good cause had been agreed.

Mary told Joan Finn who had nodded her head in Glenda's direction. The neighbour, formerly known as Net Curtain Nellie, pregnant with her seventh child and recently abandoned by her useless, bullying husband, had been helping as much as she could to get the street ready.

'She's a good cause, if ever there was one,' Joan said. 'Look at them kiddies of hers, they're eating like they're starving and yet she's done her bit and made a plate of egg sarnies for today that she could probably ill afford, bless her. She told me she has nothing for the new baby when it arrives and she's thinking it might be best if she lets it go for adoption as soon as it's born.'

Mary clapped her hand to her mouth. 'But we can't let her do that; I agree, she does need help. I think we need to put the past behind us and make her our good cause, but we'll do it in secret rather than embarrass her in front of everyone. I see even Miss Clancy is talking to her in a friendly way now.'

Joan nodded. 'Yes, she is. Glenda has apologised to her for the noise and disruption. She explained that the kids only shouted and yelled when their father was there arguing and thumping her. They were trying to protect her, not fighting among themselves as we all thought. God knows what those poor mites have seen going on in their short lives. It doesn't bear thinking about. I was wondering if we can maybe ask for donations of unwanted baby stuff from people as well. If we help her as much as we can, she can keep her baby and not feel under pressure to give it away.'

Mary sighed. 'Poor woman, I can think of nothing worse. No doubt you've heard all about our families' past history and how our Bella found herself pregnant and what happened there. But we all rallied round her. I was determined that nobody was bringing up our Levi except for his family. I fell in love with that child the minute I held him. And since his biological father decided to make Liverpool his home and married our Molly, well, just look at what a fabulous family I have now. It might seem a bit mixed up to some, and Levi calls Bobby *and* Earl, Dad, but I wouldn't be without any of them. Both of my sons-in-law say I'm the best ma-in-law ever and I won't argue with that! I love them all equally and I know we get a few stares and racist comments from the odd miserable devil, but we have learnt to ignore them.'

Joan laughed. 'I bet anyone confronting your lot would think twice with you in command, Mary. Right, I'd better collect the empty plates and fill them with cakes. Your ladies are so good; they've made umpteen giant pots of tea and haven't stopped all day.'

Mary smiled. The huge metal teapots borrowed from the church hall had been a boon today with so many wanting a drink. 'They're a very good team. Even Eva's mucking in now she's dropped her airs and graces a bit.'

'Thank the lord that flipping hat's out of the way,' Joan said with a grin. 'Last time I went inside our blooming tomcat was stalking it, probably thought it was a giant bird with all them feathers. I've lifted it up onto the top of the bookcase out of reach for now before he decides to go in for the big kill.'

* * *

Basil smiled at Mary as she handed him a mug of tea and a plate with a slice of Victoria sponge.

'We'll start to clear away in about fifteen minutes,' she told him. 'Then we can get on with the entertainment. I'll just pop into Fran's and see the young ones for a few minutes. Make sure they've had enough to eat.

'Are you kids all okay in here?' Mary called as she let herself into Fran's house. 'Have you all had enough to eat?'

'Yes thanks, Granny Mary,' Levi said and the others nodded their agreement.

'Well you all look very nice, I must say,' she said. 'Have Ruby and Dolores made your dresses?' she asked Dianna and her identical twin cousins, Ebony and Tammy, who were sitting on the sofa under the window looking like triplets in matching jade-green, V-neck, slim-fitting dresses, their hair falling in dark shiny ringlets onto their shoulders.

'Tammy – or it might have been Ebony, Mary couldn't tell one sister from the other – nodded. 'They did. We love them. They usually make stage dresses for us with sticky-out skirts, but we asked for something figure-hugging this time. Uncle Earl wants us to do more singing work so I think we look more grown-up in this style.'

'You definitely do,' Mary agreed. 'Three very beautiful young ladies. I'm really proud of you all.'

Dianna laughed. 'Thank you, Granny Mary. That's kind of you to say so.'

'And you boys,' Mary turned to Levi, Kenny and Jimmy, 'you look very smart too. Nice clean white shirts. Those ties are very thin. Is that a new style?'

'They're called Slim Jims,' Levi said and jumped to his feet from the floor. 'Do you like our jeans? We got them from the Cunard Yanks at the docks and Aunty Ruby took them in for us so they look dead fashionable. All the lads at school that are into music like us are wearing this style now; they call them drainies, short for drainpipes.'

'Ah yes, I see where that name comes from,' Mary said, looking at the jeans that were no thicker than a pipe. 'They look like they're cutting you in two, mind.'

'No they're fine, dead comfy in fact,' Kenny said with a smile.

'I'll take your word for it, Kenny,' Mary said with a grimace. 'What have you done to your curls, Levi? They look very flat today.'

Levi laughed. 'I borrowed some of dad Bobby's Brylcreem to try and flatten them down a bit. This is called a quiff. It's like the style Elvis wears. But my hair doesn't look as good as Kenny and Jimmy's because theirs is dead straight to begin with. Still,' he sighed. 'I've done my best.'

'But curls are your family heritage; look at the girls' hair, and Harry and Patti's. It's a shame to flatten them down so much.'

'All male black singers do the same,' Levi said. 'Look at Nat King Cole. His is always greased fairly flat.'

Mary sighed. 'Oh well, whatever you think looks right. But don't do it all the time. I've always loved to run my fingers through your curls.'

Levi grinned. 'Granny, stop showing me up, I'm nearly fifteen not five.'

Mary laughed. 'Well if you're all ready to go, you might as well join Basil outside to discuss a slight change of plan as he's hoping the Bryant Sisters will do two more songs. Just go and have a chat with him about timings and what have you. And make sure you all enjoy yourselves because this is a good opportunity to show the locals what you can do. You never know where it might lead. We're expecting a lot more people to turn up later from the surrounding streets so you'll have a good audience to appreciate you. And the film people are still here for a bit longer.'

'Thanks, Granny Mary.' Levi hugged her and accompanied her to the door as the others all shouted their thanks.

Mary strolled back to Joan's house and looked around at the clearing away process. The tables were being moved with the help of a couple of soldiers from the band and chairs were being set in rows in front of the stage for the audience to sit on. She smiled as she saw Basil talking to her daughter and Fran and Edie. He beckoned her over.

'They've agreed to two more songs after Dianna and the girls,' he said with a delighted smile.

'That's smashing,' Mary said. 'I won't ask what you're singing; I'll let you surprise me. Are you not going to sing a duet with Bobby, love?' she asked Bella. 'You usually do.'

Bella shook her head. 'We haven't planned to. He's seeing to Lizzie who's a bit fractious. Earl said he'd run him home with her if she doesn't settle down. I'm hoping she'll fall asleep soon and Fran said she can go and lie on Lorraine's bed if she does as Lorraine is staying with Fran's mam tonight. We'll have to see how it goes. But I think we've enough with Earl doing his bit as well. That's why he could do with not leaving the street really as he might get stuck in traffic and miss his spot.'

'Ah well, whatever you all think is best,' Mary said as people started to sit down, eagerly waiting for the show to start.

* * *

'And now, ladies and gentlemen,' Basil began from the centre of the stage, 'I would like you all to put your hands together and welcome three lovely young ladies, originally from the USA, who are delighted to entertain you tonight. I give you, Dianna and the Crystalettes.'

Amid clapping and cheering from their families and the audience, the girls walked to the front of the stage and waved to the audience. Dianna smiled shyly and spoke into the microphone.

'Good evening, everyone, and thank you so much for your warm welcome. We are going to sing you three songs and the first one we have chosen was a hit a couple of years ago for one of our favourites, the wonderful Doris Day.'

As the girls sang "Sugar Bush" the audience joined in and little kids got up and danced in front of the stage. The cheers, whistles and clapping made Dianna's eyes fill and she blinked away the tears before they rolled down her cheeks. Liverpool people were so friendly. She grinned at the twins as they bowed and blew kisses at the audience.

Ebony took to the microphone next. 'Thank you so much, everyone. Our next song was a number one hit here in England in March this year for an American trio called The Dream Weavers. It's a bit of a sad song, but I hope you enjoy it as much as we love to sing it.'

Dianna took the lead vocals on "It's Almost Tomorrow" and again the audience sang along and then applauded and cheered as the song came to an end.

Then it was Tammy's turn to introduce the next song. 'Thank you, everyone,' she began. 'Our last song was a big number one hit in 1954, both here and in America for the lovely Kitty Kallen. Please feel free to sing along if you know the words.'

"Little Things Mean a Lot" was as well received as the other two songs and again the audience sang along. Dianna and the twins held hands and took a bow as Basil walked back on stage to thank them.

'That was wonderful, girls,' he said. 'Thank you, and thank you for your appreciation,' he said to the audience who cheered and clapped once more.

The girls left the stage as Earl waited by the side for Basil to call him to perform.

'Good luck, Dad,' Dianna said and gave him a hug.

'Thank you, darling. That performance was absolutely fabulous,' he said. 'Well done, the three of you.'

'Thank you, Dad, thank you Uncle Earl,' the girls said as

they hurried over to Tammy and Ebony's parents and Molly and Aunt Ruby who enveloped them all in a big hug.

Dianna's fiancé Stewart pulled her into his arms and planted a kiss on her lips. 'You were amazing,' he said. 'That was wonderful.'

Dianna hugged him back. 'Thank you. I really enjoyed singing tonight. This is what I want to do. I always have.'

'And you will,' he said. 'You were meant to be a star and I'm so proud of you.'

'Y'all did so well,' Uncle Scotty said. 'So very proud of you girls, Grammy and Grandpa Franklin would have been thrilled with that performance.'

Dianna smiled wistfully. 'I wish they were here with us.'

'Me too, honey,' Aunt Ruby said. 'Maybe one day we can persuade your stubborn old grandpa to agree to a move. Perhaps when your Uncle Levi decides to come here for good, they may follow him.'

Dianna nodded. She loved her Uncle Levi who her brother was named after. 'That would be great, and then the whole family will be together. Right, Basil is introducing Dad now.'

Earl took to the stage like the professional he was and performed Jimmy Young's "Unchained Melody" and Dean Martin's "Memories Are Made of This". Once more the audience clapped and cheered and whistled and Earl came off stage with a big smile on his face and to pats on the back from his family.

Then Basil reintroduced the Bryant Sisters who sang Jo Stafford's "You Belong to Me" and a wartime hit that had always been a favourite. Vera Lynn's "We'll Meet Again" had the audience waving flags and singing along, recapturing the community spirit and emotional times of the Second World War.

Mary stood beside Ethel, their arms linked, and sang along

with her. 'Oh my goodness that brought back some memories,' she said as the song ended. 'Both good and bad.'

Ethel nodded. 'It certainly did, Mary. And for everybody else here tonight, no doubt.'

As the applause died down Basil announced there would be a short break before the final act of the evening. People moved away from their seats, dashing inside their homes for refreshments and a toilet break before sitting down once more.

* * *

Levi and his two dads stood by the side of the stage, chatting about their song choices with Kenny and Jimmy. Kenny spotted his mam pushing a wheelchair with his dad sitting in it and he excused himself and dashed over to greet them.

Levi smiled. 'I'm so glad they've made it,' he said, nodding towards Kenny's parents. 'He's been on pins waiting, but he knows they can't really plan anything in advance and they have to wait and see how his dad is from hour to hour.' He waved in their direction and saw Granny Mary hurrying over to get a seat sorted for Kenny's mam and helping her to put his dad's wheelchair in place next to her chair. Kenny hugged his mam, patted his dad on the arm and came running back, a big smile on his face.

'Are you ready, boys?' Basil asked. 'I'll go and introduce you, so follow me onto the stage. There's quite a lot of older kids out there now who've probably come just to see you three. Get 'em up dancing if you can. Best of luck.'

Basil thanked the audience for coming back to their seats for the finale. 'Now tonight you are witnessing the very first performance by a trio of young lads who are going to play you a few new songs of a very different kind to what you've already heard. This type of music is going to take over the world, so I'm told by the young ones. So please put your hands together and welcome on stage The Sefton Trio. Take it away, boys.'

Fired equally by nerves and enthusiasm, Levi thanked the audience for their applause and introduced the first song as he'd heard the other acts do. 'Okay, so tonight we're going to start with a number that was a big hit for Lonnie Donegan in January this year. I hope you like it.' He strummed his guitar, nodded at Kenny who was poised with his washboard, thimbles on every finger, and Jimmy, who was standing beside the tea-chest bass, and they began to sing "Rock Island Line".

Immediately some of the older kids were up dancing and people clapped in rhythm and sang along. Levi smiled with relief as cheers and whistles sounded and the boys took a bow as they finished.

'Thank you, thank you so much,' Levi said. 'Well that was called skiffle music, but now for a bit of rock'n'roll. We're going to sing two songs from an American guy who will be one of the biggest stars ever, well we think so anyway.' A cheer went up and a couple of girls near the front of the stage called out, 'Elvis Presley.' Levi smiled and nodded. "Heartbreak Hotel" and "Blue Suede Shoes" went down so well with Levi doing his best to emulate Elvis's style by curling his lips and swivelling his hips like they'd seen the star do on newsreels at the picture house.

Bella and Bobby and Earl and Molly shouted the loudest cheers as their boy took a bow, grinning all over his face. 'He's got star quality,' Bobby said proudly as the audience went mad, clapping and cheering. 'That's got to be nurtured now along with Di and the twins.'

'Definitely,' Earl agreed. 'What a fabulous day this has been. Now I'm going to get up there and make an announcement. Because the success of this day and night is down to one person and I want to make sure she gets the praise she deserves.' He went to speak to Basil, who nodded.

'She's over there with Ethel. I'll go and bring her across to the stage,' Basil said. 'While you do the thank you speeches, I'll hold onto her 'cos she'll scarper if I know our Mary. You know what she's like, can't stand any fuss. But this has to be done because she deserves it.'

* * *

Earl got back up on stage and consulted the notes he'd quickly jotted down as the evening had worn on. He stood in front of the microphone and cleared his throat.

'Well, ladies and gentlemen, may I say what a wonderful day we have all experienced. I have a lot of thank yous to dish out so I'd like to start by first saying thanks to all of you Victory Street residents who have worked very hard to make the street look so special for our royal visitors. It's a credit to you. Thank you to all who helped to prepare and serve up the delicious buffet this afternoon, the residents and the Wavertree WI ladies. I'm sure we've all eaten enough to keep us going for the rest of the weekend. Although she's actually fallen asleep now I want to say a big thank you to our little Lizzie who presented the queen with her flowers, she made us all smile with her cuteness.'

He had to pause for cheers here.

'I'd like to thank our wonderful entertainers, the military band who gave their time to support and back our singers, our own Bryant Sisters, who brought back some lovely memories with their choice of songs. To my daughter Dianna and her Crystalettes who positively sparkled on stage and gave a great performance that everyone enjoyed. And last but not least, The Sefton Trio, who ended our entertainment with a rocking good performance. Believe you me, we will be seeing more of those talented boys in the not too distant future, I'm sure. Ah, excuse me for just a moment,' he said as Molly reached up and handed him a piece of paper.

'I have here a list of the winning raffle ticket numbers whose owners can claim a prize of their choice from my wife Molly, who,' Earl continued, 'is responsible for all the lovely decorations displayed on the street.'

A ripple of applause sounded for Molly who smiled and nodded her thanks. Earl quickly read out the numbers and a few ladies whooped and dashed over to Molly to claim their prizes.

'And now it leaves me with just a couple more enormous thanks to make, so I'm going to ask Basil to step up here with my mother-in-law, Mary. Come on, you two.' He grinned as Mary, looking puzzled, was led onto the stage by Basil.

'First of all,' Earl continued, 'I'd like you to show your appreciation to Basil here, he is responsible for arranging all your entertainment today.' Basil looked abashed as a roar of thanks resounded along with clapping, cheering and whistling. 'And next but by no means least, most of you know Mary, my lovely mother-in-law, who lived on this street for many years. It is Mary who took on the enormous task of arranging this wonderful day. Her organisational skills have been fantastic in pulling all this together. Please show your appreciation for Mary and her hardworking WI team.' Earl stepped back and urged Mary towards the microphone.

'Thank you so much,' she began. 'As well as my WI colleagues whose help has been invaluable, I have my wonderful family and all the residents of this street to thank in making today such a fabulous success. I just hope the royal couple enjoyed themselves as much as we all did. Thank you, everyone, for all you have done to support me.' Mary caught Martin's eye and he stuck up his thumbs and blew her a kiss. She gave him a wave and a smile.

Basil stepped up to the microphone and added, 'Let's not

forget our Earl here for his part in this evening's entertainment. Thank you to everyone involved. It's a day I don't think any of us will ever forget.' He looked across to the Pathé News team who were getting ready to go. 'Thanks to you good people for attending too and I hope in time we'll get to see a few clips of our day that will go down in history.'

ELEVEN

Levi stared at his mother who had a letter with his recent exam results in her hand. He'd done well, she said, and had been offered another year at Quarry Bank to take his GCE O-level exams. Next year he knew they were hoping he'd be offered a place at art college if he passed at a certain level, but he really didn't want to go. Dad was smiling from his seat on the sofa.

'Well done, son,' Bobby said. 'Your mam and me are really proud of you. Why don't you go and ring Earl and Molly now and tell them your good news.'

Levi nodded and got to his feet. He supposed he was lucky as he knew Kenny and Jimmy had to leave school next week to get jobs to help support their families, but they weren't happy about it. Since the success of the street party show Levi had set his heart on singing for a living. But his mum and dad said he needed to have something to fall back on as many people came and went in the music business and it wasn't something to rely on for the future.

He supposed they were right in a way, but all the singers he admired seemed to be doing very well for themselves. However, like Lonnie Donegan and Elvis Presley, they were a few years older than he was and maybe they'd had to do other jobs first. Dianna wanted to sing for a living too but she worked alongside Molly in the shop and seemed to be enjoying herself. Although now the twins had just finished their courses at college they could all have a chance to do more musical work soon. The Sefton Trio had played at a couple of youth club dances recently and now had a following of fans who enjoyed dancing to their music.

He sighed, picked up the phone and dialled Earl's number. Dianna answered and he greeted her and told her his news.

'Oh that's great, Levi,' she said. 'It's good to get a bit more education. You never know when you'll need it. Anyway, I'll get Dad for you; I'm just off out with Stewart.'

'Going anywhere nice?'

'Just to the Abbey picture house in Wavertree to see *High Society*,' she replied. 'We're meeting up with our old friends Sally and Nigel. Not seen them for ages so be good to catch up with them both.'

Levi smiled. His sister sounded excited. 'Have a nice time. I heard the film's really good. Might go and see it myself later this week.'

'Yeah, you should. Here's Dad now, so goodbye and I'll see you soon, Levi.'

Earl's deep voice came down the line. 'Hi there, son. Everything okay?'

'Hi, Dad, yeah all is fine, I suppose. I'm just calling to let you know I've done all right with my end-of-term exams and I'm staying on at Quarry Bank to do GCEs next year.'

'Oh that's good news, boy, well done.' Earl was quiet for a moment. 'I take it you're not that impressed though? I can detect that from your tone of voice.'

Levi stared at his disgruntled face in the hall mirror before replying. 'It's not what I really want to do, is it? You know that, Dad. But Mam and Bobby think it's the best news ever.'

Earl was quiet for a moment as though considering his reply before answering. 'An education is always good to have under your belt and decent exam results will take you far. We can try and get you singing for a living but it might not last long. And what if in time you meet a girl you want to settle down with? How will you support her, and any family you might be lucky to have, if you're not skilled to do anything? Think about it. You can still sing and we'll see how it goes.'

'Okay,' Levi replied with a sigh. What his dad said was pretty much what Mam and Bobby had said too. He was lucky to be given the chance and not have to work at some mundane job for a pittance.

'And, son, you can always come into the studio when you have any spare time, learn the business from that side of things as well. It will stand you in good stead. Work with us in school holidays and Saturdays if you're not playing gigs anywhere.'

Levi smiled. 'Thanks, Dad, I'd love to do that.'

'Okay, well start next week then. We might even pay you, you never know,' Earl teased. 'I have to go now and read bedtime stories to Patti and Harry but we'll talk soon, okay. Goodbye, son.'

'Bye, Dad and thanks.' Levi hung up feeling a bit happier. He went back into the lounge with a smile on his face and a swagger to his walk. He'd be a singer one day, he was determined, but if it kept all his parents happy for now, he'd stay on at school and do the best he could to please them all.

* * *

At Friday night's meeting, Mary sat open-mouthed as the members of the Wavertree WI cheered and clapped. To her absolute shock, surprise and delight, she had just been nominated to take over as president of the Wavertree branch due to Eva Thompson deciding to resign from her post.

'I'm so shocked,' Mary said as calls of 'Speech' echoed around the room. 'For once in my life I'm lost for words.'

'First time for everything,' her friend Joyce Andrews said. 'Well as you can see by the votes, it was an overwhelming majority for you, Mary. I'm so happy for you. We all are. No one deserves the position more than you do.'

'Hear, hear,' the other members agreed. Eva Thompson was not even present at this meeting and had sent in her resignation by letter to begin with immediate effect.

'After the hard work you put in with the royal visit, it was clear to us all that you have the leadership qualities necessary in a president,' Joyce said. 'Just like your late friend Fenella had. We know we'll be in good hands if something like that is dropped on our toes again in the future.'

Mary shook her head and blew out her cheeks. 'I still don't know what to say.'

'Well can you assure us that you'll say yes, at least?' Joyce grinned. 'Then we can celebrate with a nice cuppa and biscuit.'

Mary nodded; her smile a mile wide. 'Yes, of course I will. I'm absolutely delighted to accept the position of president.'

Another cheer went up and Mary shook her head. Wait until she got home and told her family. They'd be made up for her, she was sure of that.

* * *

Dianna and Stewart ran across the road to the Abbey picture house and gave their friends hugs and kisses and got some back in return.

'Oh it's so good to see you,' Dianna said. 'It seems like ages. Are your second-year exams over now?' she asked Sally who was training to be a state registered nurse at the Royal Liverpool.

'They are,' Sally replied. 'I'm just waiting to see if I've

passed and then I've only one more year to go and I'll hopefully be a fully-fledged SRN this time next year.'

'And are you still enjoying nursing? How are the others, is Carol still there?'

'Yep, I'm still enjoying it, but Carol is leaving the hospital next week to get married first Saturday in August. I was going to write and tell you as she'd like you to come to the after-wedding party if you can. But then you suggested this night out so I thought I'd tell you when I saw you. Carol's only gone and got herself in the family way and her boyfriend wants them to get wed. Her mam's not too happy about it, says it's too soon and they've only known one another five minutes. It's six months actually, but she's being really horrible to Carol and nasty to her boyfriend, but better this than an unmarried daughter with a baby, I suppose.'

'Oh no, poor Carol,' Dianna exclaimed. 'How does she feel about it? She loved her nursing career.'

'She's fine, very happy in fact,' Sally said. 'She also loves Victor and his mam is making her front room into a bed-sit for them until they can get on the housing list and she will help out with baby-minding if Carol wants to get a job later on. She's a really nice lady, according to Carol, so hopefully she'll be a big help to them both, more than her own mother will be, anyway.'

Dianna nodded. 'Well give her our love and tell her we would love to come to her wedding party. Is that okay with you, Stewart?'

'Yeah, no problem. It will be nice for you to catch up with your old nursing pals again.'

Dianna smiled. It would. She missed them. But she just couldn't stay on and finish her training that she started alongside Sally two years ago. She'd wanted to be a nurse for as long as she could remember, but had been subjected to some wicked and cruel racist treatment and had sworn she'd never set foot in that hospital again, even though the nursing tutor responsible had been dismissed after being reported. It had soured things for Dianna and she'd started to gain her confidence back once she was away from there.

'Well the party will be at Carol's new mother-in-law's place so I'll get the address and ring you with it,' Sally said. 'She'll be really happy to see you again. They all will. We heard about the success of the show after the Victory Street royal visit last month. We saw some pictures in the *Echo*. You and the twins looked amazing, just like proper professionals in them gorgeous dresses.'

'Made by our lovely aunties.' Dianna grinned. 'We had a wonderful day. Something none of us will ever forget.'

'Right, you two, let's get in before they sell all the seats and the picture starts,' Stewart said, taking charge. 'We can have a coffee down the road after. And you can catch up some more then.'

Nigel grinned. 'We'll never get a word in, mate. You know what these two are like once they start gabbing.'

'Hoy, cheeky,' Sally said. 'You two are just as bad once you start on about motorbikes and football.'

* * *

Dianna settled back into her seat to watch the British Pathé newsreel before the start of the main picture but she wasn't paying too much attention as her mind was on Carol's wedding and meeting up with her former nursing colleagues again. She and Sally had first met Stewart and Nigel on a night out with them at the Rumblin' Tum Coffee Bar in the city centre.

She smiled, thinking back to how she had fancied her fiancé the first time she'd set eyes on him. With his dark hair and big brown eyes he'd looked so handsome, perched on a bar stool alongside blond-haired Nigel. Love at first sight might be a cliché, but it applied to her and Stewart and also to Sally and

Nigel. But Sally wasn't allowed to get engaged or married while she was training. She and Nige would have to wait for now. Dianna was interrupted from her thoughts by Stewart shaking her right arm gently.

'Look, Di,' he whispered and pointed at the screen where short clips from last month's royal visits of all the cities were being played and it was now showing Liverpool.

Dianna held her breath as a clip of little Lizzie with her arm in a sling was up on the screen. She suppressed a giggle as the commentator made an amusing remark about her stealing the show when Lizzie did her curtsey and a twirl after handing the queen her flowers. Then a shot panned onto the stage from later that night and there in all their glory were Dianna and her cousins. She held her breath as the clip finished and the Bryant Sisters appeared singing the last few lines of "We'll Meet Again". The camera then panned over the street residents all waving flags and singing along. The commentator was saying something about that old wartime spirit still being alive and well in Liverpool. A cheer went up from the picture-goers and Dianna smiled.

Sally, sitting to her left, gave a little squeal and said, 'Oh my God, Di, how exciting; my famous friend. Practically royalty!'

'Hardly,' Dianna said, laughing. 'But it was lovely to see that. We can report back and then the family can take turns in seeing the film and catching up on the newsreel.'

Stewart reached for her hand and squeezed it. 'Well done, girl,' he whispered. 'That won't be the last time we see you on a screen, I'm sure. Right, here we go. The main feature is just about to begin. They're predicting this is going to be *the* film of the year.'

'Well with Grace Kelly, Frank and Bing in it, as well as Satchmo, that's hardly a surprising statement for them to come up with.' Dianna turned her eyes back to the screen and was quickly lost in the developing storyline. As *High Society* ended she sighed and turned to Stewart. 'Oh that was lovely. I tell you what; the song "True Love" is fabulous, just the sort of ballad that Bella and Bobby could do together. I'll tell them about it tomorrow. It would suit them down to the ground,' she finished as everyone got to their feet for the national anthem.

'It would,' Stewart agreed as the anthem ended. He smiled as the audience started to file towards the doors, some beginning to sing "Well, Did You Evah!" as they made their way out. 'And that one's catchy as well,' he said with a grin. 'Bet it'll be popular.'

Outside on the pavement Dianna stared up at the Abbey name in colourful neon lights and smiled, remembering her first time here with Stewart a couple of years ago. They'd come to see *Doctor in the House* with Sally and Nigel that time too. They'd giggled at the grumpy usherette who threatened to chuck them out if they weren't quieter. They'd hardly been noisy when all was said and done.

'Right then,' Stewart said. 'Frothy coffee time, I think. And a bit more of a catch-up for these two.' He smiled at Dianna and Sally who were nodding enthusiastically.

TWELVE

WAVERTREE, AUGUST 1956

'Don't forget to remind Basil about tomorrow,' Molly said to her sister who had popped round to have a catch-up on Saturday evening. 'And tell him to bring Aunty Et,' she added. Molly had arranged a surprise tea party to celebrate their mam's good news about her WI promotion and to say well done to Levi for his end-of-term exam results.

'How did you get on with Lizzie at the hospital this morning?' she asked, handing Bella a mug of tea and a freshly baked scone from the batch she'd made for tomorrow's tea party.

'She's absolutely fine,' Bella replied. 'She was so funny though. She keeps looking at her arm and stroking it. It must feel a bit odd to her after all those weeks in plaster. Most of the nurses had seen her on the film clips at the picture house. She's quite a little star in the accident and emergency department. They made a big fuss of her and so did the doctor.'

'Oh that's so nice of them,' Molly said. 'How kind people can be sometimes.'

Bella nodded and laughed. 'She showed them her twirl so many times I had to ask her to stop or she'd get dizzy, fall over and break her other blooming arm.'

Molly grinned. 'Bless her. Have you any idea what the weather forecast is for tomorrow? Be nice to have our party in the garden as long as it doesn't rain.'

'It's supposed to be a nice day tomorrow. Does Mam think she's coming on her own, well just her and Martin anyway?'

'She does. It won't be a big party as I just haven't the time to cater for more than us lot and your lot, including Basil and Aunty Et of course. And Dianna has invited Stewart along.'

'Where is she tonight?' Bella asked.

'I gave her the afternoon off. She and Stewart have gone to a wedding reception,' Molly replied. 'It's that nursing friend of her and Sally's, Carol, that's ended up in the family way. She's had to leave the hospital but at least her boyfriend has stood by her, which is something I suppose. More than her own mother's done anyway, according to Dianna.'

'Miserable devil,' Bella muttered. 'Thank God our mam's not like that, or God knows what would have happened to me and Levi back then.'

Molly nodded. 'Talking of being in the family way, I've got a big bag of baby stuff for that Glenda on Victory Street. I put a little poster up in the shop to ask for babywear donations for a family in need and so many people have dropped off clothes their babies have grown out of. I need to take them to her at some point but I'm so short of time.'

'I'll take them to Fran's for you and then she can pass them on,' Bella offered. 'I know Mam said the WI has got a few items to take over as well. Hopefully she'll have everything she needs by her due date, which I think is in a couple of months. She was so grateful for that money the raffle made, you know. Fran said she tears up when she talks about how kind everyone is to her now that bullying so-and-so has gone.'

'What about Miss Clancy, are things okay between them now?'

Bella nodded and took a sip of tea. 'They're much better,

but she still wants to move when an offer of a new flat comes her way. It's not so much Glenda and her brood now, but she's got a bad hip and is struggling with the stairs and feels she'll cope much better all on one level.'

'Oh she will,' Molly agreed. 'And it will be so nice for her to have everything all new as well. That kitchen in there has never been improved since the houses were built and she's still got no bathroom, just the outside lavvy that she shares. The landlord only modernised a few of them and we were lucky he chose to do the ones on our side of the street. Fran and Edie have both got nice bathrooms. Miss Clancy can't manage to lug a tin bath in and out of the house now at her age.'

'She'll be much better off with a new place,' Bella said. 'I think the landlord will sell it once it's empty. He's sold quite a lot of his houses since we moved from there. As soon as a family gets moved away to the new estates, he's stopped re-letting. Maybe he's getting ready to retire and can't be bothered managing them anymore. He is getting on a bit. He always seemed to be old when we were little girls.'

'Hmm, he probably is nearly ready to retire,' Molly said. 'Get Fran to let you know when Miss Clancy is offered anything and we'll keep an eye on the house to see if he puts it up for sale. Dianna and Stewart have been saving up for a deposit for ages to buy something so they can get married. But most houses are too expensive for them at the moment. They need what Dianna calls a doer-upper. That's what they call them in America, she tells me. It'll be much cheaper to buy and they can work on it in their spare time before they decide on a date for the wedding.'

'Yeah, okay,' Bella said. 'That would be nice. She'd have Fran and Edie living opposite so she wouldn't be without someone to talk to. I can't see them two moving anytime soon. Edie's been saying for ages that they're going to buy a house but it's not happened yet and Fran and Sam can't afford to move.

They were hoping for a new house on one of the estates after little Gary arrived but there's nothing been offered them yet.' Bella finished her tea and tucked into the scone. 'That was lovely,' she said. 'Thank you. Well I suppose I'd better get off while it's still light and I'll see you tomorrow afternoon. Is there anything you'd like me to bring?'

Molly shook her head. 'We've got everything in, I think. Just bring yourselves. Remember to keep quiet about it if Mam phones you though.'

'My lips are sealed,' Bella said. 'I'll see you tomorrow then.'

* * *

Dianna smiled as Victor's dad asked everyone to raise a glass to toast his son and new daughter-in-law. 'To Carol and Victor,' he said, lifting a small glass of something fizzy in the air. 'Wishing them all the very best for a long and happy marriage.'

'To Carol and Victor,' everyone said, knocking back the pretend champagne which sent bubbles up Dianna's nose and made her cough and her eyes water. She blinked away tears and smiled at Carol, who came over to her and thanked her and Stewart for coming.

'It's really good to see you again,' Carol said. 'You look so much happier than you did a year or so ago, Di. Life and Stewart are obviously treating you well.'

'We're doing okay,' Dianna said. 'And congratulations to you and Victor and your little bump. Hope it all works out for you.'

'Me too,' Carol said, raising her eyebrows. 'It's been a nightmare keeping it a secret while we saved a bit of money up for the wedding. I'm already five months as I tried to keep working as long as I could before someone realised I was up the duff. Once they did they wanted me to leave as soon as possible. Anyway, here we are, start of a brand new life and thanks to

Vic's mam and dad we've at least got a roof over our heads. We can register with the housing department now we're official so might get a nice new flat in time. We'll see. We're taking small steps, but hopefully in the right direction. Not quite the future either of us had planned, but you have to take what life chucks at you sometimes.'

'You do,' Dianna agreed. 'I'm sure you'll be fine. But you must keep in touch with me. I'll write down my phone number before we leave here. By the way, you look lovely.' She admired Carol's knee-length ivory-coloured empire-line dress that flowed neatly over her baby bump. A little circle of cream rose-buds trimmed with ivory ribbon sat on top of her red hair which hung in soft tumbling waves to her shoulders. 'You look every bit the blushing bride.'

Carol laughed. 'Thank you. And keeping in touch will be lovely, Di. I need all the friends I can get right now, and me, you and Sally used to be so close before you left.'

'And we will be again,' Dianna reassured her. 'That much I promise you.'

* * *

'You're very quiet,' Dianna said to Stewart as they left the wedding party and walked arm in arm to the bus stop. 'You okay, love?'

He nodded. 'Hmm, I was just thinking. Maybe it's time for us to set the date. What do you reckon?'

Dianna frowned. 'I wish we could. I can't wait to be married to you. But we have nowhere to live and not quite enough money to buy a house yet.'

'I think my parents would help us out,' Stewart said. 'If we could find something to do up we'd be fine. And it takes time to get a wedding organised so if we say book a date for the end of the year we can stay with Mam and Dad while we work on the house. What do you think? Shall I have a word with them? I really don't want to wait much longer; we've been engaged two years already.' He pulled her into his arms at the bus stop and whispered into her hair. 'I can't wait to make you mine, Di. You have no idea how hard it is to say goodnight to you and leave to go home.'

Dianna snuggled into him. She *did* know and *she* couldn't wait much longer either. She also knew that if they didn't make plans soon they may well find themselves in the same position as Carol and Victor. Stewart had been so patient with her wishes to wait until they were married before going all the way, but it was getting more difficult to do that.

'Okay, let's set a date then,' she agreed. 'Everything else can fit around it. The house and what have you. What I'd really like is a Christmas wedding. It's only five months away but that's plenty of time to make plans.'

Stewart hugged her tight. 'That makes me so happy. And you'll be a gorgeous Christmas bride. Shall we tell your family tomorrow at the surprise tea party?'

Dianna grinned. 'We might as well, while we have them all under one roof. And then we can tell yours later in the evening.'

* * *

Mary handed a cake in a tin that she'd made to Molly and gave her a hug. 'It's the usual, Victoria sponge. It's quiet in here, chuck. Where are the kids and Earl?'

'Er, they're in the back garden, Mam. It's such a lovely day so we thought we'd sit outside. Go on through.'

Molly followed her mother and Martin into the kitchen where every surface was covered with plates of sandwiches and cakes.

'You've been busy, love,' Mary observed. 'Looks like you're planning to feed an army, not just us.' She stepped out into the beautiful garden where all the plants and bushes were colour co-ordinated and in full bloom.

'Surprise,' yelled a multitude of voices, making Mary jump backwards.

'Oh, my God! What the devil are you lot doing here?' She smiled at Bella and Bobby and their family and Basil and Ethel as well as Earl, Dianna and her fiancé, and Molly's kids. It was only once she got over the shock that she noticed the sweet 'CONGRATULATIONS' bunting from Molly's shop hanging behind them.

'We wanted to do something special for you to honour your WI presidency,' Molly told her, 'and also to celebrate our Levi's exam results. Well done to you both, we're very proud of you.' As everyone cheered Molly saw Stewart look at Dianna who smiled and nodded her head. He stepped forward and cleared his throat.

'Er, we have one more thing to celebrate,' he began. 'Dianna and I would like to get married at Christmas this year, if that's okay with you?' He looked at Earl.

'That is great news,' Earl said, going over to shake Stewart by the hand. 'You have my blessing to go ahead with your plans, young man.'

'Thank you, Dad,' Dianna said, rushing to him and throwing her arms around his neck.

'My pleasure, princess,' Earl said. 'That is something else to really look forward to. This family goes from strength to strength. I am so proud to be a part of it.'

Molly caught Bella's eye and winked as her sister nodded with understanding. Miss Clancy's house would definitely be needed now.

THIRTEEN

WAVERTREE, DECEMBER 1956

By the beginning of December all the plans for Dianna and Stewart's wedding on Saturday the 22nd were firmly in place and Molly and Bella accompanied her to Uncle Scott's house for a final dress fitting. Dianna's aunts, Ruby and Dolores, were making her dress and two little Flower girls' dresses for Patti and Lizzie, as well as bridesmaids' dresses for Tammy and Ebony.

Sally had accepted the position of being her maid of honour and was meeting them here tonight for *her* final fitting too. Dianna was looking forward to a real girls-only night, Uncle Scotty having been banished to Earl's for a couple of hours, and she couldn't wait to see the dresses on her family and best friend. The two little girls were at home asleep so would have a fitting another day, but at least she could have a look at their dresses tonight. Molly was in charge of making all the bouquets and church and hall flower displays.

'Come on in,' Ruby greeted them and took their coats. 'Go down to the dining room and help yourself to a glass of sherry and some nibbles. We thought we would make a bit of a party of this. After all, it's not every day our beautiful niece gets married, now is it.'

Dianna laughed and hurried down the hallway with Bella and Molly in her wake. Her cousins and Sally were already in the dining room and greeted them all with hugs and kisses.

'Mom's upstairs getting changed,' Tammy said. 'She's just off her shift. Grab a drink and have a seat. Isn't this exciting? We can't wait to try our dresses on.'

'I can't wait to see them,' Dianna said, picking up a small sherry glass and sitting down on the sofa by the marble fireplace where a log fire blazed and crackled in the grate. It felt so cosy and warm in here and a large pine tree in front of the bay window glowed with fairy lights, tinsel and colourful baubles. The scent of Christmas was all around. Dianna loved it. Christmas would always be a special time of the year for her and Stewart to celebrate now. Sally came to sit beside her and smiled.

'You okay, Di?'

Dianna nodded. 'Yes. I can't believe the day's nearly here. I'm so nervous but I'm excited at the same time.'

'I bet you are,' Sally said. 'Isn't this house fabulous? I would love to live somewhere like this when I'm married. Ha, I should be so lucky. Be more likely to be a shoebox on a new estate with mine and Nigel's wages. But still, a home is what you make it.'

'It is,' Dianna agreed. 'We've got nothing lined up to buy yet but Stewart's mam and dad are letting us live with them while we get a bit more money saved up for the deposit. Then, like you say, it'll no doubt be a shoebox somewhere. But as long as we fill it with love, it won't matter. How are Carol and Vic by the way? And is the baby okay now? I know they had a few problems with her at first.'

'They're fine and so is little Amelia,' Sally replied. 'She's lovely and she's got Carol's red hair. She's settling well now. They kept her in the special-care baby unit for an extra week while they sorted her feeding problems out. They've given Carol a special milk feed mix that's more suitable.'

Dianna nodded. Carol and Victor's little daughter had been born with a problem that caused her to projectile vomit each time she was fed and her birth weight had dropped dramatically. A small operation to repair an umbilical hernia and then the change of feed mix would help get her weight back up again.

'I'm so glad they got her sorted out. That must have been so frightening for them. Give Carol our love and tell her I hope they can make the wedding, but we understand if they can't and we'll catch up with them in the New Year.'

'I will do,' Sally said. 'She's determined to come though. She's bought a new dress and Vic's mam has said she will look after Amelia for them.'

Dianna smiled. 'Oh that's good. It'll be really nice to see them again. I just wish my Grammy and Grandpa Franklin could have come over for Christmas and our wedding day but Uncle Levi called Dad when they got our invitations and told him that Grandpa isn't at all well at the moment and hasn't been for a few weeks. *He* can't come either as he doesn't want to leave them on their own right now. Maybe they'll all visit next year when Grandpa is fully recovered.'

'That's a shame,' Sally said. 'What's wrong with your grandpa?'

'He had pneumonia in the summer and it's complications from that apparently.'

'Flying wouldn't be good for him then with chest and breathing problems,' Sally said. 'The air pressure in the plane cabin wouldn't be right for him. Maybe they'll be able to sail here on the *Queen Mary* when he's well again. That would be nice and relaxing for them both.'

Dianna nodded and looked up as the dining room door swung open. She smiled as Aunt Dolores came into the room.

Her aunt always looked so lovely in her flamboyant and bright-coloured clothes that were just perfect against her dark skin. Aunt Dolores lit up every room she walked into. Dianna loved being in her company and Aunt Ruby's too. Ruby had brought up Dianna for a big part of her childhood when Dianna's dad's first marriage ended.

On his divorce he was granted sole custody of Dianna due to her biological mother's drinking problems that led to the subsequent neglect of her small daughter. Once they moved here and he married Molly, she took over caring for Dianna and was a caring and supportive stepmother who Dianna loved very much. Dianna felt herself so lucky to belong to this wonderful mixed family.

'Okay, ladies,' Aunt Dolores began, clapping her hands to gain their attention. 'Have you all got a glass of sherry? In that case,' she continued as they all nodded, 'I'd like to raise a toast to my beautiful niece, Dianna. May she and Stewart be blessed with many happy years together. To Dianna.'

'Dianna,' everyone toasted.

'Thank you,' Dianna said and smiled round at them all. 'That means such a lot.'

'Okay, well let's get the dresses tried on before we get a little tipsy. I don't want any falls downstairs tonight. Ebony, Tammy and Sally, off you go. Ruby will take you to the rooms your dresses are waiting in and help you with the zips. Meantime, I think we should have some seasonal music playing on that radiogram to get us in the Christmas spirit.'

As the girls left the room, Dolores rooted around in Scotty's music collection, pulled out a record and placed it on the spindle where it dropped down, the arm swung across and the pleasant voice of Dickie Valentine started to sing "The Christmas Alphabet". Dolores joined in, singing along, and so did Bella. They all clapped as the song came to an end and was replaced by Bing Crosby's dulcet tones and "White Christmas".

Molly got up to answer a tap at the door and the twins swanned in and did a wiggle or two like models on a catwalk.

Dianna clapped a hand to her mouth. 'You both look fabulous,' she said, her eyes filling. Her cousins were dressed in red, tea-length, satin, slim-fitting A-line dresses that they favoured over full skirts. Over their shoulders were little half-moon-shaped cream fur capes fastened at the front neckline with matching red satin bows. Dolores clapped her hands as everyone started talking at once. She cleared her throat and, with a twinkle in her eyes, began, 'Now here we have the lovely Tammy and Ebony modelling our red satin numbers. Over their shoulders, to keep out the chill in a draughty church, goes a little cream fur cape made from Ruby's cony fur coat that she never wears anymore and kindly donated to the cause.'

Dianna laughed. 'Well I hope you don't decide you want it back, Aunty, when the weather gets really cold very soon.'

'Too late now,' Dolores said with a grin. 'It's all cut up. She'll have to wear an extra vest if she's cold.' She went to the door and opened it to let in Sally who was waiting in the hall. 'Next we have Sally modelling our full-length maid of honour dress in cream satin with a red satin panel down the front of the skirt. Sally's cape is made from matching red velvet with ivory ribbon trims. All winter weddings need that little extra layer to keep warm.'

Sally sashayed in looking elegant and Dianna smiled and nodded.

'That suits you so well,' she said to Sally. 'I love the reds and creams, it's all so Christmassy.'

'I love it too,' Sally said, smoothing her hands down the front of her dress. 'Never had such a posh dress in all me life before. Mam will be dead proud when she sees me in this.'

Ruby came in carrying two little short cream silk dresses with full skirts and two tiny red velvet boleros. Bella and Molly smiled their approval.

'Those are just gorgeous,' Molly said. 'Absolutely beautiful. Lizzie and Patti will look like two little proper princesses walking up that church aisle. And they'll carry little white baskets that I'll trim with red ribbon to match. Proper little flower girls, bless them. I've cut some red petals from crepe paper as red flowers to dry are in short supply at this time of the year. I've managed to source some to be delivered nearer the day for the bouquets and church flower decorations, but there will be none left over to play around with.'

Bella grinned. 'Good idea. Lizzie's still not got the hang of dropping petals as they walk. We cut bits of newspaper up and popped them in a little bag for her to keep practising up and down the hall with. She's not great, but I think we're getting there.'

'Well she managed to present the queen with her bouquet and made us all laugh,' said Dianna. 'I'm sure she'll do just fine.'

'Right, ladies,' Dolores said. 'Well I think all the dresses fit perfectly, which is good as that means we don't have to start messing about altering them. If you'll go and take them off and leave them hanging from the picture rails in the bedrooms.'

The girls left the room and Dolores topped up everyone's glasses with more sherry and offered around a plate of spicy chicken pieces to nibble on. 'We've got some freshly baked mince pies for later,' she announced, as the twins and Sally came back into the room.

'Dianna, it's your turn now, my love, up you go,' Dolores said. 'Ruby will help you if you need anything.'

Dianna got up and hurried out of the room. The excited butterflies in her stomach were almost dancing up to her throat as she walked into the bedroom at the top of the stairs. She stopped and stared at the stunning white dress that hung from the picture rail. She'd already had two fitting and measuring sessions when the fabric was just pieced together but this finished dress was beautiful beyond her wildest dreams. It was a slightly flared, full-length style, of delicate white floral lace over white satin with a pearl-button-fastening bodice, three-quarter-length lace sleeves and a sweetheart neckline. She was conscious of Aunt Ruby standing behind her.

'Stunning, ain't it?' Ruby said softly. 'You sure are going to look a million dollars in that, my girl. My brother will be so, so proud of his princess.'

Dianna's eyes filled and Ruby pulled her into her arms. 'Now come on, we don't want to stain that lace with tears,' she teased. 'Let's get it on you and you can go and swank it off downstairs.'

Ruby helped her on with the dress and as Dianna walked into the dining room everyone looked up and fell silent as they paused chattering. She smiled at their shocked faces. 'Do I really look that bad?' she teased with a smile.

'You look absolutely beautiful,' Molly said, a catch in her voice. 'Oh my God, your dad will be in bits when he sets eyes on you.'

Bella nodded her agreement. 'He certainly will. What a gorgeous dress. You two should go into dressmaking seriously, never mind nursing,' she aimed at Ruby and Dolores. 'All of the dresses are just fabulous.'

'There is a veil which we have yet to finish trimming with tiny pearls,' Ruby said. 'That will sit on top of Dianna's hair, held in place with a little coronet. Have you decided on a hair-style yet, Di?'

'I like it loose on my shoulders, so don't think I want an up-style. We did chat about it, me and the twins, and we love our ringlets so will probably all go for the same longer look.'

'I'm going to leave mine long as well,' Sally said. 'Might just get the ends curled out. I do wish mine was a rich dark colour like you threes though instead of this boring mousey brown shade I'm blessed with.'

Dianna laughed. 'At least you've got nice shiny straight hair,

Sal. Don't knock it. Ours takes some taming, I tell you, and mine can be so wild at times.'

'Right, Di,' Ruby said. 'Let's get that dress back upstairs so it stays safe. No alterations are needed either which is good news for us. We'll keep them all here until the Friday before the wedding, and then get them over to your houses in the evening, ready for the morning.'

Molly nodded. 'Earl will be in that night if me and Dianna are not,' she said. 'I'll be down at the church and the hall with Mam and Bella doing the flowers. Mam's got the WI ladies helping with the buffet and we're having a bit of entertainment from our Levi and his pals on the night as well.'

Dianna turned to Bella. 'Why don't you and Bobby sing a couple of songs for us? I doubt me and the twins will be able to do much dressed in all our finery. You could do that song I told you about from *High Society*, "True Love".'

Bella grinned and shook her head. 'Trust you,' she said. 'We've been learning it and that song was going to be our surprise for you and Stewart. We *had* planned to get you up for your first dance to it.'

Dianna laughed and clapped her hand to her mouth. 'Oh, I'm sorry, me and my big mouth. I had no idea. Well pretend I never said that just now and I'll act all surprised when you do sing it.'

Bella nodded and smiled. 'Go on then, it's our secret. It was Bobby's idea to sing it for you so act dead surprised for him when he announces it. Right, one more little drink and maybe one of those mince pies you mentioned, Dolores, and then I'd better ring Basil and get him to come and pick us up. He *did* offer and I told him we wouldn't be too late. Thanks for your hospitality Ruby and Dolores. It's been so lovely to get a preview of the dresses.'

* * *

Fran frowned and ducked back behind the curtain she was just drawing at the front room window. She was a bit late tonight and had usually closed them by now. She stared at the man wobbling his way down the street and then stopping right opposite and banging with both his fists on Glenda's door. Surely it wasn't that Reg, her useless ex? There'd been no sign of him for months and Glenda had been really settled and happy and had welcomed her new son into the world six weeks ago.

What on earth did *he* want now? The door opened slightly and Fran recognised young Michael, one of Glenda's twins, peering out. Fran gasped and called for Sam to come quickly as Michael, who was trying to stop the man from entering, was pushed roughly to one side and Reg went into the house, slamming the door closed behind him.

'What is it, love?' Sam asked, hurrying into the room. 'You look worried to death.'

'That bloody ex of Glenda's has just barged his way into her house. He's slammed the door shut but he shoved poor Michael out of the way to get in.'

'Oh bloody hell. Shall I go over and make sure her and the kids are all right?'

Fran nodded. 'But don't go on your own. He's a nasty vicious swine. Get Stevie to go with you. Go out the back door here though then Reg can't see you. Their curtains are open across the way so he'll be able to see what's going on over here if you leave by the front door.'

Sam nodded and hurried out to the back. He rapped on Edie and Stevie's door. Edie answered and he asked for Stevie.

'He's upstairs, come on in, Sam.' She shouted up for Stevie. 'What's up?' she asked Sam. 'You look proper mithered.'

Sam told her what Fran had seen and she gasped. 'Oh no. Glenda's not in the best of health after having the baby. She really doesn't need him causing trouble for her. And Miss

Clancy will be scared out of her wits if she sees and hears anything horrible happening.'

Stevie hurried downstairs and agreed with Sam that they should nip down the back passage in the middle of the row of their terraced houses. Edie locked her door and went into Fran's house. Dennis was sleeping over at her mam's tonight so she didn't have to worry about him.

'Fran,' she called as she went into the kitchen.

'I'm in here,' Fran called back. She was still at the window, looking out from a gap at the side of the now-drawn curtains. 'I can see Sam and Stevie standing outside Miss Clancy's house; she's come to the door so she must have been peeping out too. I can't believe that lout's had the cheek to come back here.'

Edie shook her head. 'Neither can I. He's got some blooming neck. I bet he's as drunk as a lord as well; he was wobbling as he walked down the street towards the house. Fancy him wasting good money on booze like that when he never gives Glenda a penny and she's struggling every day to put food on the table to feed his kids.'

'Oh look, Miss Clancy has asked our blokes in,' Fran said. As she spoke a loud noise of shattering glass reached her ears and she gasped as a wooden dining chair hurtled through Glenda's front window and landed in the street on the cobbles. 'Bloody hell. What is he playing at? Hope he hasn't hurt any of the kiddies. I bet they're terrified.'

'Shall we phone the police?' Edie asked, chewing her lip worriedly.

'Oh God I don't know what to do,' Fran said. 'Do you think we should?'

'Yes,' Edie replied. 'Definitely. Come on.'

In the hall Fran dialled 999 and asked for the police. As she explained to the duty policeman, who she was put through to, what was happening, she was told that a patrol car was on its way to that address already as another neighbour had already called. 'Thank you,' Fran said and hung up.

'They're on their way,' she told Edie as she rejoined her at the window. 'I bet Miss Clancy got there before us. She's our party line, so I know she's definitely got a phone. Oh my God the door's opening, look, it's one of the girls and she's screaming her head off. Poor little thing looks frightened to death. I'll go and get her.'

Fran ran to her front door and yanked it open as Sam and Stevie stepped out onto the street with Miss Clancy between them. She picked up the sobbing little girl who was only wearing a faded thin cotton nightdress and had nothing on her feet, as Sam shouted for her to take Miss Clancy inside with her as well while they waited for the police. Glenda's door was now firmly shut again but several other doors had opened along the terraced row and more neighbours were coming out onto the street to see what was going on. Fran carried the sobbing child inside her house as Edie came out to help a shaking Miss Clancy.

While Edie made Miss Clancy comfortable and made her a mug of hot sweet tea, Fran sat with the little girl on her knee while her sobs subsided. She wiped the child's tears away with a clean hanky. Miss Clancy, her own eyes moist and weary look-ing, patted the sofa for the little girl to come and sit beside her. She wriggled across and snuggled into Miss Clancy's side.

'Mammy said to get help,' she whimpered, looking at Fran with wide frightened eyes.

'Help's coming,' Edie reassured her. 'Mammy will be fine. Try not to worry. What's your name, sweetheart?' she asked, handing the child a cup of warm milk.

'Marlene,' the little girl replied. She drank the milk and handed the cup back to Edie who smoothed her hair from her eyes.

Bells clanging in the street heralded the arrival of a police car and Fran went back to looking out of the window to see what was happening. Stevie and Sam were still outside Miss Clancy's house as two policemen got out of the car. Sam waved to them and pointed at the house next door with the smashed window.

'Next door, mate. Be careful, there's broken glass everywhere and there's kiddies in there including a very young baby. My wife's taken one of the little girls into our house. She came outside screaming.'

'Thanks,' the policeman called and hammered on the door. He tried the handle but it was locked from the inside. He could hear screams and shouting from the other side. He put his shoulder against it but it didn't move. He tried again and his colleague joined in.

'It might be unlocked at the back,' Sam suggested.

'Do you know who this bloke in there is?' one of the officers asked.

'The ex-husband of the lady that lives there,' Stevie said. 'He came back out of the blue earlier and pushed his way in. He's a bullying drunkard and there are five more youngsters in there as well as their mother, plus the new baby.'

'Right, we've got to get in here, call for back-up and an ambulance. Sounds like the lady of the house might need one,' the officer said. He dashed around the back way with Sam on his heels while the other officer radioed for further help. Stevie stayed on the front ready to help the best way he could. He was aware of shouting from close to the broken window. It sounded like one of the twins.

'I'll stick this bread knife in you if you don't leave our mam alone,' the young voice shouted. 'Stop kicking her or I'll do it. I mean it.'

Stevie swallowed hard and looked at the police officer, who shook his head. 'Poor kids,' he whispered. 'He's a brave little lad to tackle him like that, but we don't want him getting into any trouble for stabbing the swine.'

As he spoke Sam appeared and beckoned to the officer to follow him. 'We're in at the back.'

The officer nodded. 'Will you stay here?' he said to Stevie. 'Send the back-up officers round to us. Sounds like they're on the next street,' he added as Stevie heard the clanging of the approaching bells.

FOURTEEN

Sam looked at Glenda's brave little tribe of kids who were piled onto his sofa and chairs, tucking into warm milk and biscuits and cuddles from Fran, Edie and Miss Clancy. He thought about their poor mother who had been rushed to the Royal Liverpool Hospital with serious injuries after fighting off the maniac she'd been married to. Glenda had gone, along with her new baby who the ambulance attendants had insisted would be better off with their mother at the hospital for the time being.

These poor kids would never forget tonight and Sam didn't think he would either. As they arrested and handcuffed Reg Clark and he'd been about to be bundled into the back of a Black Maria van that had arrived to take him to the police station, he'd turned to Sam and growled under his breath, but just loud enough for Sam alone to hear, 'My mate wants to see his kid. He wants her back. You'd better tell that bitch of a wife of yours that he'll get her as well.' His threatening words had turned Sam's stomach.

'Just going over to give Stevie a hand clearing up that glass and boarding up Glenda's window,' he said to Fran. 'It looked so nice for the royal visit, but never mind that now. We'll get it fixed with new glass before she comes home but it'll make it secure for now. I need a ciggie as well and that little 'un sounds a bit chesty so I won't smoke in here.' Marlene had coughed a lot since she'd run out onto the street but it might just be a nervous cough.

Truth was, he needed a few minutes to get his thoughts in place. He and Stevie had brought Glenda's brood across to Fran and Edie and told one of the police officers to make sure their mother knew where they were when they went to the Royal to see her and to take a statement. She'd probably be worried to death that the welfare people would step in and take them all into care. No doubt they would in the next day or so, but for tonight at least they were safe.

Sam lit a cigarette and leant against his closed front door. Their neighbour Alfie Finn was giving Stevie a hand and a couple of other neighbours were clearing up the broken shards of glass. He took a long drag on his ciggie and sighed. He didn't want to worry Fran right now with Reg's drunken ramblings, but if there was a grain of truth in what he'd said, they might be in for a bit of trouble. He knew there'd be no chance of Frankie ever getting custody of his daughter Lorraine. After all, he was still banged away in Walton Gaol for many more years, but God alone knew what was going on in that warped head with his plotting and planning. He knew he'd have to tell Fran, but would wait until she and Edie had settled Glenda's little ones for the night.

* * *

When Sam returned home, the children were all asleep, tucked up on makeshift beds and covered over with borrowed blankets from Edie. Joan Finn, who had popped over to see if she could help with anything, was there too.

'Will you walk Miss Clancy home, love?' Fran asked him.

'Make sure everywhere is locked up. She's feeling a bit better now, aren't you?'

Miss Clancy nodded. 'I am, but what an awful night. That man is an animal. These poor kiddies; what they witnessed tonight was shocking.'

'We'll see you tomorrow, Miss Clancy,' Fran said. 'I hope you manage to get some sleep.'

'I'm sure I will, and Fran, will you all please call me Mabel? It sounds so much less formal than Miss Clancy.'

Fran laughed and gave her neighbour a hug. 'Of course we will, Mabel. I'll knock on tomorrow and see how you are.' During the war she'd known all her neighbours but no longer. She was glad they'd got to know Mabel Clancy at last.

Sam held out his arm and Mabel took it. 'It's a long time since I walked arm in arm with a young man,' she said with a twinkle in her eye. 'I'll see you ladies tomorrow. Thank you so much for looking after me tonight. You're the best neighbours and I will miss you all when I get my new flat.'

'But you'll feel a lot safer,' Edie said. 'And you can come and visit us.'

'And I will do. Goodnight, all.'

Stevie looked at Edie. 'Are you ready for home, love?' He reached for her hand and pulled her close.

'I am,' she replied. 'Are you sure you'll be all right, Fran, with all these kiddies?'

Fran nodded. 'Yes of course. You two go and enjoy what's left of your night without Dennis, make the most of it, you lucky pair.'

Edie smiled. 'We will. See you tomorrow.'

* * *

After checking on Lorraine and baby Gary who were both fast asleep in spite of the drama going on under the same roof, Sam and Fran lay on their bed chatting about the night's events.

'Do you think they'll keep him locked up?' Fran asked. 'I mean, they won't just question him and then let him go, will they?'

'No, I doubt he'll be out on the streets again for a good while. I mean, I have no idea what Glenda's injuries are but she looked pretty rough when they lifted her into the ambulance. Blood everywhere and she was holding her ribs and crying with the pain. He'll be charged with assault and battery as well as breaking and entering. Even though he kept yelling at the police it was his house and his name was on the rent book.'

'Oh God. Poor Glenda, hope her injuries are not too serious, she's only just getting over the birth of her baby too. I hope he's okay. Michael, one of the twins, said she dropped the baby on the floor when Reg punched her in the face. Michael picked him up and said he seemed okay but he was screaming and Reg was telling him to shut the bloody thing up or he'd do it for him. Fancy him saying something like that to a young lad and threatening to hurt a poor innocent little baby. His own son as well. He's evil. I hope they lock him up and chuck the key away. I'm going to go and see if I can visit Glenda tomorrow and take her some toiletries and clean clothes. She'll have nothing with her; she wasn't prepared for going in. That was the last thing she'd be expecting tonight.'

Sam nodded. 'Will you take Gary to your mam's place to be minded?'

'Yeah. I'll ask her to pick Lorraine up from school if I'm not back in time as well, or Edie would probably do that for me, save Mam going out. She'll be collecting Dennis anyway. I'll sort it out tomorrow morning when I drop Lorraine off at school.'

Sam sighed. 'I have to tell you something, love. Something Reg said to me before they shoved him in the back of the police van. Please don't worry though; I'm sure he was just shouting his mouth off and it doesn't mean anything.'

Fran looked at him. 'What? You're scaring me,' she said as she stared at his worried-looking face.

He told her what Reg had said and she gasped and put her hands to her mouth. 'Frankie has no chance of getting custody of Lorraine,' she said. 'How could he possibly have? I have sole custody. And there's no way he'll be getting to see her. No one will ever take her to that place to visit him, his family has disowned him. She doesn't even know who he is. She'll be in her twenties when he gets out and I can't see her wanting to know him if anyone ever tells her that he's her father. She thinks you're her daddy, she only knew him for a very short time and she won't even remember that.'

Sam nodded. 'I know, love, but I think we should mention this to the police in case he has a contact on the outside that he sees regularly. He may have said something to them and we won't know who that is. Lorraine is very friendly and talks to everyone and anyone. We just need to make sure we know her whereabouts all the time, but without frightening her.'

Fran sighed. 'And we will. I'll sort out her being picked up by Edie tomorrow and make sure school hangs onto her until she's collected. I'll be on my way back home by then so won't be too long.' She chewed her lip thoughtfully. 'I'll bring up the subject with Glenda when I see her tomorrow. See if he's said anything to her about this.'

* * *

Fran gasped with shock as she was shown into the small single room where Glenda was being looked after. The poor woman's face was badly bruised, her lips and nose swollen, and she had two black eyes. But she smiled weakly as Fran sat down beside the bed and took her hand.

'Oh, Glenda, what the heck did he do to you?' Fran asked, patting her hand gently. She put the flowers she and Edie had clubbed together to buy on the bedside locker. 'I'll ask for a vase in a minute,' she added. 'I've brought you a couple of nighties that your Michael rooted out and some toiletries and under-wear. I'll pop the bag in the locker cupboard for now.'

'Thank you,' Glenda croaked. 'No one has ever bought me flowers before.' Her eyes filled with tears and she squeezed Fran's hand gently. 'I look a bloody mess, don't I? I asked a nurse for a mirror earlier and I wish I hadn't bothered now. I've got three cracked ribs as well on the right side. I can't let my kids see me like this. Are they all okay, Fran? The police officer said you'd taken them to yours.'

'They're all fine,' Fran said. 'The older ones have gone to school and Joan from up the road is looking after Marlene today. She'll bring her back to me at teatime. We thought it best to keep them all busy then they won't worry too much. How's the baby doing? Michael said he'd fallen on the floor. Was he injured?'

'No, thankfully.' A sob caught in Glenda's throat. 'He landed on the hearthrug and he was well padded with a blanket around him. They've checked him over when they brought us in and he's fine. He's in the baby nursery on the children's ward for now and they bring him in to me for feeding.'

'Well that's good to know,' Fran said, shaking her head. 'Poor little soul.'

Glenda nodded. 'Reg kicked the Christmas tree over and trampled on it and he threw all the little presents I've managed to get for the kids onto the fire. They were so upset. That's the first time they've ever had the promise of Christmas presents. I feel heartbroken for them. I'm dreading the welfare department coming to see me. I know they will do because the police officer told me so. Do you think they will take my kids off me?'

Fran sighed. 'I've honestly no idea, Glenda. Do you have any family that can help you?'

Glenda shook her head slowly. Tears filled her eyes and ran down her bruised cheeks.

Fran handed her a hanky from out of her jacket pocket. 'It's clean,' she said, smiling.

'My family disowned me when I got in the family way with the twins. They hated Reg, told me he was no good and not to marry him.' Glenda sighed. 'Seems they were right. He's controlled my life from the day I met him when I was seventeen. We couldn't even get married until I was twenty-one; I didn't need my parents' permission by then. But by that time we had the twins and two more. I don't even know if Mam and Dad are still alive. And I'm an only child, no brothers or sisters. And here's me with more than my fair share.'

'I'm so sorry,' Fran said. 'It must have been really hard for you coping with the little ones and no one to help you.'

'It was. It still is. But Reg was a rubbish father. He doesn't even like kids. Says they get on his nerves and always blamed me when another was on the way. I hate him, you know.'

Fran nodded. 'I'm not surprised. Why did he suddenly turn up last night? Had he been in touch before that to let you know he was coming?'

Glenda sighed. 'No. He just turned up out of the blue. Believe it or not he came back because his new floozy has chucked him out and he said he wanted to come home. The blooming cheek of it.'

She shook her head. 'I told him to bugger off. He wasn't welcome there and the kids didn't want him back either. Then he said I had to take him back as he had no roof over his head and he had a job for me to do.'

She paused and looked up at the ceiling for a second or two before continuing. 'He asked about your Lorraine. Said Frankie wants to see her and he's got a plan to get her back. I told Reg he was stupid and Frankie can't look after a kiddie when he's inside. Reg said he's got another girl now who visits his cellmate. She's the cellmate's sister and writes to Frankie. Apparently he said he wants to marry her and she will look after Lorraine and bring her to see him if she's allowed. Reg wouldn't tell me who she was or where she lives, so I can't even tell you that much.'

Fran felt her jaw dropping as Glenda spoke. 'Bloody cheek of it,' she said. 'I'm going to go to the police and tell them this. No one is having my daughter. Least of all him and whoever that woman is.'

Glenda nodded. 'You must do. The plan they'd hatched so far was that I entice Lorraine to play with Marlene in our house and this woman and Reg would take her back to hers by getting her out of our house the back way so no one would see them. Of course, when I told him he was being stupid and there was no chance of me doing that, he started beating me up. Said he was getting good money for taking the kid from you. It was horrible, Fran, and I told the police officer what Reg was planning to do, but I was in such pain last night that I can't remember what I told him properly. So you must go and see them as soon as you can.'

'I will.' Fran stood up, feeling shocked to the core. 'Glenda, I'd love to stay but I'm going to leave now so that I can be at the school gates when Lorraine comes out. Just in case the woman is hanging around. Not that we'd know who she was, but even so. Edie was picking her up but I'll be there too. Better to be on the safe side. The police will know who the woman is if, as you say, she's Frankie's cellmate's sister. Plotting a kidnapping is surely against the law. Thank you for telling me. She could have taken her off the street or the park, or anywhere that she plays out, and we'd have been none the wiser where she'd gone.'

Glenda nodded. 'Thanks for coming to see me. I do appreciate it, and thanks again for looking after my kids. I hope I'll see you again soon. I hate that Reg can still try and control me and damage the new life and friendships I've made in the last few months. I'm praying they won't let him out. I've had such a lovely time lately. It's the first time since I met him that I feel free to run my own life. And since the royal visit I've felt a real part of the community.'

'You still are,' Fran reassured her. 'Don't worry. Victory Street looks after its own. Just concentrate on getting yourself well again and you'll soon be home. I'll ask a nurse to see to your flowers. Goodbye for now, Glenda. I'll visit again as soon as I can.'

FIFTEEN

With the three of them all squeezed into Dianna's small box bedroom, Molly zipped up the back of her dress and smiled as she turned Dianna gently round to face them. Sally picked up the beaded lace veil from the bed, positioned it on top of her curls and fastened the little coronet securely to the centre to hold the veil in place. The pair took a few steps back, heads on one side, and smiled with satisfaction.

'That's just perfect,' Molly said proudly. 'You look absolutely stunning, Di. Wait until your dad and Stewart see you, they'll be knocked out. Be prepared for tears, you know what your dad's like. Right, I'd better go downstairs and make sure the other bridesmaids have picked up their bouquets from the table. I'll leave you two alone for a few minutes and I'll call you when the car arrives, Sally.'

She paused, feeling emotional. '*Your* car will follow as the bridesmaids leave, Dianna. Your dad will be waiting in the hall for you and he'll have your bouquet ready to pick up and he's got Sally's too. I put them on the chair in the hall so the twins wouldn't get them mixed up. Basil is coming to collect me and Harry very soon, so I will see you at the church in a little while.'

Molly hurried down the stairs and into the sitting room. The twins were dressed and waiting, clutching their bouquets of red and white flowers and seasonal greenery, fastened up with trailing matching satin ribbons. Patti and Lizzie were twirling around the sitting room, dancing together, holding their dresses out at the hem.

'You all look really lovely,' Molly said, straightening the little ones' headdresses, pulling up socks and handing them the small white baskets, also decorated with trailing red and white ribbons. 'Just make sure these two don't throw their petals all over the car, please.'

Ebony grinned. 'We'll do our best. They're just very excited at the moment.'

Earl called from the hallway, where he was keeping an eye out for the cars arriving, 'Okay, ladies, the bridesmaids' car is here and so is Basil, for you and Harry, Molly.'

'Right you are.' Molly nodded and shouted up the stairs, 'Sally, your car's here, come on, love. See you at the church shortly, Dianna.'

Sally gave Dianna a last hug as they both came out of her bedroom and stood on the landing. 'Phew, here we go. I'm as nervous as you and I'm only a bridesmaid. Look at my hands shaking,' Sally said, holding out her hands in front of her. 'See you at the church, Di, you do look lovely.'

Dianna smiled. 'You're not just a bridesmaid; you're my maid of honour. That's really special for me, Sal. I can't quite believe it's happening at last. I'll see you soon.' As they all left and Dianna heard the front door closing, the house seemed to go suddenly very quiet. She took a deep breath and called to Earl, 'I'm coming down, Dad. Are you ready for me?'

'I am, princess,' he replied. 'Just take it easy, I don't want you tripping and falling down the stairs on those heels.' Earl caught his breath as his first-born walked slowly down the stairs towards him, looking for all the world like a real princess, her big brown eyes sparkling.

'Wow! You look absolutely amazing,' he said, choking slightly on his words. He blinked rapidly and held out his hand. She took it and he held her close for several seconds while he composed himself. A car horn sounded outside and he handed her the bouquet Molly had made. Beautiful imported red and white roses interwoven with greenery and ribbons. Dianna linked his arm and he led her out to the waiting white car that was also trimmed with red and white ribbons and bows.

* * *

In St Mary's parish churchyard, Sally made sure the little ones were behaving and left them for a few minutes with Tammy and Ebony while she caught up with Stewart and his best man, her boyfriend Nigel, who were just getting ready to walk into the church.

'Everything okay, Sally?' Stewart asked anxiously, pulling at his tie. 'God, I'm terrified. What if she doesn't come? She might change her mind at the last minute.'

'No, she most definitely won't,' Sally reassured him, smiling. 'She wants this as much as you do. And yes, everything is all going according to plan. You two had better get inside now. Di's car was just arriving as we were leaving, so she won't be long.' She reached up and straightened Stewart's tie and did Nigel's as well. 'Go on,' she said, giving Stewart a gentle push. 'I'll see you both shortly.'

She smiled, watching them hurry inside, and then went back to wait beside the other bridesmaids for Dianna's car. She took a deep breath as she saw it turning slowly into the road and stopping by the gates.

'You all ready?' she said to Pattie, and Tammy quickly signed 'Ready?' to Lizzie who nodded eagerly and beamed.

Every one of the invited guests was now inside and a few of the Victory Street neighbours were standing by the church wall, waiting to catch a glimpse of the bride.

Sally spotted a couple of men with large cameras near the gates as well and she frowned. The hired photographer was standing on the church steps and had been snapping willy-nilly while the guests arrived. She nodded slowly as it dawned on her that they were probably from the local newspapers. After all, Dianna and the Crystalettes were celebrities in the area, since their appearance at the royal street party that was now being shown in newsreels all over the place.

As Earl helped Dianna from the car, and taking her role as maid of honour seriously, Sally hurried forward to straighten Dianna's dress and tweak her veil into place.

'Deep breaths,' she said, squeezing Dianna's hand, and followed them down the church path, collecting the other four bridesmaids on the way. As they entered the vestry the organist stopped playing his background music and struck up with the opening chords of 'Here Comes the Bride'. The congregation rose to its feet and turned to look at the little procession as they walked down the aisle, a proud Earl with Dianna on his arm, leading the way.

'Can we throw these now?' Patti asked, waving her little basket around. 'Mammy said when we're inside the church we can do it.'

'Yes,' Sally whispered, and smiled as the two little girls giggled and plucked handfuls of red paper petals from their baskets, scattering them along the aisle as they followed Earl and Dianna to the alter. Sally could see the anxiety leaving Stewart's face as Dianna arrived beside him, which was replaced by a wide relaxed smile that lit up his handsome features, his brown eyes sparkling.

Sally and the bridesmaids stood to one side and the vicar welcomed everyone to his church and began to read from the

Service of Marriage. As he looked at Dianna and Stewart, he asked, 'Who gives this woman to be married to this man?'

When Earl stepped forward slightly, Sally could see he was almost bursting with pride as he replied, 'I do.'

* * *

Mary, Bella and Molly made their way to the church front doors, boxes of colourful paper confetti at the ready, as Stewart and Dianna came out to stand on the steps, both beaming happily from ear to ear. Laughing, they ducked the shower of confetti as it was thrown over them.

'What a beautiful wedding that was,' Mary said. 'The little ones were so good and they loved it, even though our Lizzie went running back to pick up her petals so she could throw them again.'

'Trust her to do that,' Bella said, laughing. 'I couldn't believe it when she piped up "Just a minute" to the vicar just as the service should have been started. Trouble is, she can get away with it; because she's deaf, people don't realise she *can* and *does* understand what's right or wrong. She's a little monkey. Good job the vicar has a sense of humour.'

'It is.' Molly laughed. 'But her antics made the day for a lot of people, so no harm done, and I'm sure Di and Stewart will have seen the funny side.'

'Oh, I know they will,' Bella said, nodding her head as Bobby came to stand beside her. 'Where's Levi?' she asked, looking around, trying to spot his head of thick dark curls among the crowd of people now spilling out of the church. Their son had been sitting on a pew beside her and Bobby in church but had then disappeared as soon as the service ended.

'Gone to see if he can find Kenny,' Bobby replied. 'He'll probably be down by the gates looking for him.'

'He'd better come back for the photographs,' Mary said.

'Earl wants to organise all of his parents' grandchildren on one together to send over to them.'

'There he is.' Bobby pointed. 'He's with Kenny, but who are the girls they're with?'

Bella frowned. 'No idea, I've never seen them before. But the four of them seem to be quite pally,' she said, raising an eyebrow as Levi and Kenny, each hand in hand with two fashionably dressed teenage girls, strolled towards them.

Bella smiled at Kenny and the girls as Levi cleared his throat. 'Do you think our Di will mind our friends coming to the buffet?' he asked. 'She said it was okay for Kenny to come after the service.'

Bella chewed her lip. She was pretty certain that Dianna had meant for Kenny to come for the evening party as The Sefton Trio were part of the entertainment. But how could she say no now? The two girls seemed nice enough; all dressed up in their best, and looking a bit embarrassed now they realised that Levi had invited them without checking it was okay to do so first. But there was enough food ordered to feed an army anyway, and the hall was plenty big enough for a few extra guests.

She nodded her head. 'I'm sure it will be fine,' she said. 'Are you going to introduce us to your friends, then?'

'Oh, yeah,' Levi stuttered. 'Er, this is Mandy,' he said of a short girl with a slim figure, her long blonde hair caught up in a ponytail, and big bright blue eyes that looked adoringly at Levi's face as he spoke. 'And this is Valerie, but she prefers to be called Val, don't you, Val?'

The girl holding onto Kenny's hand smiled and nodded at Bella. Her auburn hair, a good match for Kenny's red locks, was also fastened up in a ponytail, a style that seemed to be all the rage now with the young ones. They both wore smart dresses in warm winter shades and matching jackets with little fur collars.

Black patent shoes, suitable for dancing, adorned their feet and they carried matching handbags.

'We met at the last youth club dance we played at,' Levi explained. 'This is my mam, Bella, my dad Bobby and my stepmam Molly,' he began, 'and that guy over there standing beside my sister Dianna, who is the bride, is also my dad, Earl. Those little bridesmaids are my half-sisters Patti and Lizzie, and those two older bridesmaids who look alike are my twin cousins from America, but they live here in Liverpool now. My family is a bit complicated, but I'll explain later,' he said as a confused expression crossed Mandy's face.

She nodded and smiled politely. 'Nice to meet you all.'

'You too, Mandy,' Bella said, stifling a grin. She turned to Bobby who was also doing his best to hide a laugh.

'God help the poor girl getting her head around that lot,' he muttered to Bella. 'Takes *us* all our time to remember who belongs to whom, never mind a stranger dumped headfirst in the middle of us all.'

'Yep, she'll be wondering what the devil she's let herself in for,' Bella agreed. 'But she seems a nice girl so we can live in hope she's also understanding.'

Mary came over and rounded up her family and sorted them into groups. 'Come on, you lot. The photographer wants our side all in one big family photo and then all the children next for Earl's mam and dad, including the older ones. Oh, they'll be so thrilled when they get that photo; I know I would if I lived that far away.'

Earl stuck his thumb up in a thank you gesture. 'Leave it to our ma-in-law, eh, Bobby? If you ever need a job doing, Mary is the best sorter-outer there is.'

Bobby grinned and nodded his agreement, taking his place next to Bella for the family photo. 'She certainly is, Earl.'

SIXTEEN

Mary looked admiringly around the stunningly decorated church hall as she helped to show the guests to their tables for the wedding buffet. Molly had done them proud again. A tall, well-decorated pine tree stood by the side of the stage, and swags of red-berried holly and ivy hung from the beamed ceiling, tied up with red and white ribbons. She breathed in deeply.

The heady scent of fresh pine and Christmas hung in the air. The tables were beautifully dressed with crisp white cloths, white china and red napkins, and hand-made decorations of red and white candles, circled with glitter-sprinkled pine cones, sat in the centre of each table. Sometimes she had to remind herself that the war was truly over at last, after so many broken Christmases full of worry during those years.

Following the afternoon buffet and toasts and speeches, the later guests started to arrive. First to hurry in and bringing a blast of freezing air with them were Fran and Edie and their husbands.

Fran whipped a silky headscarf from around her carefully waved auburn hair and shook delicate snowflakes from it.

'Snow?' Bella asked. 'Blimey. It's a shock to see that.'

'It's just starting,' Fran said to Bella after greeting everyone with hugs. 'Mind you, it's gone very cold out there now. The wedding couldn't have been better timed this afternoon. They've forecast heavy snow showers for the rest of the week-end. How did it all go? Doesn't she look beautiful?' She waved to Dianna and Stewart. 'I'll go and congratulate them in a minute. But first me and Edie have some good news to tell you that might be a big help to those two in the not too distant future.' She inclined her head in the bride and groom's direction.

'Ooh, what's that then?' Bella asked as Edie sat down next to her looking excited.

'Miss Clancy, er, Mabel, popped over this afternoon.' Fran placed a prettily wrapped parcel on the table, fastened up with a yellow ribbon bow. 'That's a present off her for Di and Stewart. But she also came over to tell us that she got a letter on Thursday from the housing department. She's been offered a new flat at last and she went to look at it yesterday afternoon. It's not all that far from Wavertree and her friends, she loves it and she's accepted it. She told her landlord this morning that she'll be leaving in the New Year. He accepted her notice and told her to take her time and to move out when she's ready. He also said he's definitely not going to re-let the house and will sell it when she leaves. But not only that, Glenda's going too. *She's* been offered a four-bedroomed house in Allerton and she's been told she will get some help with paying the rent from the social security. And she's keeping all her kids thank heavens.'

'Oh that's really good news for them both,' Bella said. 'Glenda needs the space desperately and she'll be much better away from that house and the horrible memories of living there with *him*. How's she doing now?'

'She's getting there,' Fran said. 'Her injuries are healing well. The neighbours all helped get her house back into shape for Christmas, and we had a whip-round and replaced the tree and decorations and the presents for the kids that he'd chucked on the fire. So hopefully they'll have a nice enough Christmas Day next week. He's banged away for a good while now and she feels much safer. And so do me and Sam. The woman that was supposedly helping Frankie has been questioned by the police about her part in his plans to take Lorraine away.'

'Oh that's a relief,' said Bella.

'Isn't it just. The police have told us that she will no longer be allowed to visit her brother or Frankie, and any letters she sends to either of them will be returned to her unread. Frankie will not be allowed any contact at all with her, either by phone or letter. God knows why any woman in her right mind would want a dangerous prisoner for a future husband. It really beggars belief. If she steps out of line again she'll end up in prison, so that might make her think twice.'

'Well let's hope so,' Bella said. 'Some women are just plain stupid though and *she* certainly was for getting involved with him in the first place. So does that mean Glenda's house will also be going up for sale soon as well?'

Edie nodded. 'Apparently it is, yes. Now what we need are lovely new neighbours as they'll be living right opposite me and Fran. So we don't want any horrible trouble-makers.' She looked across to where Dianna's friend Carol and her husband Victor were sitting with the bride and groom and Sally and Nigel. 'Don't those two need a house of their own?' she asked. 'Young Vic and Carol, I mean.'

'They do,' Bella said. 'They have a baby daughter now as you know and are growing out of living in Vic's mam's front room. Dianna said there's just not the space to swing a cat with the cot in there too. I know they've been saving up and looking out for a bargain to do up but haven't found anything yet. Glenda's house would be just the job and if our Di and Stewart get Miss Clancy's place she would be thrilled to have her old pal living right next door. I'll be seeing them tomorrow at our

Molly's as we're all going for a family Christmas party and to celebrate a bit more, so I'll tell Di and Stewart the house news then and she can let Carol and Victor know next week when she sees them.'

She glanced across to the stage area where Basil was taking charge of the evening's entertainment. He seemed to be busy organising the band that would be backing the singers. Sam and Stevie had joined him and were up on the stage putting Sam's drum kit together. Basil looked across, caught her eye and beckoned for her to come over.

'Looks like I'm needed. I'll catch up with you two a bit more, later,' she said and hurried across to Basil who was now chatting to Earl and Bobby.

* * *

'The boys in the band are going to start playing a bit of background music and then I'll announce the bride and groom's first dance in about ten minutes,' Basil said to Bella. 'So will you and Bobby get yourselves behind the curtains at the back of the stage in readiness to sing "True Love" for them?'

Bella smiled. 'Of course we will. I'll just pop to the ladies to brush my hair and redo my lippy,' she said. 'Be back in a jiffy.' She hurried away and picked up her handbag from the floor by the table she'd been sitting at.

'You and Bobby getting ready to do your party piece?' Fran teased.

Bella laughed and nodded. 'We are, but nature's calling me first.' Out in the foyer she bumped into her mam who was talking to Aunty Et and Stewart's mother. 'Can't stop,' she said, dashing past them. 'I'll catch up with you ladies later.'

Peering into the mirror on the wall above the sink in the ladies toilets, Bella was shocked to see how pale she looked. She didn't remember looking like that this morning. She rooted in her handbag for her Crème Puff compact and lipstick. She looked really tired, but she didn't particularly feel it – well maybe just a bit, she supposed. It had been a very busy day so far. She fluffed the powder puff over her face and managed to conceal her pale colour a little.

Maybe it's the lighting in here, it isn't the best, she thought, gazing up at the single shade-less light bulb that dangled from the ceiling on a length of flex. She slicked her lips with dark pink lipstick and dabbed a little onto her cheekbones, blending it in with her fingers. There, that was much better. She looked a bit brighter now. Perhaps it was all the late nights of reading in bed she'd been doing lately that had made her look tired. An early night or two was needed once this weekend and Christmas were over. She hurried back to Bobby, after first dropping her handbag at the table with Fran to look after.

'You okay, love?' he asked as she slipped behind the stage curtains with him. 'You look pale.'

'I'm fine, just a bit tired. It's been a busy last few weeks for us all.'

He squeezed her hand. 'I know, especially for you women. And our Lizzie is waking up really early as well lately. I suppose it's all the excitement of the wedding and she knows Father Christmas is due soon too.'

Bella laughed. 'Oh, God help us on Christmas morning. She'll be up before we've even gone to sleep.'

Bobby cocked his ear and said, 'Basil is asking the bride and groom to take to the dance floor. That's our cue to go on stage. Are you ready?' He took her hand and led her through the gap in the curtains as one of the band struck up with the opening chords of "True Love" on a small squeezebox accordion.

Bella took a deep breath and smiled as Bobby sang the first lines of the opening words to her. It was such a lovely song and just perfect for a newlywed couple's first dance. As she and Bobby finished singing the floor was full with couples joining

Dianna and Stewart for a dance. With cheers from the audience and shouts of 'More' they left the stage after promising to come back later for another duet.

Basil came back onto the stage and asked the band to play a couple more numbers to dance to while The Sefton Trio got themselves ready to play.

Back at the table with her friends Bella took a sip of Babycham, her new favourite drink that was all the rage with her friends. She loved the way the bubbles tickled her nose. 'This is so much nicer than sherry,' she said to Edie.

'Definitely,' Edie agreed. 'All our mams and grannies drink sherry. It's an old woman's drink. I'm glad we've found something else to enjoy.'

'Don't you let Bella's mam hear you say that about old women,' Bobby warned, grinning. 'Mary's into her Babycham as well now, thanks to her daughters and Dianna leading her astray.'

Fran laughed. 'Good for Mary. Ah, it looks like your boy is getting ready to do his bit.' She pointed at the stage where Levi was in discussion with Kenny and Jimmy.

'Hmm,' Bella said. 'Wonder what they did with the two girls they brought?' She glanced around the room and spotted Mandy and Val standing alone by the back wall. 'Oh, there they are. I'll go and bring them to sit over here with us. Poor girls look a bit lost.'

She hurried towards them and was pleased to see a look of relief pass over Mandy's face as she realised Bella was heading their way. 'Girls, come and sit with us while the boys do their stuff,' she said.

Fran moved over and let Mandy sit down next to Bella while Val sat the other side of the table next to Edie. 'Would you like a drink, girls? I know you're not old enough for a Babycham but I can get you an orange squash, unless they sell Coca-Cola here, although it's usually a limited bar in this hall.'

Mandy smiled. 'Thank you. I'd love a Coca-Cola if they have some and I think Val would too, but otherwise a squash will be fine,' she said as Val nodded her agreement.

Bella came back to the table with two glasses of cola and three more small bottles of Babycham. 'You're in luck with the cola, girls. That'll keep us going for a while,' she said to Fran and Edie, handing them their drinks as Basil thanked the band for playing a few instrumentals.

'Ladies and gentlemen,' he began. 'Now have we got a treat for you tonight. Can I ask you all to please put your hands together and welcome on stage, three local boys. I give you, our very own, The Sefton Trio.'

Cheers and clapping erupted as Levi took his place behind the microphone and, with a smile a mile wide, announced the first song. 'Thank you, Basil, and thank you all for the very warm welcome. We'd like to start tonight with a song that was a hit by Guy Mitchell, but has just been recorded by a new singer from London. His name is Tommy Steele and the song is called "Singin' the Blues". This is tipped to be number one in the New Year. Hope you like it.' The audience cheered and sang along with the song and when the boys finished they cheered and clapped once more. An elated Levi took a bow and blew kisses of thanks.

Dianna smiled as her grinning brother announced the next song was called "Why Do Fools Fall in Love" by Frankie Lymon and the Teenagers, and that his dad Earl would help them with the deep-voiced 'do-wah's that started the song. A smiling Earl popped his head around the curtains and obliged. He left the stage with a wink and a wave as the boys carried on singing. People got up to dance and sing along. Dianna knew that many young black boys aspired to be like Frankie Lymon and Levi was no different, emulating the young singer's energetic dance moves around the stage.

'Shall we?' Stewart asked, holding out his hand. Dianna

smiled and took it and he led her onto the floor. They were quickly followed by Sally and Nigel and Vic and Carol who jived together until the song ended.

Everyone clapped and whooped, and Dianna could see how much Levi was enjoying himself; strutting around like the star he was promising to be. The boys threw themselves into a couple of skiffle numbers next and then the group finished their set with Bill Haley's "Rock Around the Clock" and Elvis Presley's "Hound-Dog". Cries of 'More' and clapping and cheering meant that Basil asked them to do a couple more songs as an encore. Levi nodded that they would and after a quick discussion among themselves they performed 'Blue Suede Shoes' and 'Heartbreak Hotel'. He held up his hand to a smiling Basil standing in the wings and indicated they'd do one more to finish the night.

Levi bowed and thanked everyone for the tumultuous applause that was echoing around the hall. 'Now just so you can all have a nice slow dance to end the night, we're going to sing you a smoochy love song. It's new to us and this is the first time we've performed it live. But it's one that we love and it's Elvis's latest single release that will no doubt be his next big hit. We want to dedicate this song to my sister Dianna and her new husband Stewart.'

Dianna felt her eyes fill as Levi sang "Love Me Tender" with such passion in his young voice. Stewart dropped a kiss on her lips as he held her tight while they danced. They'd had such a perfect wedding day and there was no better way to end it.

Bella smiled at the two mesmerised young girls sitting alongside them at the table. 'What do you think?' she asked as The Sefton Trio walked off stage to tumultuous applause.

Mandy smiled and shook her head. 'God they were amazing; even better than they were when we saw them at our youth club the other week. We've really enjoyed ourselves today, haven't we, Val? I'm so glad Levi invited us. Thank you, Bella, for looking after us as well.'

Val nodded, almost lost for words. 'Yes, thank you so much.'

'They're gonna be dead famous, you know,' Mandy said, grinning. 'Levi told me that. He says it's all he wants to do, sing and write songs.'

Bella smiled. 'I know he does. We're doing our best to encourage him, but we also want him to finish school and maybe go on to college for a while so that he has other skills up his sleeve for the future if singing doesn't work out the way he'd like it to. Although I've got to say, after that little performance tonight, I think it's something he was born to do. It's in his genes, I suppose. I'm feeling so very proud of my boy right at this moment. But don't tell him I said that or he'll never get his head through our front door,' she teased.

SEVENTEEN

WAVERTREE, MARCH 1957

'Do you think you'll be interested in purchasing the property then, young lady, young sir?' landlord Brian Clark asked Dianna and Stewart after they'd taken two trips around the terraced house Miss Clancy had vacated last week.

'Di?' Stewart raised his eyebrows in her direction. 'You happy with it, love?'

She nodded; a big beam on her face. 'Yes, I certainly am. It's just right for our first home.'

'That's good to hear,' Brian said with a smile.

'We've saved up a good deposit,' Stewart told him, 'and my dad is lending us the balance to save us messing about getting a mortgage. He said he'd give us a bit of breathing space to get the refurbishments and decorating done how we want it before we have to start paying him back.'

'Sounds like a good idea to me,' Brian said, rubbing his chin thoughtfully. 'That's how I started out in property, you know. I inherited a bit of capital from my father, bought my first little house and used that to help me buy another. I now own fifty terraced houses around Liverpool, but I'm taking a step back now. Getting ready to retire and selling up as a lot of my tenants are being rehoused into new council properties now. A lot of the houses will be declared as slum clearance in time and the council will buy them from me at market value so they can knock them all down and build new roads and more housing estates. I think this little area will be around for a good while yet though,' he assured them.

'Well that's good to know,' Dianna said. 'Stewart works for my Uncle Scott who is an architect and he does a lot of work in the city refurbishing big old houses, mainly turning them into flats now. But he'll be able to give us some advice on how best to spend our money on this place.'

Brian nodded. 'Get the roof and chimneys checked first. That's what I always tell people. Start from the top and work your way down. It needs a bathroom but there's space to do that, and I got the electrics done when most houses had the gas lighting removed. So it's quite sound to move into really while you do the final works. She's kept it nice and it's very clean.'

'Sounds good to me,' Stewart said. 'Will you draw us up a contract and then we can get the money side of things out of the way as soon as possible. I can tell just by looking around that I don't need a structural survey doing as I trained under Dianna's Uncle Scott so have an eye for anything major.'

'I'll get that sorted for you and I will be in touch early next week,' Brian said. 'You'll need a solicitor to finalise the sale, make it all legal, but I bet your dad can get that arranged for you. We've no estate agent involved so that makes it a bit easier. Now I know this is slightly irregular, but seeing as I've known Mary and her family since the year dot and her daughter Molly is your stepmum, young lady, not to mention an ex-tenant of mine along with her husband, your father Earl, I'm going to let you keep a set of keys so that you can show your family around this weekend. Perhaps bring your Uncle Scott down to have a quick look and just make sure he's happy before you sign anything. Now I can't say fairer than that, can I? Oh, and Fran and Edie opposite have put in a good word and told me to make sure you buy it.' He laughed. 'I daren't let them down, it's more than my life's worth.'

'Oh well, there you go then,' Stewart said, grinning. 'Trust them two. But it's very kind and generous of you, are you sure?' he asked as Brian handed a set of keys to him.

'Perfectly sure,' Brian replied. 'I'm a good judge of character and I can tell right away when I can trust someone. Right, I'll get off. Go and collect some rent money in before my tenants go and spend it all at the shops,' he said. 'I'm meeting a young couple next door to here as soon as Glenda gives me her keys back. She tells me she'll be gone by Tuesday to her new house which will be a lot better for her; there'll be more space for the kiddies to sleep and a nice safe garden for them to play in as well. The young couple tell me they are friends of yours.'

'They are,' Dianna said. 'Carol and Victor. It would be lovely to have them as our neighbours. Fingers crossed.'

'Indeed. I'll be in touch next week. Give my regards to Mary when you see her.' Brian raised his trilby hat and went on his way. As Stewart stepped onto the street to wave him off someone called his name and he looked across to see Fran beckoning from her doorstep.

'Kettle's on,' she called. 'I'll just knock on for Edie. You can come and tell us how it all went.'

'Okay, thanks.' Stewart waved to her and stepped back inside. 'Brew at Fran's with Edie?' he said to Dianna who nodded.

'Ooh, please. Edie always used to bake cakes and scones on a Saturday morning if I remember rightly. Let's hope scones are on the menu today.'

Locking the front door, they made their way across the street to Fran's house. She'd left the door ajar for them and Stewart closed it as they went inside.

'Have a seat,' Fran said, indicating two comfy brown tweed

fireside chairs in the back sitting room that also doubled as a dining room. 'Edie's on her way. I'll just bring everything through from the kitchen.'

Dianna could hear Lorraine and Dennis playing outside in the shared back yard, Lorraine's voice shouting above Edie's little boy's quieter tone.

'Lorraine,' Fran yelled from the open back door. 'Let Dennis have a go. It's his turn!' She shook her head as she carried a laden tray into the dining room and put it on the table. 'Wish I'd never got her that scooter now. She knows it's to be shared between the two of them. Dennis lets her play on his bike.'

Dianna smiled. 'Where's baby Gary?'

'Asleep in his cot, but he won't be for much longer if madam doesn't shut up.'

Edie popped her head around the door, bearing a plate of scones. 'Fresh from the oven,' she announced. 'They're cut and buttered and here's a little dish of home-made strawberry jam; courtesy of me mam.'

'Oh yum,' Dianna said. 'I love your scones. And your mam's jam is always so nice. I did say a little silent prayer that you'd made some as we were walking across the street. I remember you were always baking when we lived next door. It still looks lovely out there, doesn't it? Everyone has kept their window boxes nice and colourful and the cobbles are still weed-free.'

Fran smiled. 'Yes, it's surprising. They all seem to be staying on top of things to keep it looking smart. Everybody has been taking such a pride in how their houses look since the royal visit. So anyway, you two, how did it go? Are you having the house?' she said.

Stewart screwed up his face and shook his head. 'Nah, don't think so. Too small for us and we've heard that the neighbours are right nosy devils,' he teased as Dianna play-thumped him on the arm. 'Yeah, of course we're having it. We loved it and can't wait for it to be ours.'

Dianna grinned. 'The owner has even given us a set of keys so we can show the family. It's very kind of him.'

'Well Mr Clark knows if he treats you right you won't let him down,' Edie said. 'And he's known your extended family for many years and that he can trust them. So he must have that trust in you two as well. That's great news. We're so happy for you.'

'I just hope Carol and Vic buy next door now,' Dianna said.

'I'm sure they will. They were very keen when we told them about it,' Stewart said. 'They won't get anything else as cheap in the area.'

'Fingers crossed,' Fran said. 'It'll need a fair bit of work to bring it up to scratch but they can do it as they go. Well good luck to your new home and future. Here's to our new neighbours.' She held up her mug of tea and they all followed suit.

* * *

Bella sat at the dressing table, brushing her hair. She took a deep breath and turned as Bobby walked into the bedroom. He took his suit jacket from the wardrobe and straightened his tie before slipping his jacket on. He bent close to Bella to look in the mirror and patted his blond quiff into place.

'Will I do?' he asked, smiling.

'You'll do just fine,' she said, putting her hairbrush down and turning to face him. Lizzie was so like her daddy, and her Granny Mary, blonde hair and blue-eyed.

'You okay, love?' he asked, frowning. 'You don't look too good.'

Before she could reply, Levi popped his head around the door to say goodbye.

'Right, I'm off to catch the bus to school. You all right, Mam, you look a bit pale?'

God, she thought, *the pair of them were fussing now*. 'Yes, I'm fine, both of you. Just a bit tired, that's all. Have a nice day. See you later, son.'

'I'll get off now as well,' Bobby said. 'Basil's outside waiting for me. I can hear the car engine running. Will I see you this afternoon at the studio?'

'Erm, if Mam can pick Lizzie up from school for me you will. Monday's a bit of a busy day for her. She likes to get her washing done. So I won't make any promises. I'll see you back here later, if not.'

'Okay.' Bobby dropped a kiss on top of her head and left the room.

Bella breathed a sigh of relief and closed her eyes. Just Lizzie to sort out now and then she could have a bit of peace and quiet before she kept her one thirty doctor's appointment. The appointment was a follow-up to one she'd secretly had last week so she was hoping the news would be good news and not that she was suffering from some horrible illness. She got to her feet and went into the kitchen to sort out Lizzie who was just finishing her cereal.

'Let's get your face washed and you can brush your teeth,' she signed to her daughter who nodded, her blonde curls bouncing on her shoulders.

On the walk to Lizzie's school Bella's thoughts tumbled around in her head. Since her mam had told her she seemed a bit peaky the week after Christmas and remembering how pale she'd looked the night of Dianna's wedding Bella had eventually admitted to herself that she might 'need a tonic' as her mam had put it. She'd felt a bit strange for a few weeks but with the wedding and everything else that had been happening she just thought she was tired out and needed more sleep.

When she eventually went to see her doctor at the end of

February, nearly two weeks ago, he had examined her and told her that there was probably nothing to worry about. Her blood pressure was fine but she seemed to be a bit run-down and he'd asked the surgery nurse to take some blood samples. He'd also asked Bella to bring a urine sample into the surgery, which she had done last week. The only other time she'd been asked to do that, the results had confirmed she'd been expecting Lizzie, but much as she would love it to be, it was highly unlikely to be the same scenario this time.

Lizzie was seven years old now, and Bella and Bobby had done nothing to prevent her conceiving another baby, but with his internal injuries from his wartime accident, they both knew that Lizzie had been nothing short of a miracle. To be lucky a second time would be near impossible. Bella wondered if she might be a diabetic and the results would confirm it. Tiredness and needing the lavvy a lot could account for a number of things. Not all of them a baby.

She didn't feel sick for one thing and since having Lizzie her monthlies had been very irregular so she'd have to think long and hard to remember exactly how long ago her last one was. Definitely before Christmas and Di's wedding, and that was ages ago now, and she'd not put any weight on as far as she could tell. None of her clothes felt tight anyway. Ah well, she'd soon know once and for all what was going on with her body.

Bella left Lizzie in the hands of her teacher and turned to walk back home. She popped into the bakery in the row of shops near to the school and her mouth watered at the tray of vanilla slices that were just being placed in the window. Dare she be greedy and get one to guzzle with a brew when she got back home as well as have one after tea with everyone else? She smiled at Hilda White who had run the popular bakery with her husband for many years.

'Morning, Mrs White. Erm, I'll take six white rolls, and five of your vanilla slices, please.'

'Morning, Bella love,' Mrs White replied, placing six bread rolls into a white paper bag and handing them to Bella. 'How are things with you and yours on this fine spring morning? And how's your lovely mam?'

'We're all fine thank you. And yes it is a fine morning. I love this time of year when the daffodils are coming out and the trees are all sprouting greenery. Not to mention the birds making their nests. Feels like the world is finally waking up after a long, cold winter.'

'It does indeed.' Mrs White nodded and arranged the order of vanilla slices into a cardboard box. She passed them to Bella who placed both the box and bag of rolls into her shopping bag and handed over a ten-shilling note. She waited for her change and said her goodbyes.

She walked away with a renewed spring in her step, feeling more awake now as she looked around at the gardens she passed by, smiling at the little birds flying in and out of the hedgerows with twigs and bits of straw in the beaks. Building their new homes and getting ready to welcome new broods of fledglings. It made her smile thinking of how like the human world the animal world was really.

Back home Bella switched on the wireless to listen to *Housewife's Choice*, made herself a cuppa and sat down at the dining table to devour her secret treat. She smiled as she cleared away her plate and mug and sang along to Doris Day's "Que Sera, Sera, (Whatever Will Be Will Be)", a song that she and Fran and Edie loved to sing. She wished she still lived closer to Fran and Edie and could pop round for a natter but it wouldn't have been possible to live on Victory Street as the stairs were too steep for Bobby to cope with. She was so pleased she'd been able to be a part of the royal visit, even though she no longer lived there.

They were better in their bungalow for his sake but it was such a pain having to get buses to catch up with her pals. She

envied Dianna and Stewart who were definitely buying Miss
Clancy's house and had been full of excited plans for their new
home when they'd popped in on their way back to Molly and
Earl's yesterday. Dianna was already planning colour schemes
and getting ready to rope in her clever aunties to help make the
soft furnishings. The little house would be a palace when they'd
finished with it.

A sudden thought occurred to Bella and she went to get the
telephone directory from the sideboard cupboard. She turned to
the business section and looked for a driving school number.
She wrote the number down with the intention of giving them a
call later. When she walked past the post office on her way to
the doctor's she would ask for a driving licence application form
and get it on its way.

If she had a car she could go anywhere at the drop of a hat.
What was the point in promising herself that she'd do it and
then keep putting it off? It would make their lives so much
easier and they wouldn't need to rely on Basil too much. She
could borrow a copy of the *Highway Code* from Molly and
make a start on studying it this week while she waited for her
licence to arrive.

By the time she arrived at the doctor's surgery she was fired
with enthusiasm and the application form for a driving licence
was safely stashed away in her handbag. She picked up a well-
read *Woman's Weekly* magazine from the table under the
window and sat down to read it in the waiting room until her
name was called.

'Mrs Harrison, please take a seat,' Doctor Jackson greeted
Bella as she walked into the surgery.

'Thank you.' Bella took a deep breath, wondering what the
devil he was going to tell her. Doctor Jackson had been their
family doctor for many years but she'd hardly ever had the need
to see him apart from with Lizzie when her deafness had been
diagnosed.

He looked up from his notes and smiled. 'Don't look so worried, Mrs Harrison. There's nothing serious going on, all your blood samples were fine, just a little anaemia which is not unusual given your diagnosis. We can fix that with a course of iron tablets.'

Bella frowned. 'My diagnosis?' she questioned worriedly. Was this where he told her she had a life-changing condition? Would she need to take tablets for the rest of her life? 'What's wrong with me then?'

'Well, your urine sample came back with a positive result so I am very happy to confirm that you are expecting a baby. Now we need to work out some dates and get you booked in with our midwife who will look after your needs for the next few months.'

Bella stared at him, her mouth open wide. Although she'd secretly hoped for this she hadn't dared to let herself think it possible for one moment. Tears filled her eyes and she shook her head. 'Oh my God! Are you absolutely sure? I mean, I don't feel queasy like I did with Lizzie or anything. Just very tired and a bit weary all the time.'

'No two pregnancies are the same. Pop up on the couch and I'll just check your tummy,' Doctor Jackson said, getting up from his chair.

Feeling a bit shellshocked, Bella lay down on the couch and made herself comfortable. Doctor Jackson gently palpated her tummy and checked her breasts. He nodded and smiled at her. 'You are without doubt pregnant, Mrs Harrison. Congratulations.'

'I can't believe it,' Bella said, a sob catching in her throat as she adjusted her clothing and he helped her to sit upright. 'I'd given up all hope that we'd ever have another child. Oh God, I can't wait to tell Bobby, he'll be so thrilled. He really will.'

'I'm sure he will. Now do you have any idea at all when

your last period was? I know you told me they were very infrequent.'

Bella sighed as she tried to work it out. She'd felt a bit tired and weary at the wedding, but those were the only signs she could think of. 'It must have been sometime around the middle of November maybe,' she said. 'Which could fit in with me getting caught and feeling a bit grotty at the end of December and over the last few months, I suppose? But I've got no noticeable bump or anything.'

'You've definitely got something going on in there and it's possibly dating further back than Lizzie was. I estimate you to be about eleven weeks which will give us a date mid-September. So we'll use that as a guide for now and our midwives will be able to give you a more accurate date when they see you.'

'Thank you,' Bella said. 'I'm in shock, but it's very happy shock. No wonder I fancied a vanilla slice this morning and had to force myself not to think about eating all the others that were waiting in the box for after our tea.'

The doctor laughed. 'That's a nice craving to have. Better than some I've heard of. I mean, who on earth gets a craving for eating lumps of coal, but it's not unheard of, so I'm led to believe.'

'Rather them than me.' Bella got to her feet, beaming. 'Well, I'd better get off home and plan how to tell them all my news. Thank you so much. You have no idea how happy I feel.'

'I think I do. Until we meet again,' Doctor Jackson said, smiling as he saw her out of his surgery.

Bella grinned as she strolled back home. A new baby, what an absolutely blooming and totally unexpected miracle this was. She knew that Bobby had often blamed himself as the years went by for them not being able to have more children; it was something that played on his mind, even though he tried to hide it.

It upset her so much when he told her it made him feel less

of a man. This little surprise would bolster his confidence no end. And wouldn't it be marvellous if they were to have a boy. She knew he would love a son of his own now that Levi was growing up. It would be the best thing she could ever give him.

* * *

Although she was bursting to say something, Bella waited until they were in bed that night before she told Bobby her exciting news. Lizzie had been a bit fretful this evening and Levi's mates had been round and singing in the music room so there hadn't been the right time until now. She lay on the bed reading while Bobby took a quick shower in his special walk-in cubicle with a seat attached to the tiled walls. He called for her to help him hop to the bed after he'd dried himself. Bella helping to support him saved him having to reattach his false limb. He flopped down onto the bed and sighed.

'Are you tired?' she asked him.

'Not really,' he replied, pushing himself up the bed so that he was propped up against his pillows. 'I feel like I've hardly seen you today with you not coming down to the studios and then it's been a bit chaotic here tonight.'

'Did you miss me?' she said, moving across and snuggling close into his naked chest as he put an arm around her. She breathed in the scent of the Imperial Leather soap he'd used and smiled.

'I always miss you when we're not together,' he said. 'Did you have a busy day?'

She nodded. 'I had a few errands to run. I called in to the post office and got a form to apply for a preliminary driving licence. I just think it's time I shaped myself up and learnt to drive so I can take us for days out.'

'Oh that's great news, love. As soon as you get it we'll book you some lessons. Meantime we can go and look at a few cars so you can see what model you would like. Be great for us to have wheels of our own. Lizzie will love that. We can take her over to the beaches at Formby and New Brighton. Have some lovely family days out with her.'

Bella nodded. She reached up and kissed him. 'We need a second set of wheels as well. And we'll need them before September.'

He lifted her chin up and frowned. 'We only need one car, love. I'll never be able to drive again, you know that. Why do you say we need two? And why September? What do you mean?'

She grinned and reached for his hand. She laid it across her tummy and patted it gently. 'I didn't mean another car. I meant a pram for this little one. Although, if it's a boy, he may in time want a pedal car to drive.'

She watched as a million expressions chased one another across his handsome features. From shock to total disbelief to pure joy, and then the tears came and he held her tight.

'Are you happy?' she asked, her tears mingling with his.

'My darling Bella, you will never know how much.'

Levi stared up at the poster fastened to the wooden noticeboard outside St Peter's church. He'd been strolling home from his evening boxing club after jumping off the bus on Church Road when the poster had caught his eye. He studied it for a while and smiled. The garden fete and crowning of the rose queen was this coming Saturday the 6th of July. He remembered his mam talking about the rose queen thingy last week but he'd not really taken in what she was saying. Surely they'd had enough of royalty last year?

His mam had just said something about how Lizzie might enjoy it and that they should all go as a family for an afternoon out. It wasn't really his cup of tea but what he'd seen on the poster had made him think it might not be a bad idea. Although he'd rather go with Kenny and Jimmy, and he was certain they'd want to give it a go as well. He hurried on his way, deep in thought. He was starving and looking forward to eating his tea in peace. Lizzie would be in bed by now and his mam and dad Bobby would be watching the telly no doubt. Mam's favourite drama, *Emergency Ward Ten*, was on tonight.

Levi reached his bungalow home and dropped his bag onto

the hall floor. He kicked off his shoes and popped his head around the living room door. Mam was half-sitting, half-lying on the sofa under the window with a bag of white wool beside her, her legs stretched out across all three seats. Her needles clacking as she finished her row of knitting, she looked up and smiled at him.

'Hiya, love. Had a good session at your club?' she greeted him and swung her legs down.

Levi hurried across to help her as she lumbered to her feet. She laughed and shook her head. 'God knows what's in here,' she said. 'But it's a lot bigger than either you or Lizzie was at this stage.'

He smiled and gave her a hug. 'Club was okay, thanks. Kenny couldn't come tonight though; he had to help his mam with something at home.'

The unexpected and very surprise baby that his mam was carrying had been a shock to them all. When they broke the news to him both she and Bobby were excited and Lizzie was looking forward to having a new brother or sister, but Levi hadn't quite got his head around it yet. He had to admit that deep down he felt a bit like an outsider when they were all talking about what it might be, where it would sleep and choosing names.

But that's what he was really, an outsider; neither white nor black. He didn't feel that he belonged to either Bobby or Earl, even though he called them both Dad. Mam and Bobby's family and Earl and Molly's were normal and they each had children that equally belonged to them. And though Harry and Patti were mixed-race like him, they had the same mam and dad. But he and Di were somewhere in the middle. He shook his head, he shouldn't be thinking along those lines. He knew he was loved just as equally by both families and that was more than some kids ever got.

'You okay, Mam?' he asked, following her into the kitchen.

She took a tea towel from a hook by the sink and reached into the oven for a covered plate that contained his tea.

'Smells good,' he said, sniffing the air. 'What is it?'

'Lamb scouse,' she answered. 'Doesn't dry up like some meals so it's easier to make this on the days I know you will be late home for your tea. And yes, love, I'm just fine thanks. A bit tired but that's to be expected at my age.'

He nodded and sat down at the kitchen table as she poured him a glass of orange squash. 'Where's Dad?'

'He's popped round to Basil's while I watched *Emergency Ward Ten*. He doesn't like hospital dramas. He spent such a long time in hospital while he recovered from his injuries after that wartime plane crash. I think he feels he had his fill of it.'

'Bet he does,' Levi said, shovelling a forkful of his tea into his mouth. 'I just saw a poster near the church about the garden fete on Saturday. I'm going to see if Jimmy and Kenny are free. We should go and watch the group who are playing. Are you going, Mam?'

'Yes,' Bella said. 'Bobby's working so Fran and Edie are coming over with their kiddies and we're going to take a picnic. There's all sorts going on so it should be a nice afternoon. What group are playing? I saw the poster but can't remember all the details. I know there's a police dog display and a fancy-dress parade; we said we'd dress the kids up a bit. Lizzie can wear her bridesmaid dress from Di's wedding and go as Princess Anne. She likes that idea. I'll find her a little tiara to put on her curls.'

Levi laughed. 'I bet she'll love it. Prancing around as a princess is right up her street. The group are The Quarrymen skiffle group. That John Lennon whose group it is was at our school but he's going to college to do art later this year, I believe.'

'Oh I know who you mean,' Bella said. 'Mimi's lad from Menlove Avenue down the road. Well she's his aunty of course, not his mother.'

Levi smiled. 'He's lived with her for a long time though.' He finished his scouse, deep in thought, and smiled as Bella placed a dish of apple pie and custard in front of him.

'Enjoy that,' she said. 'I'm dashing to the lav.'

As she hurried away, Levi thought how good it would have been if his group could also have played at the fete. Apart from a few youth club dances this year they'd done very little. He knew that was down in part to their work and school commitments, and John Lennon's group were a few years older and more established than The Sefton Trio.

But even so, whenever they did play a gig the audience always had a good time and seemed to like them. Now he'd finished school and was starting art college in September he felt ready to do more. It was time to have a serious chat with Basil and his dad Earl about the future of his group.

He'd see Kenny and Jimmy at youth club tomorrow night and, with a bit of luck, Mandy and Val would be there too. He hadn't seen Mandy properly for the last few weeks because he'd been so busy with his studies for his GCE O-levels and so had she. But the exams were behind them now and the school summer holidays loomed, so time for a bit of fun.

* * *

'Why don't you come with us, Di?' Fran said as she stood out on the street with Edie and Dianna who had come outside to wipe down the windows of her new home. She and Stewart had made good progress with the work they'd chosen to do and they had wasted no time in moving in and making the house their home. Fran had just invited her to join them at the Woolton church fete that afternoon.

'Oh, I've just arranged to go to Paddy's Market with Carol,' she said. 'But thanks anyway. They're moving in next week.' She inclined her head towards next door which now belonged to their friends Carol and Victor. 'They've finished the decorating and put some nice flooring down, so she's hoping to get some decent second-hand curtains that Vic's mam said she'd alter if they don't quite fit. Then we said we'd treat ourselves to a nice coffee and cake at The Kardomah.'

'Sounds like a very good plan to me,' Fran said. 'I feel almost envious of your freedom to do things for yourself, although I know it will be short-lived for Carol of course.'

Dianna smiled. 'True enough. Our Levi was talking about the fete yesterday. He's going with a couple of mates and their girls. The Quarrymen are playing and he wants to see them in action.'

'Is he still seeing that nice little blonde, Mandy, who he was with at your wedding?'

'He is,' Dianna replied. 'She's a lovely girl and seems to be besotted with him at the moment. But he's a bit too young for anything serious and he's got college in September for two years if his grades are good enough and he gets offered a place. We shall have to see what happens meantime.' She waved at the postman who was delivering mail on the other side of the street, hoping he'd got something for her from Grammy Franklin.

She'd written to her last month to tell her the new address and as a rule Grammy wrote back right away. Even allowing for the airmail service sometimes being a bit slow, it was unusual to have a long gap in between letters. If there was nothing in the next few days Dianna decided she'd write again on the off-chance her letter had gone astray or ended up in the surface mail system, which took forever.

No wonder Aunt Ruby called it snail mail. It was Grandpa's birthday in two weeks' time and today she would choose a nice card for him and then post both card and letter on the same day.

'I'd better get on with my little jobs,' she said to Fran. 'Then I'll be ready when Carol calls round for me. Have a good time at the garden fete and say hello to my brother for me.'

Back inside her house, Dianna plumped up the cushions on her wine-coloured velvet sofa and straightened the cream linen antimacassars on the backs of the matching armchairs. The suite had been a housewarming gift from her dad and Molly and she loved it. They'd never have been able to afford such beautiful furniture and had been quite prepared to buy a second-hand sofa and chairs until Dad told her to stop looking and to expect a delivery.

Aunt Dolores had gifted them a dark wood coffee table she no longer needed and a matching side table that Stewart had applied a fresh coat of varnish to. Her aunt had also made the curtains and matching cushion covers in dark pink fabric dotted with cream flowers and she'd given them a plain fawn wool carpet square for the floor. Stewart's parents had donated a radiogram that his mother had told her would never be played anyway now he'd left home so they may as well take it with them.

It sat in pride of place in one of the chimney breast alcoves, with a lamp on top, and one side of the radiogram had a small cupboard in which they stored their records. In the other alcove was the television they had got on a rental agreement from Epstein's store in the city centre. Dianna loved her new home and liked nothing better than to curl up on the sofa with Stewart after a working day and relax to music or a favourite telly programme.

With a coal fire lit and burning brightly in the cream-tiled fireplace on colder nights, the room felt so cosy and Dianna felt very lucky that they'd finally got a home they could call their own. If she could find a wine-coloured fireside rug at Paddy's Market today the room would be complete. A knocking at the door took her out of her reverie and she went to let in Carol.

'Come on through,' Dianna invited her friend who followed her down the narrow hallway into the back room. 'I'll just get my jacket and handbag. I'm really looking forward to going shopping.'

'Me too,' Carol said. 'It's good to have a break and get out of our little bed-sitting room for a while. I can't wait to move into our own house now. I'm so excited. You've got this place looking so lovely, Di. It's a credit to you both.'

NINETEEN

On Saturday afternoon Levi and Kenny waited for Mandy and Val by the church gates, Levi glancing anxiously at his watch. 'Where the devil are they? It's half two now and the fete is being officially opened at three by some doctor bloke.'

Kenny shrugged and looked up and down Church Road in both directions. 'Don't know, but we'll give them ten more minutes and then go in. They'll have to come and find us.'

Levi nodded. His mam and her friends and the kids had passed by them ages ago now and gone to the field at the back to watch the rose queen procession which had been at two o'clock on the dot. The Quarrymen skiffle group, as they were billed on the poster, had been a part of the procession and had arrived on the back of a lorry with their instruments.

There was all sorts of stuff going on before the live music was due to start but, even so, he wanted to get in and bag a place as close to where the group would be playing as he could. He needed to see for himself just what made John Lennon's group so popular and how they could work on expanding The Sefton Trio to get a few more gigs. They needed more members and that would mean a change of name; that much was certain.

The only time they'd had a drummer was when Fran's husband Sam played with them, like when they were doing a show for Basil and they had the full backing band. Apart from his own guitar, and Kenny's washboard and Jimmy's tea-chest bass, they had nothing. Money, or lack of it, was the main problem. If only he was working other than just doing odd hours helping out at the studio he'd have a bit to invest in further instruments.

Kenny and Jimmy were always skint so they had nothing to spare. He really could do without going to college and maybe work full-time for his dads and Basil instead. All he could do now was keep his fingers crossed that he got poor O-level grades and then there was no chance he'd get a college place. But somehow he had a feeling they'd be fairly good because he had worked hard to keep his parents off his back. Kenny broke his train of thought by whooping loudly down his ear and waving. Mandy and Val were just getting off a bus on the opposite side of the road. They looked a bit red in the face and flustered.

The girls dashed across to the gates, breathing heavily, as though they'd been running for ages.

'So sorry we're late,' Mandy gasped. 'We missed the earlier bus, or rather we thought we had, and decided to walk as it was quicker than waiting for the next one.'

Then Val took up the tale while Mandy took a few deep breaths. 'Then we got so far up the road and realised that the bus we thought we'd missed was actually late and we could see it coming towards us in the distance.'

'So we legged it like crazy to the next bus stop but it was a heck of a way off and the blooming bus sailed right past us,' Mandy continued as Val took another few deep gulps of air. 'Then we still had to wait for the next one and that was late too. Anyway, we're here now.'

'So you are,' Levi said and pulled her into his arms. He dropped a kiss on her lips and she flung her arms around him and kissed him full on. 'Not here,' he said, pushing her gently away as an older couple walked past them and the bloke muttered, 'There's a time and a place for that sort of carry-on.'

'Let's get inside and we can find a spot to sit down,' he said, grinning after the old bloke. He took her by the hand and pulled her through the gateway, Kenny and Val following. They paid their entrance fee and strolled inside the grounds of the church. The police dogs were getting ready for their display and being put through their paces by a couple of uniformed officers. Children were lining up at the top of the field waiting for their fancy dresses to be judged and somewhere in the distance Levi could hear a brass band playing.

There was a holiday mood about the place and people were smiling and exchanging friendly greetings. Little kids were enjoying the freedom of running around; a few small boys were marching up and down, saluting like soldiers, to the tunes of the brass band. There were stalls set up around the perimeter of the field, selling crafts and home-made cakes. Levi hoped his mam would remember that she'd promised to buy a nice cake for after their tea tonight. He spotted Lizzie near the hoopla stall with Dennis and Lorraine so that meant his mam would be close by.

He saw her waddling her way towards Fran and Edie and she looked a bit weary. He'd be glad when that baby arrived. He couldn't recall her having such a huge bump when she was having Lizzie, but he'd been much younger then so his memory might be deceiving him and maybe she had. She spotted him looking her way and waved. He waved back and pointed to one of the cake stalls. She held up a bag she was carrying. 'I've got one,' she mouthed and he grinned and stuck up his thumb.

Kenny nodded towards the lorry that had transported The Quarrymen onto the field. 'Let's go over there so that we can get close enough to watch them play properly.'

'Who are they, this group?' Mandy asked. 'Are they mates of yours?'

'No, not at all,' Levi replied. 'A few of the lads were a couple of years above us at Quarry bank, but they've left now. Not sure about the others but John's going to art college soon, so I was told.'

Mandy nodded. 'So which one is John?'

Levi pointed to a lad wearing a checked shirt, his dark hair fashioned into a stylish quiff and a guitar hanging around his neck.

The foursome strolled across to where the lorry was parked up. Levi could see that John was now talking to a boy who was setting up a drum kit. 'That's what we need,' he said to Kenny.

'What, the kit or a drummer?'

'Both.'

'I'd get one if I could afford it,' Kenny said, his eyes shining. 'I'd love to play the drums. Bit more exciting than the washboard. Mind you, there's not an inch of space spare at home so God knows where we could store it, even if I did get one.'

'There's room in my dad's studio at the bungalow,' Levi suggested. 'Or down at Bold Street. I'm sure Basil would let us keep it there.' He paused for a moment as an idea came to him. 'You could always learn on the studio set, Kenny. They wouldn't mind. It doesn't belong to an individual guy, it belongs to the business.'

Kenny nodded. 'Shall we ask? See what they say.'

Mandy pulled on Levi's arm to gain his attention. 'What's up?' he asked.

'That lad over there that's talking to one of the group,' she began. 'I know him, is he one of The Quarrymen too?'

'No idea.' Levi shrugged, staring at a dark-haired boy wearing a white jacket, black drainies and of similar age to him. 'I've never seen him before. He's not from our school.'

'No, he goes to The Institute. He's called Paul McCartney,' Mandy told him. 'He lives around the corner from us on Forthlin Road in Allerton. Val used to fancy him, didn't you?'

'Just a bit,' Val admitted, grinning. 'But it was when we were at primary school. He has lovely eyes, sort of brown but not as dark as Levi's.'

'He's got a guitar with him,' Levi observed. 'Maybe he's just come to watch. There are five of them already up on the lorry and three have guitars so I don't suppose they need another.'

'They're playing tonight as well, you know,' Val said. 'There's a Grand Dance at the church hall. Shall we go to that?' she asked Kenny.

He shook his head. 'Sorry, I can't. I'm skint and I'm needed at home later.'

'Okay,' Val said, sighing. 'Mandy, do you fancy the dance tonight?'

Mandy shook her head. 'I can't either. I've got to babysit my little sisters while Dad takes Mam out to the pictures. He's been promising to take her for ages and it's their wedding anniversary today so there's no getting out of it. That's where she said she wants to go.'

'Ah well, never mind.' Val shrugged. 'We can watch them here. They might not be any good anyway. Bet Levi's group's better.'

Levi laughed. 'I don't think we are, but there's always room for improvement and we've not been playing together for as long as they have. Ah look, they're getting ready to play.'

The band tuned up and following an introduction of the Lonnie Donegan song "Puttin' on the Style" by John they started to play and sing. Levi noticed that Paul definitely wasn't getting up onto the makeshift stage on the back of the lorry. He was standing to one side, nodding his head, tapping his feet and watching every move John Lennon was making, following his fingers as they flew up and down the frets on his guitar. Levi smiled, thinking that maybe the lad was hoping John would ask him to be in his group one day.

TWENTY

WAVERTREE, JULY 1957

'Who the hell is knocking on the door at this time on a Sunday morning?' Stewart said, groaning as he rolled out of bed. He peered blearily at the clock on his bedside table. 'Ten past bloody six,' he muttered, reaching for a t-shirt and his pants from the floor.

Dianna sat upright and ran her hands through her wiry curls. She shook her head. 'It's a bit early for visitors. Look through the window and see if you can spot anyone. They might have knocked on the wrong door by mistake. We're not expecting anyone today and definitely not at stupid o'clock.'

Stewart pushed one of the curtains out of the way and looked down. 'Your dad's car is outside, Di. You'd better get up. I'll go and let him in before he wakes next door up too.'

Dianna climbed out of bed and pulled on a pair of jeans and a white blouse. She hurriedly did up the buttons and followed Stewart down the stairs. She could hear her dad's voice apologising for waking them as he was shown into the front sitting room.

'Dad, what's wrong?' she asked, pulling him to sit down

beside her on the sofa. 'Why are you here so early? Are Molly and the kids okay?' Her words tumbled over one another.

Earl nodded and took a deep breath. 'Molly and the kids are all fine, love. But I'm afraid I've got some bad news to tell you, sweetheart.' His eyes filled as Dianna looked at him. She reached for his hand and he held hers and squeezed it gently. 'I've had an early morning call from my brother, your Uncle Levi in New Orleans. The line was quite bad and I couldn't tell what he was saying at first. Anyway,' he paused and choked on a sob, 'I'm so sorry to have to tell you this, Di, but Grandpa Franklin passed away in his sleep last night. He went very peacefully, Levi told me.'

Dianna's hands flew to her mouth and tears splashed down her cheeks. 'Oh no, Dad. No. He wasn't even ill, was he? I've been waiting for a letter from Grammy for ages. Oh, my poor Grammy, she must be so upset. I wish we had a phone and then I could talk to her.' Dianna sobbed and Earl wrapped his arms around her and held her tight. Stewart sat on the arm of the sofa and reached over to stroke her curls, shaking his head, lost for words.

Earl took a deep breath. 'Well you can, speak to her that is. Get yourself properly dressed and come with me. I'm going to your Uncle Scotty's house. Levi couldn't get through to them so he's asked me to break the news and then we've to try and call him back later today. He's not going to bed because of the time difference, although he's made Grammy go for a lie-down, until he hears from us.'

'Okay,' Dianna said, getting to her feet. 'Would you like a cuppa meantime, Dad?'

'No thanks, love. I'll wait until we get to Scotty's house, your aunties will sort us out.'

Stewart shook his head as Dianna left the room and ran upstairs. 'I'm so very sorry to hear this sad news, Earl,' he said. 'I know Di's been worrying because she's not had a letter for a while. Was he ill, or was it unexpected?'

'Not ill as far as we know. It was sudden. He was quite elderly, late seventies, a few years older than my mother, so I guess it's to be expected at his time in life. And to go peacefully without pain is as much as anyone can wish for. Just makes it hard, them being so far away though and most of the family living in the UK. And the fact we never got to say goodbye one last time is heartbreaking.'

Stewart nodded. 'Will you go out there for the funeral?'

'I guess so. I'll wait and see what Scotty thinks.'

Dianna ran back down the stairs. 'I'm ready,' she announced. 'My hair's a mess, but it's not that important right now, is it?' She touched the top of her head where she'd piled all her curls up and fastened them in place with bobby pins. 'Are we going to go and tell Levi too, Dad?'

Earl nodded and sighed. 'On the way back we will. No doubt Molly will ring Bella and tell her, but it's so early that she won't have done it yet. I told her to make sure Bella doesn't say anything to Levi until I'm there. As his father, breaking that sort of sad news should come from me.'

'It should,' Dianna agreed. She kissed Stewart goodbye and followed her dad out to the car. 'See you later,' she called to Stewart as they pulled away.

* * *

Earl pulled up on Prince Alfred Road and killed the engine. He looked up at his brother's house and sighed. All the curtains were still closed and there wasn't a soul about apart from a paperboy on a bike who waved as he rode past them. 'Right, are you ready, princess? Lucky will have them up barking as soon as I knock on the door.'

Dianna chewed her lip and nodded. There would be plenty of tears shed in the next few hours. She felt herself filling up again at the thought and dashed her hand across her eyes. If only she could have seen him one last time. She couldn't bear the thought that Grandpa Franklin would never tease her again. She'd never again hear his deep throaty laugh when they found the same things funny. He'd always sung along with her when she had danced and sung for him as a little girl. He'd taken great care of her, along with Grammy, while Dad was over here during the war.

They always looked after her when her own mother couldn't be bothered, and had their own song and dance act, sometimes taking her along to the bars and salons where they were performing. She'd sit quietly behind the bar with a glass of juice and a packet of chips while they entertained the customers. That was when she'd first decided she also wanted to sing and they had encouraged her. She'd missed them both so much when she left New Orleans with her dad and Aunt Ruby to move to Liverpool.

She'd only seen them just the one time since, when they came over for Christmas three years ago. She would have loved them to be here for her wedding day. So many regrets and now it was too late. How would her Grammy manage without him? Uncle Levi lived close by, but it was his plan to move over to England very soon. Maybe Grammy would come too now that she was alone. All her family were here now and she had her youngest grandchildren to enjoy as well as her older ones. And one day hopefully there would be great-grandchildren too if she and Stewart were ever blessed.

Her dad coming to help her out of the car broke her reverie. He put his arm around her and led her up the garden path and the few steps to the front door. He took a deep breath and rang the bell. Lucky the little dachshund began to bark immediately. They could hear him clattering up and down the wooden floor in the hallway. Then a male voice called for quiet and a bleary-eyed Uncle Scott opened the door. He stared at the pair with a puzzled expression.

'Di, Earl, what on earth brings you two here so early? Come on in.' Scott led the way down the long hall and into the dining room. 'Have a seat. I take it from the early hour and the sombre look on both your faces this is a bad news visit? Mom or Pop?'

Dianna burst into tears and Earl nodded slowly. 'Pop, I'm afraid. He passed away peacefully in his sleep last night. Our brother Levi tried to call you but had a struggle with the connection. He managed to get hold of me a couple of hours ago.'

Scott puffed out his cheeks. 'I'm so shocked. I know he was no spring chicken but he was in reasonably good health. Do they know how, why, what caused his death?'

Earl shook his head. 'Levi said there would be an autopsy next week. They think it was most likely a heart attack.' As he finished speaking he was aware that their sister Ruby, looking puzzled, had walked into the room.

'Ah, so it's you lot making the noise,' she said. 'What's going on?'

Scott took her arm and led her to sit down next to Dianna on the sofa. 'Earl's brought bad news, sis. I'm sorry to tell you this, but Pop passed away in his sleep last night.'

Ruby's eyes opened wide and she shook her head slowly. 'No. Oh my God. How, what happened? Is Mom okay, have you spoken with her?' she aimed at Earl.

Earl shook his head. 'I've spoken with Levi. Mom was resting. Levi wants us to call the house after I've spoken with all of you. We can speak with her then.'

Scott sighed. 'I'll go and wake Dolores and the girls. Will you fill the kettle, Earl? I think we're going to need plenty of tea with extra sugar.'

* * *

Bella dropped the phone back onto its cradle and made her way slowly into the kitchen. She chewed her lip as she brewed a pot of tea and poured a mug for herself. No one else was awake yet. The baby had wriggled and kicked all night and her poor bladder couldn't take any more of being used as a football. Molly had just called her with the sad news that Earl's father had passed away and that Earl would call round later today on his way back from Scotty's place to tell Levi.

Molly had asked her not to say anything to him until Earl had spoken to him. She'd agreed. It was definitely better the news came from Earl. She wondered if she should tell Bobby. After all, he would wonder why Earl was suddenly turning up at their home without a prior arrangement. She poured a second mug of tea and took both drinks into their bedroom.

Bobby stirred as she put his mug on the bedside table beside him. She closed the door so they couldn't be overheard, although Levi would be flat out for hours yet after his busy day at the garden fete yesterday afternoon and then out with Kenny to goodness knew where last night. She'd heard him come home and lock the front door just after midnight.

She propped herself up on her two pillows and wrapped her hands around her mug of tea. Bobby opened his eyes and shuffled up the bed so that he was level with her.

'There's a drink on the bedside table for you,' she told him.

'Thanks, love,' he said, reaching across to pick up the mug. 'You're up early. Is Bobby junior keeping you awake?' He grinned and patted her huge belly. 'He's a whopper for sure.'

'You're sure it's a "he" then,' Bella teased. 'I think it's more likely to be Nelly the baby elephant.'

He laughed and then frowned as she shushed him and looked meaningfully towards the door. 'Why shush, what's up?'

She took a deep breath. 'Our Molly just called,' she began in a low voice. 'Earl's father passed away during the night. Earl's gone to get Dianna and then was going to tell Scott and Ruby and the family as his brother Levi couldn't get them on the phone earlier. Later today he is going to come here and tell our Levi that he's lost his grandpa. He'll be so upset. I know he only met his American grandparents that one time when they came over, but he loved them immediately and they him. Grammy is always writing to him and sending little cards and things.'

Bobby shook his head. 'Oh God. He's going to be devastated, love. I'm glad Earl's going to tell him and he's not leaving it to us to do that. It's not going to be easy for him. He'll be so upset himself. It's horrible when you lose your father, as both you and I know.'

'We do,' Bella agreed. She still missed her much-loved dad Harry and she knew Bobby missed Charles Harrison too, even though he had a great stepfather in Basil. It was that blooming Hitler's fault they had no dads. Such a sad waste of their short lives.

'Do we know what time Earl will be here?' Bobby asked. 'We need to make sure Levi stays in until he's been. You know what he's like at the weekend, can't stand being in the house for more than five minutes at a time.'

'No idea. I expect he'll be at Scott's for a while, comforting his family. Ruby and Dianna will be so upset, they lived with Grammy and Grandpa Franklin and I know they both miss them very much.' Bella finished her tea and slid out of bed again. She placed her hands on her back and sighed. 'I'm going to use your shower, love, as I can't get in and out of the bath on my own now and you can't possibly lift me or we'll both get stuck.'

Bobby smiled. 'Okay, love. But give me a shout if you can't manage. Although you should be safe enough in there; just mind you don't slip.'

* * *

Levi had spent most of the morning in the music room with dad Bobby who had asked him to help with some lyrics he was working on that he felt weren't quite right. He loved to be involved with anything that went on in the studios and was delighted to be asked to give his opinion.

The as-yet untitled song was a catchy number and as Bobby played the melody on the piano and Levi sang along, he could see where a change of lyrics in the second verse would help. He wouldn't mind giving this song a go with Jimmy and Kenny when they got the chance. It would suit them and would appeal to the youngsters they played to at the youth clubs. Maybe Earl and Bobby would agree it was a good one for them.

As they came to the end of singing it with the new words, he heard his mam calling out that he had visitors and to come through to the sitting room for a moment. He hurried through with a big grin on his face, expecting it to be his mates, and was surprised but delighted to see his dad Earl and big sister Dianna sitting on the sofa.

'Hello, you two. Everything okay?' he asked as he realised that neither of them appeared too happy and Di looked as though she'd been crying a lot. Her eyes were red and swollen.

'I'll leave you alone for a few minutes,' Bella said. 'I'll make us all some tea.'

Earl nodded. 'Thanks, Bella. Sit down, son,' he said as Bella left the room.

Levi sat down on a chair under the window and stared worriedly at the pair. Dianna blew her nose on a hanky she pulled from her jacket pocket and tears began to tumble down her cheeks as Earl explained to Levi the reason for their visit.

As Levi dropped his head into his hands and started to sob Dianna got to her feet and went to sit on the chair arm beside him. She put her arms around him and pulled him close. Earl jumped up and held both his children in his arms while they cried. Tears tumbled down his cheeks too and dripped from his chin onto their heads. Thank goodness they had each other. Patti and Harry were too young to understand and the twins had one another for comfort. But Dianna needed Levi and he needed her.

* * *

Earl left Dianna and Levi alone for a few minutes while he went to seek out Bobby and Bella. He found them both in the kitchen wearing concerned expressions.

'Is he okay?' Bella asked. 'Are you all okay? What an awful shock for you, Earl.' She made to give him a hug but couldn't get near him with her baby bump. 'I can't even hug you, my bump's too big to get close to you,' she said, tears running down her cheeks. She stroked his arm instead and squeezed his hand.

Bobby patted him on the back and shook his head. 'So very sorry, Earl. Believe me, we both know how painful it is to lose your dad. If there's anything we can do to help, please let us know.'

Earl nodded. 'Thanks, guys. I haven't said anything to him yet but, if it's okay with you, I'd like to take Levi to the funeral with me and Di. Does he have a current passport?'

Bella nodded. 'He does. I got it for him because he was supposed to go on a trip to France with school last year but he changed his mind about it because Kenny's mam couldn't afford to pay for Kenny to go. And you know how joined at the hip they always are. I'll dig it out later.'

'Oh that's good. Ours are all in date thank goodness, even though we haven't used them since we got here. I had them all renewed just in case anything like this should happen and we had to fly home pretty quickly. So you don't mind me taking him with us then?'

'Not at all,' Bobby replied. 'He needs to be there for his own sake. Your family is his family too and he loved his grandpa.

He'd be so upset if he couldn't go. It will be good for both he and Di to see Grammy again too. Do you have any idea when you'll be going?'

'Not yet, but it will be pretty soon. We spoke to my brother Levi and my mom while we were at Scott's and they have to wait to see why he passed away and then the body will be released for burial. They think it was a heart attack. He hadn't been ill as such but Mom said he'd had a few chest pains lately and was being treated with pills for mild angina. So it seems pretty conclusive it was a heart attack, but with a sudden death in an otherwise healthy guy they do an autopsy. Bit like your post-mortems over here.'

Earl wiped away tears. 'Scotty will come down to Bold Street tomorrow to meet me and we'll go see about flights. What we do know is that we have to go to New York first from Heathrow as BOAC don't fly direct to New Orleans at the moment and then we get a connection from there.'

'Are the twins going as well, and Ruby?' Bella asked.

Earl nodded. 'Yes, the lot of us. Hey, I don't suppose you guys could help out with looking after Lucky for them, could you?'

Bella grimaced. 'Not me right at this moment as I can hardly move never mind look after a dog, but I'm sure my mam and Martin would oblige. I'll phone her later and double-check that's okay and I'll call our Molly with the answer and then you can tell Scott.'

'Thank you. That will put Dolores's mind to rest. I'd better get off back to Molly and the kids now. I'll be in touch with regards to dates and what have you.'

Bobby nodded. 'Let us know how much money you'll need for Levi's flight.'

Earl held up his hands. 'That's on me,' he said. 'You two just find his passport.'

'If you're sure. Thanks, Earl,' Bella said. 'And I'll call Mam and sort out the dog situation.'

Earl went back to the sitting room and told Dianna that he was ready to take her home to Stewart. He turned to Levi. 'I'll see you soon, son. And your mam and dad have said that it's okay for me to take you to New Orleans with us for the funeral. That's if you want to come, of course.'

Levi stared at his dad, his mouth open wide. His big brown eyes filled with tears again and he flung his arms around him and hugged him tight. 'I wasn't expecting that, but wow, really?'

Earl nodded. 'Yes, really. Come on then Di, say goodbye to your brother. We'll see you soon, Levi.'

Levi stared out of the small window as the plane landed with a slight bump. He let out the breath he'd been holding and uncrossed his fingers, relaxing slightly for the first time in over a day as the aircraft taxied towards the allocated unloading bay. That had been some journey to say the least, and thankfully they'd arrived safely and in one piece. It had taken a long time, travelling to London Heathrow first by train and then a taxi to the airport. Flying to New York had been thrilling and he wished there had been time to take a look around the most exciting city he had read so much about.

But the long wait at the airport for the delayed connecting flight to New Orleans had taken ages and Dad wouldn't let him and Di out of his sight in case they got lost and missed their flight. Dad was a nervous wreck as it was so they didn't want to upset him any further and Uncle Scotty told the twins to stay put as well so at least they weren't on their own and could have a bit of a wander around the airport to stretch their legs. They played a game of spot anyone famous but the guy they thought was Elvis wasn't after all. It was just a bloke who looked similar with a dark quiff and sultry eyes. It was the guitar in a case he was carrying that made them look twice, so Levi concluded it was an easy mistake to make.

It had been a funny week since Grandpa's death had been announced. Kenny and Jimmy had thought he was joking at first when Levi told them he was off to the USA in a few days. They said they were sorry to hear about his grandpa of course, but still envious of the fact he was going to what they considered to be the most exciting country in the world and where all the best music was currently coming from.

Levi had told them there wouldn't be much time for doing anything other than going to the funeral as they were only away for a week and the funeral was in the middle of their time there. Mam had packed him a smart new black suit and tie, along with a crisp white shirt to wear on the day. Dianna had since told him that funerals in New Orleans were rather colourful affairs and most people didn't wear black, although she said it was still considered to be a mark of respect if one chose to dress like that. He guessed they'd have to wait and see what other people were doing. He didn't really have anything else suitable in his case, just jeans and t-shirts.

'You all ready?' Earl said, standing up and looking over the back of his seat at Dianna and Levi. 'Don't leave anything behind. Make sure you have your hand luggage with you. Uncle Levi and his friend should be here waiting to take us to Grammy's place. We'll call on her first and then take our stuff across to the hotel later.'

Levi nodded and he and Dianna followed Earl down the aisle. Uncle Scott and his family and Aunt Ruby had been sitting up closer to the front of the plane and had already vanished from sight as they alighted. Once through passport control the family met up in the crowded meeting and greeting area and looked around for Uncle Levi.

'There he is,' Earl said, pointing to a tall man who was very similar in height and looks to both him and Scott. He was accompanied by a man a bit shorter than he was and more olive-skinned than dark. Both men waved excitedly as Ruby dashed towards them and was enveloped in a bear hug by them both at the same time.

'That's our childhood friend Albie,' Earl said. 'He lives next door to Grammy and Grandpa. Well, to Grammy now, of course. He's like you Levi, has a white mom and a black pop.'

Earl caught his brother in a hug and Albie grinned as Dianna squealed and ran towards him. He swung her round and round. By the time they'd all finished greeting each other and Levi had been introduced to Albie, who he learnt was a professional musician, the crowds had dispersed and they collected their baggage from a carousel and followed Uncle Levi and Albie to the waiting vehicles.

Scott and family, minus Tammy, squeezed into Albie's pick-up truck after loading their bags onto the back, and Earl, Levi, Dianna and Tammy piled into Uncle Levi's shiny bright red Cadillac with a white roof and lots of chrome trims. Levi loved the car on sight and admired the white leather seats as they set off. He'd have a car like this one day, he promised himself.

Levi stared fascinated out of the window at the cars driving on the opposite side of the highway to what they did at home. He'd had no idea that Americans did that although he must have known deep down as he'd seen enough American films with cars in. Maybe it had never dawned on him. God, his mam would have a fit if she saw this. She'd had a couple of lessons just after she learnt the new baby was on the way, but had found it hard to concentrate due to her mind being on other things, she'd said. She intended to carry on once the baby arrived.

So in the meantime they still had no family car. Well it wouldn't be long now until he could learn to drive. Just a couple more years and he'd be applying for his first licence and then there'd be no stopping him. He'd probably be driving before

Mam at the rate she was going. He jumped as four large and noisy motorbikes flew past, almost like they were racing each other. *Now that looked like fun*, he thought. Just like James Dean. The riders were all clad in black and looked like they may be part of a gang.

As Uncle Levi pulled off the main highway and drove through Jefferson Parish to the suburb of Metairie, Levi could hardly keep his eyes open. He felt overwhelmingly tired. He was aware of Dianna speaking to him as she jiggled his arm to keep him awake.

'Nearly there, Levi. Not long now. Grammy's house is on the next block. Here we are, Sturgis Street.'

Levi forced his eyes open and looked at the little cottage-style homes with shutters that they were passing. Uncle Levi pulled up outside a white-painted wooden single-story house with blue shutters. Albie was already here parked outside his own house and his passengers were standing on Grammy's porch.

'Home sweet home,' Uncle Levi announced, switching off the engine. 'Now leave all the large baggage in the car and just take your small stuff inside for now as there won't be a lot of room when we all get in there. We'll take your big bags round to the hotel on the next block later. But first of all, let's feed and water you. Mom has been cooking all day and will want to spoil everyone.'

Dianna squealed excitedly as she spotted Grammy Franklin standing on the porch in front of all the others, waiting to greet the rest of her family. She hurried across the front lawn and threw her arms around the elderly lady, holding her tight.

'It is so good to see you again,' she sobbed as Grammy rubbed her back and held her spare arm out to greet Levi who felt his eyes filling as he walked towards her and was enveloped in a warm embrace.

'It's so good to see all of you,' Grammy said. 'Oh, my darling children and grandchildren, I am so glad you could make it home to say goodbye to him. Come on inside, all of you.'

* * *

Bella sighed with relief as she put down the phone. Molly had just called her to let her know they had all arrived safely at Grammy Franklin's and that Levi was absolutely fine. She went into the sitting room where Bobby was reading a story to Lizzie. Well he was trying to, but Lizzie kept interrupting him with her hands, signing to ask him questions after lip-reading but not always getting it right. It was a work of art sometimes and he had the patience of a saint.

'Lizzie,' Bella signed. 'Go to your room for a minute. I will come to you soon.'

Lizzie nodded and ran off and Bobby let out a deep breath. 'Thanks, love.'

Bella laughed. 'You're very welcome. That was Molly on the phone. They've arrived safely. Levi's fine. Dianna has asked that I let Fran or Edie know and they can pop over to tell Stewart. I won't be a minute, and I'll just call Mam while I'm at it and see how Lucky is as well in case they ask Molly when they next call her. I know Dolores will be worrying about him. She treats that dog like her baby. Which I suppose he is; but knowing Mam he'll be getting spoiled something rotten.'

Bobby's laughter followed her as she left the room. God it was so quiet without Levi, too quiet. Not that he was in a lot these days but, even so, she was missing him. Still, another five days with him away and she would have the time to gut his bedroom as it needed a damn good cleaning. It was an untidy mess after all his faffing around to take the 'right' clothes with him.

She'd reminded him he was going to a funeral not gadding about all over the place so he wouldn't need much, but he'd insisted on getting himself a checked shirt like he'd seen that John Lennon lad wearing at the fete and another pair of black jeans that she'd asked Edie's mam to quickly take in a seam down the legs to resemble the 'drainies' he seemed to think everyone would be wearing out there. Dolores would be able to do them properly for him when she came back to Liverpool. Bella hadn't liked to bother her this week when she knew she would be so busy getting her own brood ready to go away.

She dialled Fran's number but got no answer so dialled Edie's.

'Hello,' Edie gasped and then stuttered out her number as an afterthought.

'You okay?' Bella asked. 'It's only me.'

'Oh hiya, Bella. Yes, I'm fine thanks. I was just on my way downstairs with my arms full of bedding for the washer. What's up?'

'Sorry to interrupt your housework. Can you do me a favour? When you see Stewart coming in from work will you let him know that they've arrived in New Orleans and Dianna is fine? I know he's holding the fort at the office for Scotty this week so he might be home a bit later and it's possible he'll go to his mam's for his tea before coming back to Victory Street.'

'Yes, of course I will. I bet you're so relieved to hear from them.'

'Well it was Molly who rang me after speaking to Earl, but yes, it's such a relief to know they're safe. I hate the thought of flying anywhere and obviously so does Bobby after his wartime accident. But Earl and Scott are experienced pilots so they have no nerves but to think of my precious boy up there in that plane made me feel sick all day.'

'Well you can relax now and stop worrying. It's not good for your blood pressure. Anyway me, Fran and the baby will see you tomorrow for a brew. That's why I'm loading the washer now then it's out of the way for the morning. We'll be with you about half twelve, is that okay?'

'That's smashing,' Bella said. 'Basil is taking Lizzie to school tomorrow when he picks up Bobby from ours, and if she doesn't kick off then he said he'll do it until I've had the baby, so that's something I hopefully don't need to do for the next few weeks. I can have a bit of a daily lie-in. Not long now, less than six weeks. I can't believe how quickly this pregnancy has flown by.'

Edie laughed. 'That's because you were nearly halfway there before you found out, you daft thing.'

'I suppose so,' Bella agreed. 'Right, I need to pay a visit and then I've got to phone my mam. See you tomorrow.'

She hung up and dashed to the lavvy as fast as she could. She was never off the bloody thing lately. 'Roll on September,' she muttered, waddling back down the hall.

Mam assured Bella that Lucky was doing just fine. 'He adores Martin. He won't leave his side. And he loves sausages, bless him. No wonder they call this breed a sausage dog. It's got nothing to do with the shape, it's the appetite for them.'

Bella hung up laughing and went back to sit with Bobby. She told him what Mam had said and he laughed with her.

'Basil is popping over in a while,' Bobby said. 'He'll just want an update. I did say I'd call him when we heard something but he said a stroll up the road after his tea will stretch his legs and do him good. He gets a bit lonely when Aunty Et's not with him.'

'Bless him. It'll be nice to see him,' Bella said. 'Right, I'll go and get madam ready for bed and then we can relax with Basil when he arrives.'

'Now you're all familiar with the procedure,' Earl began as the family gathered in Grammy Franklin's house on the day of the funeral. 'So I'll just brief Levi then he won't be too shocked. This isn't the way they do funerals in England, so it's all new to him,' he explained as he took Levi to one side. 'When the coach and horses arrive, carrying the coffin and all the flowers, the family will follow it to the end of the street where the local jazz band will be waiting. They will then lead the procession around the neighbourhood and along to the church for the service. Neighbours and friends will join us along the way and people will sing along to the music.'

He smiled at Levi, who looked bemused by the whole thing. He was wearing the black suit and white shirt that Bella had packed for him, but Uncle Levi had given him a brightly coloured tie to wear with it.

'That tie's a nice choice,' Earl said. Everyone else in the family was used to the more flamboyant style of dress New Orleans people chose to wear to celebrate the life of their lost family member. 'You okay with all that, son?'

'Yep, thanks, Dad. Shall I walk beside Dianna?'

'She can walk in between me and you,' Earl replied. 'Uncle Scott will walk with his wife and the twins and Aunt Ruby and Uncle Levi will accompany Grammy and they will take the lead behind the carriage.'

Levi nodded as Scott called from the open front door, 'Okay, we're ready for off. Take your places while I lock up.'

Outside the house, the shiny black carriage, carrying Grandpa's coffin, was filled with bright summer flowers. Aunt Ruby led Grammy to the front of the family line-up and Uncle Levi joined her. He took Grammy's right arm and Ruby took the other. The carriage driver gently flicked the two chestnut horses on the flank and they set off at a trot down the street.

* * *

Dad had been right, Levi thought, as throngs of people lined the streets and joined the procession along to The Tabernacle Church. The jazz band leading them all played uplifting tunes and people swayed along as they followed the family. And although it was a sad occasion, it was also joyous and Levi was sure that if Grandpa Franklin could have been here he would have enjoyed himself. At the church the coffin was lifted down and carried inside with the family following.

At the top of the beautiful church that was lit by sunlight dancing through the stained-glass windows and making patterns on the walls, an organist played softly while the family and mourners came inside to find seats. A tall black man in robes, which were far fancier than the vicars at home wore, greeted everyone as they came into his church. Levi looked at Grandpa's coffin which was covered in colourful sprays of family flowers, and was now on a stand in front of the altar.

The vicar, who introduced himself as Pastor Michael Moore, came to stand beside it and welcomed everyone, then asked them to kneel for a prayer if they were able and if not to stay seated. When he finished he bade them to take a seat again and began the tale of Grandpa Franklin's life. Levi listened intently as there were sure to be things he didn't know about.

Grandpa's full name was Otis Leroy Franklin and he had emigrated to America from South Africa many years ago with his wife Blessing Mary Franklin. They soon settled into their new homeland and as entertainers had worked on the circuit, gospel singing and dancing in many bars and African-American clubs all over the state as well as their family church. In spite of the arrival of their four children, Ruby, Scott, Earl and Levi, they still carried on with their show business careers as the children travelled with their parents from venue to venue and often sat in makeshift cots made from old sets of drawers while their parents entertained.

As soon as they were old enough the kids were taught to sing and dance and did their own little routines to entertain the audiences. Levi and Earl were also taught to play the piano and eventually had their own gigs and, until joining the air force, they and Uncle Scott, who played drums, were a popular jazz trio who performed all over New Orleans with their father managing them. Music was the life and soul of the family and the talent had now been passed proudly on to the next generation of Franklins.

As Pastor Moore finished his funeral service Levi saw Grammy looking proudly down the front-row pew at her family. She smiled at him and he smiled back. As the choir started to sing "Take My Hand, Precious Lord" Levi found the hymn in a small book and sang along with the congregation. Dianna and the twins were singing better than the choir, he thought as people around them nodded and looked at the girls. No wonder Grammy was proud of her family.

After the next prayer and hymn the coffin was carried outside to the freshly dug grave and carefully lowered while the Pastor said a committal prayer. Grammy picked up a handful of earth from around the graveside and threw it onto the coffin and everyone else followed suit. Dianna linked Levi's arm as they walked away towards their dad who was talking to Grammy and Ruby.

'You okay, Levi?' Dianna asked, squeezing his arm.

He nodded. 'I'm fine thank you. I actually enjoyed that funeral. It wasn't all sad and weepy like my Granny Fen's funeral was at home. Everyone was crying at that one. But this one made my spirits lift.'

'Yep, I know what you mean. I almost felt Grandpa's presence was with us.'

'Me too,' Levi said. 'It's made me think, too. I want to be a Franklin like all of you are. I *am* a Franklin and I want to have the name. How do I get my name changed from Harrison?'

Dianna stared at him. 'Are you sure? Won't it upset Bobby and Bella if you change your name?'

Levi shrugged. 'Probably. I'm going to ask our dad what he thinks.'

Dianna nodded. 'Okay, but maybe not today. Wait until we get home to Liverpool. That will give you time to think it over a bit more.'

* * *

Grandpa Franklin's wake was held in a club he and Grammy often went to. The manager of The Lounge, an African-American club in Metairie, welcomed the family and some of the friends and neighbours who had been invited back, and took them to a private room where hot and cold drinks and a hot buffet was being served. A couple of smart uniformed waitresses were on hand to help and Grammy was given a comfortable chair to sit on while a hot drink was brought over for her.

Earl made sure everyone had a drink in their hands before he raised a toast to his father. 'Wherever you are right now,

Pops, we know that you are with us in spirit and you live on in your wonderful legacy, your family. To our amazing Pops, Otis Leroy Franklin. Sleep peacefully, but knowing you, it won't be too quietly.'

People smiled and after glasses were raised and the toast was taken up by everyone in the room, Grammy got to her feet and clapped her hands to gain attention. 'Thank you all so much for coming to Otis's funeral. Your support sure means a lot to me. And to my lovely family, thank you for flying all this way to say your final farewells to your father and grandpa. I couldn't have got through this without you all by my side. I'm sure going to miss you when you go home. Now please everyone, help yourselves to the food. There's plenty for you all, so don't skimp on your portions.'

A ripple of laughter sounded around the room. Levi knew that Grammy loved to feed people and today was no exception. She'd ordered enough to feed an army, as his Granny Mary was fond of saying. He looked over to where his dad and Uncle Levi were deep in conversation. Grammy's neighbour Albie beckoned him over. He went to sit beside him and smiled.

'You okay, son?' Albie asked. 'I know it's not easy saying goodbye to a grandparent and I also know you haven't known old Otis for too long, but let me tell you this, he loved to get your letters in his later years and he talked about you a lot. You're his first grandson and that meant a lot to him after having the three girls first. Before Earl emigrated, he used to get regular letters from your mother with photographs of you, and your grandpa would show everyone the photos down at the club. He was very proud of you, Levi. You can carry that fact around in your head now. Take some comfort from it, boy.'

Levi could feel his eyes filling. 'Thank you, Albie. That really does mean a lot to me. It makes me feel like a real part of the family to know my grandpa actually talked about me like that.'

Albie patted him on the shoulder. 'I might just take a trip over to Liverpool next year. You can show me around the city Earl's always talking about. He loves that place. What's the music scene like there at the moment? I expect you've heard a lot of the stuff we've got going on over here right now: rock-'n'roll, Elvis, Little Richard and Frankie Lymon and the Teenagers. They're all quite hot and I believe there are loads of others giving it a go. It's going to take over the world if what I've heard is true. If you get the right mix of guys together, a good vocalist, a couple of decent guitar players and a drummer, it would appear you can't go wrong. It's worth thinking about. Your dad tells me you have a trio on the go at the moment. Get yourself a couple more members and jump on the bandwagon while you can. Be one of the first in Liverpool to make it big.'

Levi grinned. Albie was on the same wavelength as he was, that was for certain. 'It's been on my mind to expand as soon as we can. You've given me something to think about now on the flight home.' And Levi also knew what he was going to do as soon as he got back to Liverpool. If he'd been offered a place at college he was not going to take it, no matter what Mam and dad Bobby said. He would ask Basil for a full-time job at the studios and get some money saved up so they could get cracking on forming that group.

And the name change he wanted to do would sound much better as Levi Franklin and 'the something or others'. Or whatever name he and the others chose for the group. He could tell Mam and dad Bobby that was the main reason he wanted to change, so he could use it as his stage name.

Bella heaved herself up from the floor of Levi's bedroom, using the wooden foot board of the bed as a support. She'd just finished cleaning and tidying the room as he was due home this evening and she couldn't wait to see him. She'd really missed her boy. She rubbed her aching back the best she could reach it and tried to straighten up. As she made her way to the kitchen a slight twinge below her bump made her gasp.

'Ouch! Little monkey, keep still.'

Her mam was coming round later to help her and to bring Lizzie home. Her daughter had been dropped off at her granny's by Basil to give Bella a little break with it being school holidays. Mam had promised to bring a casserole over to save Bella cooking tea. The phone rang in the hallway and she went to answer it. It was Kenny asking what time Levi was expected home.

'He'll be here about seven, Kenny,' she replied. 'Why don't you come here after tea and wait for him, he'll no doubt be really glad to see you.'

Kenny thanked her and she hung up as another twinge crept up on her but this one felt more like a severe cramp. She took a deep breath and went back to making the cup of tea she'd promised herself half an hour ago while she was still on her knees. By the time her mam arrived Bella had dozed off on the sofa. She'd left the door unlocked so Mam could let herself in and she had a spare key anyway for when the bungalow was empty.

She opened her eyes and blinked as she heard her mam calling out. 'Bella, I'm here, chuck. Where are you?'

'Here, Mam, just shutting my eyes for five minutes.' She smiled as Mam popped her head around the door.

'I'll just put this casserole in the oven on a low light. It'll be ready by teatime. There's an apple pie here as well. I'll put it on the worktop and you can warm it up later.'

'Oh, Mam, what would I do without you?' Bella heaved herself to her feet.

'You stay there and I'll put the kettle on,' Mam said. 'I'll just see Lizzie into her bedroom to play with her dollies for a while.'

'Okay, Mam, thanks. I need the lavvy, again. I'd better go; I can't hold it, I'm afraid.'

Mam nodded. 'I remember being like that with our Betty,' she said, a faraway smile on her face as she mentioned her late daughter. 'Bless her. Biggest of the three of you she was. Ruined me bladder for life, I tell you.'

'Oh don't say that, Mam. I can't stand this for much longer.' Bella grimaced as she waddled to the bathroom while her mam settled Lizzie down in her room with her toys. As she washed her hands at the bathroom sink she felt another twinge and a wave of pain around her back took her breath away. 'Oh no, not today, please. Levi's coming home; I want to be here for him, not in the hospital.' She made her way to the kitchen where her mam was brewing a pot of tea. 'Mam, I'm getting a few twinges and a pain around my back.'

'Oh, don't worry, love, it'll just be what they call settling pains. It's too early for labour pains yet. Go back and sit down in the sitting room and I'll bring the tea through. Have you had anything to eat for your dinner yet?'

Bella shook her head. Not totally convinced or reassured by Mam's quick diagnosis. 'I'm not really hungry. I'll just have a couple of biscuits maybe. There's some custard creams in the biscuit tin.' She lumbered away and winced as another sharp twinge took her breath away. 'Mam,' she called out. 'I really do think it's coming. Shall I phone Bobby?'

Mam carried a tray of mugs and biscuits through and put it down on the coffee table. 'Let's have these and wait a few more minutes. No point in worrying him or dragging him away from work until we're sure. I'll get Martin to go and pick him up if we think it's on its way. Basil will have to stay put in case they've got anyone in using the rehearsal rooms.'

By the time they'd finished their tea and biscuits, Bella was more than convinced her baby was eager to make an appearance sooner rather than later. 'Mam, we'd better call the doctor and Bobby,' she said, biting her lip and wincing with discomfort.

Mam got to her feet. 'Right, I'll get Martin on his way to pick up Bobby and give him a quick call and then I'll speak to the doctor and see what he'd like us to do. I know you'd planned to have this baby in hospital, love, but they're not expecting you just yet. Bear with me.'

'I need to go to the lavvy again and I'll get my little case ready.' Bella heaved herself up and made her way to the bathroom groaning with the pains that were coming more frequently now. By the time she came back to the sitting room with her case and handbag, her mam was pacing up and down the floor.

'There's an ambulance coming shortly. I've told them how often you seem to be getting the pains and the doctor said you may as well as go straight in. He's letting them know in maternity that you're on your way. Martin's gone to pick up Bobby. We'll sort out seeing to Lizzie for you.'

'Mam, I wanted to be here for Levi when he gets home,' Bella cried. 'Oh God, does nothing ever go right?'

'We'll be here for Levi; you're not to worry about anything. There's no point Bobby going with you as they won't let him in anyway until after the baby arrives but he needs to be here to look after Lizzie and to greet Levi as well. We'll sort it all out, so don't you worry. Just sit yourself down for now.'

Bella lowered herself gingerly onto the sofa and turned her head to watch out of the window for Martin's car. She breathed a sigh of relief as Martin's light blue Morris Minor pulled onto the drive. She watched as Martin leapt out and hurried around to the passenger side to help Bobby out.

As she made to stand up a searing pain ripped around her middle and a trickle of water ran down her legs, followed by a further trickle and then a gush. 'Mam,' she cried out. 'My waters have broken!'

'Oh bloody hell,' Mary exclaimed. 'Let me get some towels.' She ran out of the room and warned Martin and Bobby, who were just coming into the hallway, what had happened.

Bobby limped into the lounge and Mary followed him with the towels while Martin hovered in the hallway.

'Where's that blooming ambulance?' Mary said, throwing towels and newspaper onto the sofa and helping Bella to sit back down again. 'Stay there with her, Bobby, while I go and phone that doctor again.'

She dashed out and Bella could hear her on the phone, raising her voice slightly in panic.

Bobby sat down beside Bella and squeezed her hand. 'Don't worry, love. We'll get you there if they don't hurry up.'

'I can't get in Martin's car like this, 'Bella said. 'I'm wet through and I'm in pain.' As she spoke the ambulance pulled up outside, but as Mary let in the two male attendants Bella could sense there was a problem by their worried expressions.

'We've got a flat tyre,' the tallest man said. 'We need to get help because there's no way we can risk taking you to the hospital until it's fixed.' He turned to Mary. 'Can you call Mrs Harrison's doctor and explain the situation and ask him to appoint a midwife immediately? Thank you. We have equipment on board and we can help but neither of us has ever delivered a baby before.'

Bella let her head fall back on the cushions as she let out a bellow of pain. 'I don't care who delivers it or where, just get it out.'

'We need to get Mrs Harrison settled on her bed and I'll bring in the gas and air from the ambulance,' the tallest man said.

Mary dashed back into the room from her phone call. 'The doctor is sending us the duty midwife. She won't be long and he said to ring back if we need him to attend. Come on, love, let's get you comfortable.' She took some towels and a plastic sheet into the bedroom and spread them on the bed and then helped the attendants to get Bella onto the bed.

'You okay now, chuck?' Mary said as one of the attendants left the room to get the gas and air.

Bella nodded as Bobby popped his head around the door. 'Shall I sit with you until the midwife chucks me out?' he asked. 'Martin will take Lizzie to your mam's house now. He's just getting her ready. Fortunately she hasn't heard anything so she's happy to go off with him and play with Lucky.'

'Please, Bobby.' She sighed as he pulled a small chair to the side of the bed and sat down, taking her hand. 'Thank goodness for Martin. I can't believe this. I'm so unprepared. I wanted to hear all about Levi's experience when he gets home later.' She chewed on her lip as another pain washed over her. 'Oh God. That was strong.' She blew out a long breath, trying to ride the pain until it eased off.

'You can still hear what he's been up to, but it will have to be a bit later. And anyway, think what a lovely surprise he'll have when he sees his new sibling has arrived early.'

'I suppose so. But I hope this baby will be okay. It's too early.' She looked up as the attendant arrived back with a canister that he placed by the side of the bed. Attached was a small mask that he fixed around her face.

'Just lower it while you're chatting,' he instructed. 'Pull it back up when you feel you need a good lungful. It'll help relieve the discomfort a fair bit. I think your midwife is here. I can hear voices in the hall.' He left the room and was back in seconds followed by a young uniformed midwife who smiled at Bella reassuringly and introduced herself as Duty Midwife Sister Iris Perkins.

'Right then, let's have a look what's going on, Mrs Harrison,' Sister Perkins said, removing her cap and coat and handing them to Mary. 'I need to wash my hands please.'

'This way,' Mary said, showing her to the bathroom and hanging her hat and coat on the hallstand.

'Mr Harrison?' Sister Perkins addressed Bobby. 'Could you leave us alone while I examine your wife, please?'

Bobby nodded and got to his feet. 'I'll be in the lounge, love, if you need me,' he said to Bella with a look of relief on his face. He steadied himself with the side of the bed and limped out of the room, closing the door behind him.

'She's being examined,' he told Mary who was hovering nearby, looking anxious. 'I'll go and say bye to Lizzie and Martin.'

The two ambulance attendants were waiting in the drive for someone to come and change their wheel. Mary popped her head around the door. 'Would you two lads like a cuppa?' she asked.

'We would that, thanks,' the shorter one said. 'What a palaver, eh? But your daughter is in good hands now; Sister Perkins is one of the best midwives in the district.'

'That's good to know,' Mary said, smiling. 'I'd better go and get some water on the boil then as well as make the tea. It looks like we're in for the long haul. Although our Bella doesn't take that long once she gets going properly. I'll give her a couple of hours tops with this one.'

She went to see Bobby and Martin on her way to the kitchen. 'Take Lizzie to our place now, love, and keep her there until I phone you that it's okay to bring her home. I'll sort Levi out when he gets here. He may want to stay, or depending where we're up to, he can go back to Earl's with him and Dianna. We'll cross that bridge when we come to it. Why don't you go with them, Bobby? You might as well and I'll let you know as soon as it's okay to come back.'

* * *

By the time Levi's plane was due to land at Heathrow airport, Bella was proudly cradling her second-born son in her arms. He'd certainly been in a hurry to arrive and his weight of just over eight pounds had told Sister Perkins that he wasn't as early as first thought.

'He's more or less bang on time,' she said. 'I think your initial dates must have been miscalculated.'

Bella nodded. 'I think you're right,' she agreed. 'I wasn't certain, and all the way through the midwives at the clinic did say he was either a big baby or my dates were out.'

'Well he's here now and he's beautiful,' Mary said, gazing at her latest grandchild. 'He has a look of your dad and you, Bella. Look at all that dark hair and his eyes are very dark as well, although not quite brown yet, but they do say they can change over a few weeks. He even has a look of Levi as a new-born, lighter skin of course but similar colouring otherwise. Well we'd better let Bobby know and then Martin can bring him back with

Lizzie and see his new boy now you're all done and dusted in here.'

Sister Perkins nodded. 'Everything is satisfactory. I will be back in the morning to see you. If you are worried about anything at all don't hesitate to call that number I've written on your notes. At least you can relax now, easier than if you were in hospital. Make sure you rest.'

'I will.' Bella nodded. 'Thank you so much and will you thank the ambulance men when you see them. I'm glad they got their tyre sorted out and I'm also glad the puncture happened before they got here and not when we were on our way to the hospital.'

'Indeed,' Sister Perkins agreed. 'Right, I will love you and leave you and then you can introduce Baby Harrison to the rest of his family. Maybe tomorrow he will have a name to add on his tag. Goodbye and good luck for a peaceful first night.'

'Goodbye and thank you,' Mary said, showing her to the front door. 'See you tomorrow.' She walked back down the hallway and into Bella's room again. 'Have you chosen any names for him yet, love?'

Bella shook her head. 'We've got a few we quite liked, but they were mainly girls' names. Boys we were undecided on and to be honest I thought we had another six weeks to make up our minds. I also thought we'd have another girl. We'll choose a name tonight when Lizzie and Levi are here. Then it will be a family choice.'

Mary nodded. 'I'll go and make that call now and give Bobby and Martin the good news.'

TWENTY-FOUR

Bobby stroked the soft cheek of his new-born son and shook his head. 'I can't believe it,' he said for the umpteenth time. 'A son, I've actually got a son. Oh, I wish my mum was here. She'd be so thrilled.'

'She would,' Bella said, gently caressing his hand. 'Well Lizzie seemed happy enough with him but preferred to go home with Granny Mary and Martin again. It makes life a bit easier for us, tonight anyway. They'll spoil her and I think she wanted to get back to Lucky the dog as well, but he'll be going back home later when Scott picks him up. What time is it now?'

'Just after half past six,' Bobby said. 'Levi should be home in just over an hour or so. Molly rang to see how you were as your mam had let her know you'd had the baby and also to tell us that Earl had called earlier from a phone box at Euston Station and they were just about to board a train to Lime Street.'

Bella smiled. 'Oh thank goodness for that. He's on the last leg of the journey then. I can't wait to see his face. Molly didn't tell Earl about the baby, I hope?'

'Nope, she didn't. She's not that daft, love.'

'No, of course she's not daft. I just want it to be a surprise for Levi and then we can decide on the baby's name together,' Bella said. 'Do you still like Charles, after your father?'

Bobby shrugged. 'It would be nice, but maybe something a bit more modern and less royal. People will think that because we've got an Elizabeth we might be choosing another royal name, like Prince Charles.'

'Well what about after you, Robert Charles? Bobby Junior.'

Bobby shook his head. 'Not sure, love. Two Bobbys might be a bit confusing. Let's wait for Levi, see if he's got any ideas up his sleeve. Lizzie won't mind one way or the other. A name's a name for her and she'll probably call him baby anyway. Ah, there's the phone. Won't be a minute.' He limped out of the room and was back in a couple of minutes. 'That was Kenny. He can't come round tonight after all but he'll see Levi tomorrow, he said to tell him.'

'Oh God, I forgot he said he was coming over,' Bella said. 'Mind you, I've been a bit busy this afternoon and it just slipped my mind.' She laughed. 'Can you put little Mister Harrison in his carry cot for a while please? I'm just going to shut my eyes for a few winks before Levi arrives.'

* * *

Levi let out a big sigh as the train pulled slowly into Lime Street Station. Home at last. He felt tired and weary and was looking forward to a good sleep tonight. Then tomorrow he would catch up with Kenny and Jimmy and they would learn of his plans to extend the group to a four- or five-piece. He'd been thinking over a change of name to put forward as a suggestion. Something snappy that would sound like an American group.

He'd had another chat with Albie before they'd left New Orleans for their flight home. Albie had told him about a group of lads from Lubbock in Texas who were about to record their first single, a song they'd written themselves. He said that they now had a good following so would likely have a big hit with it and to look out for the record when it was released in England. Levi liked the sound of that, writing their own songs would be a brilliant idea.

After helping Bobby with those lyrics last week he felt like he wanted to do more. The one thing that had made him smile about the new group though was the name they'd chosen. Buddy Holly and the Crickets. The lead singer's name was great, but who on earth would name their group after insects. Levi shook his head and grinned. He didn't think for one minute that the daft idea would ever catch on in Liverpool. But first he had the tricky job of telling his parents he wanted to change his surname. Levi Franklin just tripped off the tongue. Two syllables rather than the three in Harrison. Dianna dug him in the ribs and broke his reverie.

'Come on, Levi. Grab your stuff. Dad's going to the luggage truck for our cases. You were miles away then. What's on your mind?'

Levi smiled. 'My future. I'm going to make some big changes.'

Dianna shook her head. 'You might not be allowed to until you're older.'

'We'll see,' he said, an air of determination in his reply.

* * *

As Earl helped Levi unload his suitcase from the boot of the taxi the front door opened and Bobby raised a hand in greeting. 'Welcome home,' he called.

'Thanks, Bobby. I'll catch up with you tomorrow,' Earl said. 'Need to get Dianna home to Stewart now. See you down at the studios. Bye, son. See you soon.' He got back into the taxi and Levi waved them off. He lifted his case and strolled up the drive to the bungalow.

'Where's Mam?' he asked, looking round. 'And our Lizzie?'

'She's just having a rest. Had a busy day. And Lizzie is at Granny Mary's tonight for a treat. We'll give your mam a few more minutes and then I'll wake her. She can't wait to see you but was struggling to stay awake.'

'Poor Mam. Bet she'll be so glad when it's all over. Still, not long now.'

'Anyway,' Bobby said, changing the subject, 'leave your case there and you can shift it later. Come on into the sitting room and tell me how you got on in New Orleans.'

'Oh it was great,' Levi said, flopping down on the sofa as Bobby sat on an armchair opposite him. 'It's a lovely place to live, well where Grammy's neighbourhood is anyway. The people are all very colourful and musical and friendly. Even Grandpa's funeral was a happy affair. Nothing like they are here where everyone seems to enjoy being miserable and they all wear black. Uncle Scott said it's because life is celebrated there and you give thanks for it in a happy way. Can't see Granny Mary approving of that idea but that's the way they do it.'

'Sounds good.' Bobby nodded his head. 'And you're right. We should celebrate the life lost as well as mourn it. Did you get the chance to sing, apart from in church?'

Levi shook his head. 'If we'd been there longer Grammy said we could have sung as a foursome at her local club that did Grandpa's wake. Her neighbour Albie was childhood friends with dad Earl and my aunts and uncles. He's a musician too so it was good to talk to him about what's happening with the music scene over there. He's given me some good ideas about changing our group from a trio to a four- or five-piece band. I need to talk with Kenny and Jimmy about it very soon.' He stopped and frowned. 'What's that strange noise? Have we got a kitten?' The sound of mewling was coming from across the hall and then his mam's voice called out for Bobby.

Bobby got to his feet. 'Er, no, not a kitten. But we have got a little surprise for you. Follow me.' He led the way to his and Bella's bedroom and moved aside to let Levi enter.

Levi stepped cautiously into the room and stopped, his mouth wide with shock as he stared at his mam who was propped up on pillows looking weary but happy at the same time, and by the side of the bed in a small cot was the mewler. Except now it was no longer making squeaky sounds but firing up and yelling, waving its fists in the air.

'Oh, son, it's so good to see you,' his mam said, holding out her arms. Levi smiled and moved into them, hugging her tight.

He shook his head and pointed at the cot. 'You had it? Oh my God, when? What is it?'

Bobby picked up his little son and held him while Levi sat down on the side of the bed, shaking his head in wonder. 'He's a boy and he arrived late afternoon today. So he's nearly five hours old now. Do you want to hold him?'

Levi nodded and held out his arms. Bobby handed his new little brother to him and he looked down in wonder at the little face with the big dark eyes that stared at him unblinkingly. 'He looks like you, Mam. He's nothing like Lizzie or Dad. Definitely like you.'

Bella nodded. 'Granny Mary says he's like my dad and she can also see you in him a little too with the dark hair, and we think his eyes will turn brown soon.'

'He's lovely,' Levi said. 'I can't believe he's here so soon.'

'No, neither can we,' Bella said. 'But he is. Now he needs a name. We just assumed he'd be a girl so we haven't really got a boy's name lined up. We thought we'd wait until you got home and you can help us to choose. We want something different. At first I suggested naming him after Bobby's dad and then adding Robert as a second name but Bobby's not keen, are you, love?'

She smiled as Bobby shook his head. 'And Earl and Molly have given their Harry my dad's name so that's out too. Basil is too old-fashioned nowadays for a little baby. I like Gary but Fran's baby has that name. So we're back to square one. Are there any names you'd like us to consider, Levi?'

Levi smiled. 'If this little boy is anything like the rest of our family, he'll be a singer or musician before he can walk, almost. You need to give him a name that will suit him as he grows up and sound right if he ever gets famous.'

Bella laughed. 'Levi, I know you have dreams and big ideas, love, but I only gave birth to him a few hours ago. You've got him on stage with his name in lights already.'

'I know you did, Mam. But you have to think about his future too.' He was quiet for a minute as an idea came into his head. He screwed up his face. They wouldn't go for that though. After all, Grandpa Franklin wasn't *their* relative. But he supposed there was no harm in making the suggestion. His mam *did* ask after all. 'While I was away I made a discovery about dad Earl's parents' names. I've only ever known of them as Grammy and Grandpa. But Grandpa was actually called Otis Leroy Franklin. I really like those names and you never ever hear of anyone called that around here, do you?'

Bobby shook his head. 'That's true,' he agreed. 'I really like Leroy. It's different. What do you think, Bella?'

She nodded. 'I love it. We'll have three Ls then. Levi, Lizzie and Leroy. In actual fact I like Otis too. It would be a really nice tribute to your grandpa if we gave him both names, but we'll use Leroy first.'

Bobby smiled and nodded his approval. 'So, Leroy Otis Harrison it is then. Well done, Levi. Good job you're home, son. He'd have been Baby Harrison forever if it was left to us.'

Levi beamed. 'I'll write to Grammy tomorrow and tell her. She will be so thrilled and probably shed a few tears as well. I do hope Uncle Levi can bring her here when he moves over to England for good.'

'That will be lovely if he does,' Bella said. 'All her family will be here then so she needs to be close to them.'

* * *

The following day Levi struggled to get up with the time difference, but he'd promised Bobby he would go down to the studios to help as Bobby was going to stay at home to help Granny Mary to look after Bella and baby Leroy, and Lizzie too. Bobby had said to tell Earl he'd ring him later in the morning. Basil was collecting Levi at eight thirty so he had a quick shower in Bobby's unit to wake himself up and threw on his checked shirt like John Lennon's and a pair of drainies.

A quick brew and slice of toast and he was ready to go. Mam and Bobby were still asleep, but they had been up a couple of times in the night when Leroy had cried. *They must be so tired*, he thought. He went to stand out on the drive so that Basil didn't need to knock at the door. The cool fresh air woke him up a bit more. It was a nice day with a bright blue sky dotted with fluffy white clouds. Nowhere near as hot as New Orleans had been from first thing in the morning and throughout the day.

He wondered what Mandy would be doing today and if she'd missed him. He'd sort of missed her but had been so busy that the days had flown and he'd had no time to write her a post-card or letter. But then again he'd have probably been home before it was delivered anyway. And as Jimmy said, if a girl felt a bit ignored and left out it made them even keener. He smiled. He'd see her tonight, hopefully. He raised his hand as Basil pulled up outside the bungalow in his Rover car and climbed into the passenger seat. 'Morning, Basil.'

'Morning, young man. How's the new arrival and his parents?'

'All fine thank you. They're still asleep but have been up during the night.'

Basil laughed. 'You have to grab your sleep when you can with a new nipper. Have they given him a name yet?'

Levi nodded. 'Yep, they have. They let me choose his names. He's called Leroy Otis after my late grandpa.'

'Oh, that's unusual. I like it. Good names. Well chosen. You can tell me about your trip when we get to work and meet up with Earl. Bobby will need a few days off to help out at home so it will be good to have you around.'

Levi beamed. He couldn't wait to tell his dad about the baby's names. He sat back in the seat and looked out of the window. He hoped Kenny and Jimmy were free tonight for a meeting in the music room at home. Although if they *were* free then he wouldn't be able to see Mandy. Ah well, he hadn't told her the day he was actually going to be home as he hadn't been sure with the long journey and the time differences. Also he had the excuse he may be needed at home helping with the new baby and looking after his sister too. There'd be time at the weekend, maybe, he'd have to wait and see.

* * *

Earl frowned as Levi asked him for help with regards to changing his name. Basil had gone to keep an appointment at the bank and the pair were alone in the Bold Street Studios. 'You can still use the Franklin name, son. Why would you want to lose the name you've been brought up with?'

'Because I want to be a proper Franklin like *you* all are,' Levi said. 'It's just better for a stage name than Harrison is, don't you think? Also it goes better with Levi.'

Earl sighed. 'I haven't really given it any thought. It's a complicated procedure and I think Bobby and Bella have enough on their plates to cope with right now. It may upset them if you do change it. Like I say, you can still call yourself Levi Franklin for stage name purposes.'

Levi shrugged. He didn't want to upset Mam and Bobby at the moment, so he supposed he could just use Earl's surname when he needed to.

'There's another thing too,' he continued. 'I'm not going to college. I made my mind up while we were away. I don't need an art degree or anything else educational at all for what I want to do. We haven't got my results yet, but no matter what they are, I'm not going and that's that.'

Earl raised his eyebrows. 'You have got it on you today, haven't you, son? Where has all this come from?'

'Nowhere really,' Levi said. 'I just don't wanna do it. I want to sing, you know I do. I also want to write songs and perform them. I don't need art for that. I'm not wasting two or three years doing something that's going to be no use to me in the long run. I can work here until the group gets going properly.'

Earl nodded. 'I suppose you can and we could sure use your help. But you can bet your life that Bella and Bobby will blame me and say I've influenced you in all this. You'd better tell them that none of it is my idea.'

'I will,' Levi said. 'I think they'll be a bit wrapped up in the new baby right now to kick up too much of a fuss. He came along at the right time.' He laughed. 'Dad, will you please come home with me tonight and help me to tell them? We can make it sound like the best idea in the world. You can get us more gigs for The Sefton Trio as soon as possible as well so that we can earn a bit of money to put towards more instruments.'

'I'm sure we can sort that out,' Earl said. 'We have more youth clubs on the books now asking us to supply groups for their dances. If you're not planning on going to college then you won't be studying as much and that was one of the reasons Bobby and Bella didn't want you out too often late at night. And yes, I'll come home with you and speak to them. I can meet young Leroy as well. It's so good of them to choose my pop's names. I can't wait to let the other family members know.'

A month after returning from New Orleans, Levi had achieved half his goal in recruiting a lead guitarist to join the group. His brother-in-law Stewart, although a few years older than the original threesome, had jumped at the chance as soon as Dianna had mentioned it to him. He was to play lead, Kenny was to play drums following a few lessons, Jimmy the double bass guitar and Levi would play rhythm and do lead vocals.

The others would provide harmonies and backing vocals. They were all ensconced in the studio with Earl and Bobby for an evening session and to make sure Stewart was suited to their style. Earl had chosen a couple of songs they were familiar with and Bobby had finished the song he'd been working on when Levi had helped him. It was a catchy pop number that Bobby thought would suit them. The bass and drums belonged to the studio but they could have the use of them for now until they felt ready to buy their own equipment. Levi and Stewart already owned their own instruments.

'Right, lads,' Earl said as Bobby twiddled knobs at the mixing desk, preparing to record them. 'This name you've been dithering over for a couple of weeks. Have we reached any decisions yet?'

Levi smiled and nodded. He'd agreed to a compromise with his mam and dad Bobby about his surname. That he would stay a Harrison and use Franklin on stage. They in turn had agreed that he could refuse the place he'd been offered at art college last month if he was prepared to work hard to make his music career a success.

And also that if nothing came of it after he gave it his best try, he would reconsider doing a college course. Earl had smoothed the waters as best he could and things had worked out well and Levi had hurt no one's feelings in the process.

'We have,' he replied. 'We are – tada,' he threw out his arms in a dramatic gesture, 'Levi Franklin and The Blue Cadillacs,' he announced proudly. 'It sounds American, don't you think?'

Earl and Bobby nodded. 'Very. Influenced by your Uncle Levi's car, no doubt,' Earl said. 'Although his is red.'

Levi laughed. 'Influenced just a bit. I'd love one eventually. But mine will be blue.'

Earl smiled. 'Whatever you say, son. Right then, let's get on with things. Do a quick tune-up and we'll begin.'

Earl tapped his foot as they played and sang in perfect tune and harmony. They sounded great and Stewart fitted in really well with them. Kenny kept perfect time on the drums and he and Jimmy together were a tight rhythm section. Levi's vocals were spot-on. Chuck Berry's "Schooldays" was popular with the kids and all the new groups that were forming in the area. And Danny and the Juniors' "At the Hop", which they'd performed before, sounded great with an extra guitar.

'That's a real good sound, guys,' Earl said. 'You've got something special there. Lots of rehearsals over the next couple of weeks and we'll send you out on some gigs. See how it goes. Now then, let's give the new song a whirl. And if we like what we hear we may be able to get this out as a single for you eventually.'

Bobby nodded his agreement as Levi gasped with surprise. 'And because you have helped me get the lyrics just right, Levi,' he said, 'we'll share joint writing credits on the label. How does that sound?'

'Oh my God,' Levi replied. 'Really? Wow, thanks Dad, that's fabulous news.'

'Just the start of it all, son, just the start,' Bobby said. 'Come on then, give it a go. I know the song is new to you all but you've heard it a few times this week and there's sheet music here with words and dots to help with the chords.' He handed the hand-written papers out and sat back down at the desk. 'Just run through it a couple of times to see what you think.'

The new song "Don'tcha Know I'm the One for You" was a slightly upbeat number and sounded good. A few fumbled notes and the odd missed drumbeat, but all in all Bobby and Earl were pleased with the way the boys interpreted the song.

'A few more rehearsals this week and we can get that down on tape,' Bobby said. 'It's got a great beat.'

* * *

By the time the boys had been dropped off at their individual homes, and Earl had come back to take Levi and Bobby to their bungalow, the hour was late. Earl refused a nightcap and said he'd better get back to Molly. They waved as he drove away. Bella opened the door and let them in, telling them to be quiet as she'd just settled Leroy and Lizzie, who apparently had been a pest, mithering all night for Bella to play with her while she was trying to get the baby to sleep.

'She's driven me crazy,' Bella said as she greeted her menfolk with a hug and a kiss each. 'Anyway, she's zonked now, thank the lord. How did it go? I can see by your faces you're running on excitement. Go and sit down and I'll make a cuppa and fetch you some biscuits and then you can tell me all about it. I've got some news for you, as well, but yours can come first.'

Bobby and Levi sat down in the sitting room and smiled gleefully at each other. 'I really enjoyed that, Dad,' Levi said. 'I feel like we're getting somewhere at last.' He grinned as his mam waltzed into the room with a tray of mugs and lemon puff biscuits.

'Help yourselves and then talk,' she demanded, a happy smile on her face.

After they'd excitedly told her how the rehearsal had gone she told them her news.

'I had a phone call from your Aunt Ruby,' she said to Levi. 'She wanted to speak to you but I told her where you were and she said she wouldn't disturb you while you were working and also she wanted to speak to Earl so I said he was with you. She said she'd catch up with him at home later. Anyway,' she continued. 'I've got some very exciting news for you. Your Uncle Levi and Grammy Franklin are coming for Christmas again. Also they are in the throes of emigrating but it will be next year before they have all that completed. Aunt Ruby said Grammy didn't want to stay in America this Christmas now that Grandpa has gone. She wants to spend it here with her family. Uncle Levi has booked all the flights and they will be staying at Prince Alfred Road of course, so you'll be able to see them as much as you want to. Now isn't that good news?'

Levi's beaming smile lit up his face from ear to ear as his mam continued. 'She also can't wait to meet your grandpa's namesake. She's very happy that we have chosen his names for our new baby.'

'I know she is, she told me when she wrote back to me,' Levi said. 'She had a little cry about it, but she's so pleased as she feels a part of our family now too.'

Bella ruffled his curls and gave him a hug.

'Mam,' he said, ducking out of her reach and grinning. 'You used to do that when I was a little kid.'

'Well you still are, to me anyway.' Bella laughed at her boy and playfully thumped him on the arm. 'Oh, by the way, Mandy called for you as well. She didn't sound very happy that you were out again. Didn't you tell her what you were doing tonight?'

Levi screwed up his face. 'Oh no, I forgot. We've been so busy getting the group sorted, I just haven't had time.'

Bella nodded. 'Maybe girls should take a back seat for now. You've got a lot on if you're determined to get this group off the ground. Let her down gently though. She's a nice girl.'

'I will,' Levi said. 'And yes she is, nice that is, but my music has to come first.'

Bobby laughed. 'Plenty of time for women later, lad. And believe me, if you get going with this musical career, well they'll be throwing themselves at you left right and centre.'

* * *

By the time the second week of November arrived the recording of "Don'tcha Know I'm the One for You" went on sale and within a week was vying for a chart space with "That'll Be the Day" by Buddy Holly and the Crickets, the very same group that Albie had told Levi about. Levi and the boys couldn't believe it. They were being talked about all over Liverpool and the local newspapers ran an article on the Franklin family and their musical background.

On the strength of this Basil decided to put on a review show in mid-December and hired the Empire Theatre. The Bold Street Studios had put on shows at the theatre before and they were always a sell-out. Levi and the boys would be top of the bill. Dianna and the Crystalettes agreed to do a spot and

Earl said he'd sing a few songs too. Basil filled the other spots with a couple of variety acts from his books, a comedian and an acrobatic trio.

Bella and the Bryant Sisters chose to opt out this time. They were too busy with family life to perform these days, Bella told Basil. 'But we'll be there on the night to watch you all, that's if someone can look after the kids for us. Hopefully a neighbour will babysit as no doubt Mam and Martin will want to be in the audience and our Molly will have to find someone for her two as well.'

The Christmas Review Show sold out in days as everyone wanted to see Levi Franklin and The Blue Cadillacs performing.

Levi had called Mandy to ask if she and Val would like to come and sit in the circle with his family. They'd parted company amicably a few weeks ago and Mandy said she'd always be his friend and that his career must come first and she would always be there to support him. He was glad she hadn't fallen out with him and maybe at a less busy period in his life they would have a bit more time for each other.

Basil had made them appointments at a tailor in the city centre and they had chosen smart blue suits and matching ties to go with their name. Coupled with crisp white shirts, Levi thought the outfits lent them a look of some of the American groups that were starting to make a name for themselves. He couldn't wait for the show. They were all excited to be able to perform their song live in their home city. Basil had received a phone call from a London agent who had requested to book them in the New Year. He explained that he worked for the BBC and had been asked to try and book the boys for a Sunday Night at the London Palladium show.

Basil had spoken to them and to Earl and Bobby and they had all agreed that they should definitely take the booking. It was the most popular variety show on the television and a huge compliment to be asked. Basil told them it could lead to all sorts of opportunities. The book was getting full and the year ahead looked good.

The one thing Levi would have loved was for his Grammy to see the show at the Empire, but it was on the weekend before they arrived, midweek the following week, just in time for Christmas. Ah well, there would be more shows in the future, he was certain of it.

* * *

Levi and Earl stood in the wings and watched Dianna and the Crystalettes singing. The applause was rapturous. He was so proud of his sister and his cousins. They could certainly entertain. His dad was next on stage and he gave it his usual all with a selection of Dean Martin and Nat King Cole songs. He finished with a 'song for his daughter' and sang Paul Anka's "Diana".

'Love it,' Dianna said, laughing, 'even though it's a different spelling. He did a good job there. Your turn now, Levi. Good luck, little brother.' She gave him a hug and he and the rest of the group bounded on stage to cheers and clapping.

Levi greeted his audience and thanked them for the warm welcome. As he looked up to the circle to thank his family and friends he spotted a familiar face smiling down at him. He caught his breath and almost choked on a sob. He looked round for his dad who was in the wings with Dianna and who had been watching him closely.

As he pointed to the circle his dad nodded. He hadn't been seeing things. Right up there, and flanked by Uncle Levi and his dad's old pal Albie, was his Grammy Franklin. She waved both hands at him, beaming with pride, and he smiled and waved back, almost lost for words. They must have come early and the family kept it as a surprise for him. How wonderful. And now Levi knew that he and his group were about to give the most important performance of their lives. No matter how many more they did, he would never forget that precious moment he'd looked up to the circle for as long as he lived.

A LETTER FROM PAM

Dear reader,

I want to say a huge thank you for choosing to read *A Royal Visit to Victory Street*. If you did enjoy it, and want to keep up to date with all my latest releases, just sign up at the following link. Your email address will never be shared and you can unsubscribe at any time.

www.bookouture.com/pam-howes

To my loyal band of regular readers who bought and reviewed my previous Bryant Sisters stories, thank you for waiting patiently for this fifth book. Your support is most welcome and very much appreciated.

As always a big thank you to Beverley Ann Hopper and Sandra Blower and the members of their Facebook group Book Lovers. Thanks for all the support you show me. Also thank you to Deryl Easton and the supportive members of her Facebook group Gangland Governors/NotRights. Thank you to Claire Lyons and her beautiful son Riley who is my inspiration for Bella and Earl's son, Levi. As always, Claire's daily Facebook updates of Riley are a joy.

A huge thank you to team Bookouture, especially my lovely editor Maisie, it's been such a pleasure to work with you again, and also thanks to Rhian, Loma, Mandy and Billi for your help with copy edits, proofreading and everything behind the scenes.

And last but definitely not least, thank you to our amazing media team, Kim Nash, Sarah Hardy Jess Readett and Noelle Holton for everything you do for us. You're "Simply the Best" as Tina would say! And thanks also to the gang in the Bookouture Authors' Lounge for always being there. As always, I'm so proud to be one of you.

I hope you loved *A Royal Visit to Victory Street* and if you did I would be very grateful if you could write a review. I'd love to hear what you think, and it makes such a difference helping new readers to discover one of my books for the first time.

I love hearing from my readers – you can get in touch on my Facebook page, through Twitter, Goodreads or my website.

Thanks,

Pam Howes

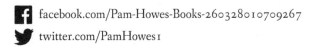

facebook.com/Pam-Howes-Books-260328010709267

twitter.com/PamHowes1

AUTHOR'S NOTE

While I was working on the copyedits of this book, our dear Queen Elizabeth II sadly passed away after an amazing reign of seventy years. When I researched early royal visits for this story, she was a new queen, much adored, and had the world at her feet. A wonderful monarch who will never be forgotten. Rest in peace, Your Majesty. Thank you for all your years of dedication to your job. In our thoughts forever.

ACKNOWLEDGEMENTS

For my lovely and supportive partner, my dear daughters and their other halves, my assorted grandchildren and their wives and partners, and my two new great granddaughters, and the rest of my family. Thanks for all your support and love. To my dear friend and Beta readers Brenda Thomasson and Sue Hulme. Much appreciated, as always. Lots of love to you all. xxx